LIVING
TOGETHER

LIVING TOGETHER

SEARCHING FOR COMMUNITY IN A FRACTURED WORLD

Mim Skinner

FOOTNOTE

First published in 2022 by
Footnote
www.footnotepress.com
Footnote Press Limited
4th Floor, Victoria House, Bloomsbury Square, London WC1B 4DA
Distributed by Bonnier Books UK
Owned by Bonnier Books
Sveavägen 56, Stockholm, Sweden

First printing

1 3 5 7 9 10 8 6 4 2

A CIP catalogue record for this book is available
from the British Library and the Library of Congress.

ISBN (paperback): 978–1–80444–003–2
ISBN (ebook): 978–1–80444–004–9
Cover design by Anna Morrison
Typeset by Bonnier Books UK Limited
Printed and bound in Great Britain by
Clays Ltd, Elcograf S.p.A.

Contents

Author's note

This book was written was written in conversation with communities around the UK. Where communities have included marginalised groups, consent was ongoing, including allowing for collaborative editing, e.g. for groups to take an active role in how their identities are described. This does not equate to approval of or agreement with their worldview.

Preface

For most of my twenties, I slept in a bunkbed in a room that I shared with my friend Nikki. We were in the process of establishing a social enterprise together, intercepting food heading to landfill and minutes of an early directors' meeting lists the meeting's location as 'top bunk'.

The beds in our community house, Number 25, were stacked together so our rent would cover a spare room for someone that needed it. Sometimes our visitor was homeless, or seeking asylum from war, and at other times, in crisis or just needing to retreat from the spin of life. There was an extendable dining table and a roll of black sacks by the door, ready for our regular midnight trips to the supermarket bins. Along with a shared vision, our life together was accompanied by a shared rhythm of mealtimes, prayer and meditation, hospitality and activism. I dressed from a shared wardrobe and ate from a communal pantry. I had only a handful of possessions that were mine alone.

It was a space where the line between personal and public was blurred, scratched at and often rubbed away completely, where community was built on local proximity rather than similarity and our dogged commitment to its best and worst sides ran deep into the fabric of our days. For the seven years our intentional community lasted, it became reflex to cook for ten or twelve – great pots of stew that could be bulked out easily for the unexpected diners we knew would come.

Over the time we lived together, my roots burrowed deeper and deeper into the soil beneath me, the tendrils of other lives in the local community entwined around my own until it was hard to tear away.

I did though, at least in part.

I found myself getting weary and when my husband, Sam, and I got married, we swapped that life for a quieter, more predictable one with our cat and loft conversion, for Farrow & Ball tester pots in eight shades of green. So did the others. We still maintained points of connection with community members and those that travelled through, but it stopped being the foundation for everything else.

The communal cooking has been the hardest habit to break. Our dinners fill our two plates and then Tupperware boxes and cling-filmed bowls with food destined for phantom unexpected guests, as though I'm still exercising an amputated limb.

Sahr Yambasu, the first Black president of the Methodist church, talks about how important it is to understand the difference between inclusion and welcome. Welcome means inviting someone into your home, but inclusion means allowing them to move around the furniture. We invite plenty of people into our house still, but the sofa is angled to my preference now. Those guests are not equal members of a shared life, entwined into our comings and goings.

I often reflect on the decision to move back into a world built for two, to drift into the version of normal we'd been so intent on disrupting. I wonder at what point that motivation was dulled by the pressures that joined it, why each of us was pulled by jobs, life circumstances, families and, ironically, the pressure of running community projects we'd dreamed up at the kitchen table, towards living more conventionally, towards dinner tables of people we know, and fridges full of Tupperware spares.

Introduction

W E HAVE, OVER THE LAST four generations, become less and less tethered to our local areas. To die in the house you were born in is now the stuff of folklore. Globalism has pulled us out of the village's orbit and into great global ellipses that spin broader with each younger generation.

Column inches and book pages all over the world are given to discussions about how our culture has become increasingly tribal, but the new boundary markers for belonging are no longer geographical, they are ideological, political, spiritual and cultural. New generations are being born into a world where we have more global connectivity than ever with our cultural tribes but are less grounded in the soil under our feet.

When we started our first intentional community, sharing meals, possessions, rhythms and duties, it felt quite radical. In the years after graduating university or starting work, most of my peers were living quite transient lives, signing six-month tenancies in locations dictated by impermanent job contracts, their stories punctuated by a cast of ephemeral flatmates. Our decision to stay still, to put our energies into the humdrum of domesticity and hospitality, spending afternoons looking after kids and sharing cups of tea with neighbours, was a marked departure from our peers.

Digital generations being in perpetual transition reflects a global trend. In the US 25- to 34-year-olds will stay in a job for an average of 2.8 years, compared to 10.1 years for workers ages 55 to 64[1] with the average North American moving house or area every five years. Here in the UK the statistics are similar, with more under-30s renting, or still living with their parents, than ever before. The effects of this are borne out in our sense of belonging and connectedness.

A survey in 2016 found that just 30% of over-45s, 14% of 25- to 44-year-olds and 5% of 18- to 24-year-olds were even on first-name terms with those living nearby.[2] The most significant reason given for this disconnect was lack of time. This will not be a surprise for many of us living under the multiple pressures of a precarious market, strained finances, work pressure, childcare, parent-care, self-improvement, physical and spiritual wellbeing, social responsibilities and professional ambitions. Of course we don't have time for a cup of tea at the community centre (which in any case has probably shut).

We know the importance of connection and we are doing our best to seek it out, but after scheduling in this catalogue of professional, social and health demands there are few remaining gaps between the Tetris-ed coloured appointment blocks we have to choreograph together into tight calendar grids. We are left little time or energy for that stationary grey space that holds the blocks in place, for the unplanned interruption of community, the inefficient background hum of other lives, the connection that happens when nothing else is happening. The grey space made up of borrowed sugar and shared childcare, of cups of tea with Barbara on a Tuesday and a Monday afternoon spent helping John with his Universal Credit form.

Incidental and interdependent social interaction used to be embedded into British life. Where I live in County Durham you can still go and see communal bread ovens built into terraces of mining towns where households from the village would bring their proven dough. The ovens became important community meeting places, particularly for women. People gathered to cook pies and cakes on celebration days and meat joints that were dropped off before church and collected after for Sunday roasts. Baking advice was shared and children met and played as they were sent to collect the warm loaves. Now, these brick ovens are consigned to history, replaced with individual kitchen appliances and supermarket loaves that we can scan through a self-service check-out or have couriered to our door.

As we've become more self-sufficient in our own homes, youth centres, local pubs, community centres, greengrocers and libraries have all closed in great numbers because funding and appetite for these gathering spaces has decreased. Churches, too, have ceased to provide communities with the cohesion they once did, the calendar of rituals which gave us weekly and seasonal gathering points in our local areas.

If we live in a society where these incidental meeting points are designed out, interdependent social interactions are replaced by those that are deliberate and intentional. We are the authors of our own social networks, making time for those we want to see or feel social duties towards rather than those interactions being integrated into our lives. If you want to avoid unplanned social interactions completely, remote working, online shopping and social media can make that possible.

I'd love to claim that, having seen the richness of a more communal life, I buck the trend. It wouldn't be true though. We grew up, got full-time jobs and built the scaffolding of our lives for two rather than twelve. Our wider community were re-cast as additions rather than woven into the fabric of our day-to-day living, the space left for uninvited interruption became slim.

In that absence of a decisive structuring of my world against the status quo, I joined the slipstream; a life structured around the preferences and demands of my unit of two. And I'm very comfortable here. Our living environment is highly tailored to our needs, complete with tools that allow the world around us to be finely optimised around our preferences. Our Spotify and Netflix accounts predict our music and film preferences, our news sources tell us what we'd like to hear, and our bathroom tiles were selected from sixteen samples of glazed brick. If there's an unexpected knock on our door, it'll be an Amazon parcel.

Our household make-up is now much closer to the UK average of just 2.4 people, a number which has shrunk significantly over the last century as households themselves are less likely to include multiple generations and household staff, and far more likely to centre on single adults or a nuclear family.

The proportion of one-person households in the UK is at an all-time high, ranging from 22.8% in London to 33.6% in Scotland and the North East of England.[3] This trend is mirrored across the globe, particularly in wealthy countries. In Sweden and Norway nearly half of all households are single-person. The number of people who live alone in the States has doubled in the last fifty years. Compared to a household average of 6.9 people in sub-Saharan Africa, the European average is just 3.1.[4]

So why does it matter? What effect is it having on us that our energies are spent in smaller circles? That our lives are less dependent on those around us? If we're happy in smaller units and managing to forge social connections where we want them, does it really make a difference?

The Loneliness Experiment, the biggest study ever completed on the topic, found that rather than being the preserve of the elderly, the feeling of disconnection now spans every generation, peaking for divorced empty-nesters in their 50s and 60s and city-living millennials, reaching its height amongst 16- to 24-year-olds, new parents, minority groups and disabled people.[5] One in five millennials reported that they could not name a single friend.[6] Conducted across 237 countries, it found that loneliness was greater in individualistic, as opposed to collectivist, cultures.

A recent Harvard study, which focused on the US, mirrors these findings: 36% of adult respondents admitted to feeling lonely 'frequently' or 'almost all the time or all the time'. This included 61% of young people aged 18 to 25 and 51% of mothers with young children.[7]

Less embedded and more virtual social interactions mean that we have to opt in rather than opt out, so it makes sense that time-poor urban millennials on the lower rungs of the professional ladder, disabled people and new parents do not have the energy for it, and are falling through the net. Given that loneliness

is one of the biggest indicators of wellbeing and longevity, disconnection – along with the pressures that cause it – could be set
to snowball into a global health crisis.[8] Perhaps it already has.

In the UK, the average age for a diagnosis of depression was
45 in the 1960s. It's now 14.[9] In the US, 15% of youth have
experienced a major depressive episode in the last year, and 4.6%
of adults report having suicidal thoughts.[10] In Canada, mental
illness is the leading cause of disability,[11] a direction which is
visible globally. The WHO reported last year that the number
of people disabled by depression increased by 33.4% between
1990 and 2007.[12]

Anxiety disorders, where worry becomes so potent as to gnaw
at your sense of self have exploded, affecting 25% of children in
the US. Reliance on mood-altering drugs has become mainstream. Hospitalisations for self-harm and eating disorders in
the UK doubled between 2013 and 2016, to the point that
self-injury became the leading cause of death for 20- to
24-year-olds.[13,14]

While I'm not going to claim to have isolated the cause of a
mental health epidemic, we cannot separate these downwards
trends from their context, from the Petri dish that enabled their
growth. George Monbiot writes that our growing mental health
crisis is the canary in the coal-mine of a toxic culture, a broken
lens through which our worlds are experienced:

What greater indictment of a system could there be than
an epidemic of mental illness? Yet plagues of anxiety, stress,
depression, social phobia, eating disorders, self-harm and
loneliness now *strike people down all over the world*. The

6

latest, *catastrophic figures for children's mental health* in England reflect a global crisis.

There are plenty of secondary reasons for this distress, but it seems to me that the underlying cause is everywhere the same: human beings, the ultrasocial mammals, whose brains are wired to respond to other people, are being peeled apart. Economic and technological change play a major role, but so does ideology. Though our wellbeing is inextricably linked to the lives of others, everywhere we are told that we will prosper through *competitive self-interest and extreme individualism.*[15]

The health benefits of communal life are well documented. 'Selfish herd theory' finds the root of our draw to one another in our origin as a hunted species. We formed packs where members had a duty to protect one another so that all members had a greater chance of survival. Social connectedness is at the core of what makes us human. Maslow, and his over-cited hierarchy of needs, put social connection and belonging as the thing we need most after personal safety. It comes before freedom, status, self-esteem, achievement or success. Conversely, the opposite of social connection, social pain, coming from loneliness or rejection, has been shown in studies of dogs and capuchin monkeys to elicit extreme distress which can even exceed that of physical pain.[16] That our bones can be broken by sticks but we are left unaffected by unkindness is, by all accounts, inaccurate. We were aware of that even as we chanted it in the playground.

Positive social interactions, though, have the opposite effect. They give us greater confidence and improved resilience. One

2010 study of 300,000 participants found that having a healthy social network was twice as likely to lead to a long life than either exercising or giving up smoking. A lack of positive social connections makes us more likely to experience stress, and in turn anxiety and depression. Loneliness literally erodes the fight in our immune system, with its effects spanning the interwoven duo of physical and mental health. One Swedish study found that those with few or no good friends were 50% more likely to have a heart attack.[17]

And it's not just our personal health that is affected by the diet of time-starved individualism that has carved up communities into individual or household units. Living more separate lives can impact our societal and environmental health too. More deliberate and streamlined communication can, if we're not careful, leave us with artificially carved communities of similarity, meaning that those we're interacting with day to day are more likely to hold the same views as us, come from a similar background and be in a similar age group. A recent discussion amongst my millennial professional friends revealed that none of their peers voted for Brexit and they couldn't name a single friend in receipt of Universal Credit or PIP payments.

If we're more siloed and don't have positive connections with those who have different perspectives, it can leave us disagreeing at a distance, via polarised online soundbites. A number of studies show that on key issues both Brits and Americans actually hold a greater consensus than we have done at previous times in history, but the way we communicate across difference from opposite sides of the room can feel like we live in times of unprecedented division.[18]

Our siloed worlds put us at a distance from those who are different from us in class, race, generation, ideology and experience. We love to do fund-raising marathons, or share black squares on our Instagram accounts for Black Lives Matter but how much difference can it really make campaigning for communities whose complications and disadvantages – unintentionally or not – are at arm's length? Whose struggles and fortunes we don't have a stake in. Being part of a community with others gives you a stake in their flourishing, it necessitates dialogue and promotes equality through resource sharing.

One of the most amazing, and admittedly most uncomfortable, parts of our communal set-up was that it disrupted the power dynamics of charity that I'd been taught were the building blocks of compassion. Volun-tourism and white-middle-class-saviourism were the norm in Surrey where I grew up. We'd give to Comic Relief and see teenage friends go on World Challenge expeditions 'helping' to build orphanages, but be advised to avoid certain parts of Croydon.

Community doesn't allow one party to be 'service users' or 'charity cases', and another the comfortable altruism of being a 'volunteer'. Or to cast one political identity as heroic and the other as villainous. 'Othering' becomes less comfortable once you become mutually dependent participants of community, whether you're in need or in surplus, young or old, conservative or liberal, Black or white, rich or poor, cis or trans. Community life didn't make me a better person – in fact, it made me more aware of how self-interested I am – but it did make it harder to choose the easy route. Marginalised voices or, even worse, the ones I'd rather cast as villainous, have to be part of the dialogue if they're sitting at the table drinking a cup of tea.

As well as sharing dialogue within our silos our individualism can shape our consumption habits too. Capitalism, the invisible framework for much of the world we live in, sees people primarily in terms of their economic value; we are producers and consumers. It is far more effective for a healthy market if our consumption habits centre on the individual. We're on a conveyor belt where there's always a better product, one that's more tailored to our individual preferences.

If we have no one, or just our own family with whom we collaborate on the day to day of life – the eating, living, and scheduling – and if we limit ownership to those groups too, then the environmental cost sky-rockets.

As individuals, our consumption rate is far higher. The 'personalised experience' is the ultimate luxury, products tailored to reflect our personality, preference and desires. An individual model of consumption is brilliant news for corporate interest, but less so for the planet. The likelihood is that most homeowners along your street or in your apartment building will have a drill, selected from the large range of drills available to meet their needs. Those expensive drills, living in their plastic carry-cases in sheds or under beds, will have been used for an average of ten minutes each.[19] Buying food in single-person units also increases overall consumption. Without others to prepare and eat meals with, those living alone waste 40% more food[20] compared with those living in groups, contributing towards the 6–10% of global carbon emissions caused by food waste. Each day thousands of cars with thousands of empty seats will be travelling in the direction that you need to go.

Drawing our circles of reliance and ownership around small household units rather than wider community groups means that our patterns of consumption are being duplicated millions of times across millions of households, each of whom are likely metres away from another similarly equipped group. It makes our time more efficient, sure, but the additional costs in carbon and resources are vastly inefficient which, at some point, is likely to become the more important metric.

If we're going to address our climate crisis then a more conjoined sharing economy will be a crucial part of the equation, redrawing our lines of ownership in wider arcs.

*

So, when connectedness is so core to human, societal and environmental wellbeing, why do the single-person, family-sized or couple-shaped households that most of us live in not reflect this priority? Why have we not sought alternatives to the individual worlds that are the path of least resistance?

The short answer, I think, is that there don't appear to be many credible alternatives. In order for something to enter the realms of possibility we need to be able to see it working well.

Communal living has yet to be seen as a large-scale credible option. The topic regrettably conjures up images of polygamous bonneted home-educators, Idaho apocalypse preppers and loinclothed ersatz gurus with a disproportionately young and female following. The popular show-reel of communal life comprises Louis Theroux looking uncomfortable at an orgy, ex-Mormon children spinning out of control after leaving coercive homes and exasperated starched nuns trying to solve a problem like Maria. Dangerous iterations aside, at best, most of us think of communal living as something for other people, a bit kumbaya.

Even my own grandma, on hearing the idea for this book, commented, 'Who will want to read this? The Russians? The Chinese?!'

In order to see these more communal forms of living as possible options we need to see people similar to us choose them, to feel assured that these other options would still allow us to still be ourselves and prioritise the things we value. But what if there were credible options that we could learn from? What if there were people radically shifting the frameworks towards communal living in successful, healthy and replicable ways?

Admittedly, our DIY model of intentional community didn't offer a sustainable solution. Despite its successes in some areas, ultimately it buckled under the pressures of modern life. The experience, though, situated me in a conversation with people across the world who've been doing it much more successfully for much longer. Groups who are, in a spectrum of different ways, rejecting the assumption that family units are the only route to connection available.

An 'Intentional Community' (IC) is the catch-all term for groups like this. As a model for living, they're much more common than we think. For many of us, our lives are book-ended by it. First in student halls and house shares and then in care homes or independent living developments. Although we see these as quite normal, beneficial to our progress and wellbeing even, efforts to live more communally in the middle section of life are often viewed with more suspicion. It's this middle section that we're usually referring to when we talk about ICs.

The following chapters will cover a range of different expressions but broadly they come under the umbrella of 'groups that have consciously designed community connection into the way they live together'. They have chosen to hold communal assets, share space in some way and to establish a set of values and practices which shape life together. There's a definite overlap with a search for utopia: ICs often attract people who have grouped together in the hope of living in better ways, improving on the status quo through critical mass. They are idealists and optimists, entrepreneurs and traditionalists, environmentalists living in forest camps and Buddhist monks sustaining centres of prayer.

The set of values and practices doesn't have to be as all-encompassing as a monastic rule of life, it could simply be an agreement that defines considerate living between members of a cooperative. Likewise, the way they're challenging the status quo could range from ensuring quality and affordability of housing in the face of soaring property markets and insufficient supply, to a radical opting out of capitalist systems through self-sufficiency and pooled income.

Thirty years ago people might have more comfortably used the word 'Commune'. The term implies a quite closely knit household – some even use the phrase 'chosen family'. Here, space and resources are shared to a greater extent. As communal living has sprouted more commercial expressions and become less associated with other subcultures, the term 'co-living' has been popularised. It has closer associations with the co-working movement.

'Cooperatives' refer to a framework of ownership where property is owned by a society or association in which residents have a stake. Life in a co-op can look more or less enmeshed.

It's a movement in flux so many people involved might disagree with how I've defined them and there are also plenty of intentional communities which don't fit easily into any of these sub-groups, and sit in their own categories. Eco-villages, where individuals can buy their own self-build plots, set alongside communal farmland and meeting rooms, rehabilitation centres where residents stay on to help newcomers and residential special interest groups, like an intergenerational disability inclusion project, are all part of the patchwork.

The terms, in any case, are often used interchangeably to fit different focuses.

The directory of intentional communities lists 764 communities in the US as well as hundreds more across South and Central America. There are more than 400 across the UK, ranging from eco-villages to intergenerational living projects, from religious and spiritual groups to traditional agri-communes.[21]

These types of living may not be the mainstream yet but they are growing in popularity, with the pandemic serving as a catalyst for change. James Dennis, who helps coordinate the UK-based network of intentional communities, Diggers and Dreamers, tells me that this is normal. That following every major disruption, whether it's the 2008 financial crash, austerity movements or wars, people get a little more disillusioned with self-sufficient living and a little bit braver about trying other options.

The trend is reflected across the spectrum of ICs: housing providers have pumped hundreds of millions in investment into developments that recognise owners' social as well as material needs; interest in rural communalism has exploded over the last two years, meaning established communities have been inundated with applicants; all over the UK and US there are campaigns to reform planning and zoning laws to reflect more conjoined ways of living; people seeking to live in greener and more affordable ways are joining together in cooperatives to provide sustainable solutions to the housing crisis. Whilst multi-family households still represent the smallest proportion of housing set-ups, the Office for National Statistics reported in 2020 they are the fastest growing household type.

Individually, these groups will not provide a blueprint for how we should all live, a one-size-fits-all answer to the mental health, climate and housing crisis, but I think, on a small scale, they are able to offer alternative options that are being modelled in beautiful, messy, small, quiet ways, outside of the spotlight.

*

I want to find out what we can learn from these groups about how to build more interdependent communities. I want to discover whether there are models for communal living that can be compatible with the pressures of modern life, sustained alongside children, full-time jobs, grief and health problems, that can work for families, business owners, younger and older people, across lines of race, class and disability. At a time when we're realising that the individualised world we've inherited and built for ourselves has contributed to our mental health crisis, divisions in society and our looming environmental emergency, I want to scope out the other options.

This journey of discovery will be a literal one, taking me to visit communities across the UK and Europe. It is a journey that, for me and my partner, is not purely academic. We're feeling the edges of our individualised life chafing at our sides, the constant time-poverty, the over-consumption, the neighbours we've never met. We often wonder whether we could be living another kind of life, a more conjoined, kinder and greener one that could help us opt out of some of the norms we've slipped into.

We once had an assembly at primary school where the teacher told a quite harrowing story about boiling a frog. 'You can't drop a frog in boiling water,' she told us, 'it'll just jump out. But if you put it in a cold water pan and turn up the heat, it won't notice the water gradually warming around it until it boils.' It's always stayed with me, that story.

It's what many of us feel like, I think, that we were swimming in cold water while the pressures of capitalism and globalism gradually increased around us. We started working longer hours, buying more, feeling more anxious and depressed, feeling too stretched to invest in the things that matter or connect with those outside of our comfort zones, pulled at on all sides. And suddenly, we're boiling frogs, warmed gradually into a reality that we didn't choose and didn't even notice had been shaping our environment.

Four weeks before the first visit is booked in, two red lines tell me that whichever type of home we build for ourselves will be the one I bring a baby into. I've seen, over the last five years, how having children has changed the shape of my friends' lives, how they have suddenly found themselves a little more alone, barred from the usual swirl of socialising by these new circumstances. The saying goes that it takes a village to raise a child, and yet new mothers score higher in loneliness statistics than almost any other group. A 2020 US study of parenthood found that 32% of parents with young children always or often felt lonely and 82% felt lonely at least some of the time.[22]

The solitude that can accompany parenting, where respite from time at home is often served up in the form of expensive baby classes, has been, for me, the biggest point of hesitation in deciding to start a family. Will losing the mobility required for opt-in community leave me feeling lonely and overwhelmed? Will it shrink my social world? Have I got enough of a support network around me to make it work? Our quickly multiplying embryo is a reflective surface, a boulder blocking the path of least resistance and asking us to question what version of home we'd like to parent in.

Despite the calm and comfort of our world of two, we miss the unavoidable hum of community life, the sense of purpose it brought being bound up more closely with the fortunes and challenges of others, the way that being part of a collective gave us the resources to be a place of safety and welcome to people that needed it. Whilst I'm writing we'll also move in, for a trial period, to a County Durham community farm where, we hope, families will live together sustainably and provide space for women in crisis.

The truth is that whilst I hope we'll find a model of communal living that will fit us, I'm nervous that it will feel like a leap too far, that my longing for a more conjoined, compassionate life will jostle uncomfortably against my parallel priorities to create a space of security and safety for our own family. In the back of my mind, I wonder whether those who chalked our communal life up to the idealism and radicalism of youth will have been right.

I've written a lot so far about why people might want to find alternatives to a status quo that doesn't work for them, but for most people living more communally, the journey towards it is far more about what they're being drawn to, than what they're leaving. I want to feel excited about the new life we could find, rather than simply dissatisfied with the one we've got.

Communal living, especially with a larger critical mass, gives you greater opportunity to shape the world you live in. Shared ownership gives members the opportunity to have fewer, or even no, possessions. Eating in a group makes it easier to shorten your food supply chains, where the time burden of ethical living is shared. You have the opportunity to step out slightly from the norms we've been given and set the culture, to imagine a new way of life. Do you want to live plastic-free? Take the climate crisis seriously? Create space for disabled members? Celebrate and include queer folk? Renounce individual ownership? At its best, communal living can help you step off the carousel. With enough people, it can be a blackboard on which you can redesign what is of value and live in a way that reflects that.

Even though our intentional community only lasted for seven years, looking back, I'm amazed at the number of ideas, projects and campaigns that grew out of conversations that took place in that kitchen. We regularly ate with people we'd never have had cause to meet otherwise. We painted protest banners on the dining table, held our own version of TED Talks in local cafes sharing ideas on social justice and community change. We joined political campaigns. Those who chose to join the community had in common the audacity of believing that a better, different world is possible, and the even greater audacity of believing we could help to bring that world about.

More than half the ideas failed, but it didn't matter. Our bin-diving turned into a food intercepting organisation founded on our top bunk with a bitten-ended biro. REfUSE CIC now runs a large warehouse, cafe and catering company that collects around 13 tonnes of food each month and redirects it to local communities. It's run by almost 200 volunteers and provides training for people who have come through the criminal justice system or have faced long-term unemployment or poor mental health.

Discussions about ethical media spawned a grass-roots tabloid, training citizen journalists to tell their own stories. Men were empowered to become full-time parents and women, managing directors. My partner Sam helped to found a refugee choir with Syrian refugees that went on to tour the UK, perform in Parliament and release an album. We planted an allotment together with young people on a nearby estate and registered others to vote for the first time, wearing fancy-dress in the market place. The collective 'Yes We Can' spirit expanded our perception of what was possible. It was what the entrepreneurial communities I spoke with called a 'bias to action'.

Of course then we had organisations to run, funds to raise and safeguarding policies to write and so the violently fizzing chemical reaction of enthusiasm, passion and possibility simmered down to a slow buzz. But the feeling that it left us with, that a better world is ours to create, has never gone away.

Whilst we visit groups, newly formed or upholding thousand-year-old traditions, I want to learn how we can all live in more conjoined and locally connected ways, how we can shift the building blocks of life in different patterns. I want to ask those that are in the business of designing more connected, resilient and less divided micro-societies, what life can look like if we throw the cards in the air and shuffle the pack of priorities back together in a different order.

CHAPTER I

How we got to where we are

I N ORDER TO THINK ABOUT what kind of communities we want to build, we should probably start by asking how we got to where we are. In two generations we have moved from having active community centres, Blitz spirit and mixed generational living, to corporate care homes, anonymous neighbours and M&Ms that can be personalised with a photo of your own face.[1]

It would be easy to paint younger generations as more selfish, we hear it a lot, and the generation below me even more so: 'People these days just don't care about their neighbours like they used to, they're too busy taking selfies, watching the Kardashians and buying avocados.' But these tropes reflect little of a generation who have sought to be aware of the issues facing their near and global neighbours, a generation who are often engaged and compassionate.

Billions of individuals didn't just wake up one day and consciously choose to construct a different set of norms; we were pulled towards an individualised version of normal by political, cultural, technological and economic currents much stronger than the sum of the individual choices that created them.

In philosophy, the 'cosmopolitan' school of thought, dictates that our primary regional identity should be as a 'Citizen of the World'. It advises that when we think about our responsibilities ethically, we should think about what we owe humankind rather than be biased towards our families or local communities. Although the theory has its roots in fifth-century Greek cynicism, it has been, until the last two decades, more or less just a theory. It's a nice idea being a citizen of the world but in reality our identities and sense of duty are moulded by those we see and spend time with. That's why people can obsess over the wellbeing and development of their own children but demand the imprisonment of Syrian children crossing the channel in RIBs.

The age of the internet has turned the slightly niche philosophical idea of Cosmopolitanism into an achievable reality. Younger people often see regional or national pride as parochial, a closed-minded preoccupation of the boomer generation. If we look at the points of social connection for digital natives – the 18- to 24-year-olds that have grown up with the internet and know nothing different to global connectivity – we might get some way towards explaining why 95% of them don't know the names of their neighbours. They know, instead, neighbours of experience and preference all over the world.

Of course, that can be a really good thing. Climate activism, political movements and traditionally marginalised groups have found strength in numbers when their connection is not tethered to proximity. It is, though, a framework which can leave us more connected to those we seek out, but less connected to those on our doorstep. We may have billions of people available to us, but they can't visit with a casserole when we're grieving or bring round shopping when we're sick.

We don't have endless social energy and financial resources. In the same way that being able to access thousands of retailers at the click of a button has drawn financial spending away from our local high streets, spending our social energy more widely across the country and world cannot help but leave a deficit of local connectedness.

Of course, the internet cannot totally be to blame; it reflects change as well as creating it. Its frameworks can manipulate our social habits or change our focus and priorities, but can't easily be separated from a tangle of other factors that have made our generation and the one to follow, slower and more reluctant to put down roots.

Younger generations have infinitely more opportunities than previous ones. The number of options available to the average person in 1970 or 2010, compared with those in 1870 or 1910, are incomparable. We can move anywhere, can choose to not have children, live on a barge with cats if we want to, take photos of our beautiful lifestyles and call it a job. The world has become our oyster, so why would we sit at home eating fish fingers?

It's also true that when it comes to some crucial categories, we have fewer opportunities. In 1996, 90% of 25- to 34-year-olds would have been able to afford a house in their local area. The unprecedented house price inflation in the following decades, with wages not following suit, meant that by 2017 the Institute for Fiscal Studies reported that just 35% of 25- to 34-year-olds owned their own homes.[2] These figures starkly correlate with the likelihood that a person would know their neighbours.

You cannot separate feeling ownership and responsibility towards your local area from literally having some ownership of it. Why should people invest in a place they can't afford to stay in, where they have to work fifty-hour weeks for a room in a shared house of mis-matched mugs and tired Ikea furniture, employing fairy lights and Blu-tacked posters by way of personalisation. It might seem a small thing, but something as simple as being able to change the colour of a wall or put up a shelf can be significant in engendering belonging. So much so that at Handcrafted, the charity where I've worked with the women's team, it's a key part of how we disrupt cycles of homelessness or unstable housing. New trainees who are often deemed difficult-to-house and stuck in cycles of chaotic living, start off by choosing a paint colour or coming to the wood-workshop to make a piece of furniture to personalise their new house. The dividends this pays in the form of stability and belonging are far more than the sum of paint, brushes, time and timber.

When we talk about belonging, the idea that people need to be 'stakeholders' is really central. In order to be a stakeholder, to state the obvious, you need to be holding a stake. In other words, to have a personal investment in something larger, like a place, business, community or society. If the business or community gains, you gain, and if it loses, you lose. This mutual fortune is the currency on which communities operate. As younger generations increasingly cannot afford to buy their stake, the barriers to belonging are built higher. It is one less point of contact with the ground, one less meaningful tie to physical place.

Along with home ownership, for many people, employment has failed to provide anchorage either. In a dramatic change from the 'Jobs for Life' that characterised careers starting in the 1950s, people now change employers on average every five years and re-train into different sectors multiple times, leaving professional lives far less static. Recent research by the female-only members' club AllBright, found that of the club's members, mostly well established in their industries, one-third felt anxious about job uncertainty.

For those without permanent contracts, the treadmill is running faster. Zero hours contracts, freelance work and side-hustles in the same breath allow flexibility and instability. 66% of people on zero hours contracts would prefer the increased job security brought about by fixed hours.[3] People are not choosing them.

But it's not just that a rocky jobs market itself makes employment feel less binding, it's part of a bigger reality that the rise of free market capitalism has inducted us into a system obsessed with growth and success, that always asks us to focus on the next step rather than the spot we're standing in.

Rowan Williams, former Archbishop of Canterbury describes the social problems that arise when an over-centralised market becomes our norm.[4] Our instinctive sense that we need balance between productivity and rest has been written over by a narrative of constant and relentless growth, projected loudly by advertising firms and political leaders. Growth is the measure of our country's economic health through the tracking of Gross Domestic Product (GDP). If we're not growing, we're told, it is cause for concern, ignoring the reality that it's a growth-centred mindset that is squeezing the planet dry of its resources. We can't keep on going forever.

This cult of progress did not even let up during the Covid lockdowns with mummy bloggers posting about how their six-year-olds had got to grips with permaculture and nutrition whilst being home-schooled, Duolingo users increasing by 300%, and we endured relentless posting of inspirational encouragement on social media as people felt they needed to emerge from the global crisis like a butterfly from a chrysalis with some sort of meaningful learning or attained goal.[5] In this framework our rest too becomes a reward we earn and a means to an end, attaining mindfulness to optimise productivity.

Our cultural commentary even encourages us to leverage trauma for personal growth. We buy inspirational books from people that have turned pain into success as though that were the most appropriate response. We share viral images of disabled people completing Herculean feats captioned with 'Don't let anything stop you achieving your goals' as inspiration porn. I've done it myself, writing a positive think-piece about what I learnt from the early death of both my parents when what I mostly learnt is that I could barely cope.

Talking about personal, professional, social and fitness goals in a public setting has never been more culturally mainstream. #friendshipgoals, #travelgoals, #bodygoals, #careergoals, #couplegoals and #stylegoals have been tagged hundreds of millions of times on social media by individuals sharing their achievements. Even #squadgoals, perhaps the most mainstream of these hashtags, reframes our social connectedness as personal attainment.

The cult of capitalist ambition, sponsored by Reagan's tax cuts and Thatcher's free market policies may have changed its branding since the 1980s but its centralisation of the individual and the family unit has remained embedded in our cultural consciousness. The millionaires of the eighties boom, in pinstripes with brick phones, have swapped places with tech billionaires in hoodies trading NFTs and flying to space, but they're telling us the same thing – that we can have anything we want if we work hard enough, that we deserve success, and should design out inconvenience and inefficiency to achieve it. This focus consumes huge chunks of our time and then tells us to strictly boundary the rest of it. 'No one is entitled to your time and energy except those you choose', it announces before draining us dry.

Individualism has co-opted ideas and language from the world of mental health, wellbeing and psychology, and stretched them to its demands. Boundaries, protecting energy, surrounding yourself with good vibes and positive thoughts, and even safe spaces when repurposed to serve the priorities of capitalism can be a get-out-of-jail free card for individualism, unchallengeable because of their origins in healthy communication even when they isolate the people they were designed to serve. If we buy into it, we can be the masters of our own destinies, our lives never more tailored and individualised, but never more disconnected to one another.

Seeking a life that's better, faster and stronger is premised on some dissatisfaction with the lives we have. It's left us working incredibly long hours to prove our worth professionally, to qualify ourselves for the next thing, and to afford the higher costs of housing, interesting holidays and leisure activities that make our jobs seem worth it. People in the UK now work longer hours than any other European country, an average of forty-two hours a week.[6] Adding on a fifty-six-minute commute, or eighty-one minutes for Londoners, it leaves us with precious little time and energy to invest in the costly business of building and sustaining local communities that we're renting in. Our American counterparts are working similar hours but are entitled to just ten days holiday a year, compared to twenty-eight days in the UK.

We are, I think, pretty exhausted.

As with financial capital, social capital is invested, returned and invested again. The more we have, the more we are able to have, connections spawn connections, belonging engenders belonging. The feeling of being less grounded then, unless interrupted, only breeds more of the same feeling. It makes us less likely to invest in our communities, receive support from them, and see value in them. It makes us build our lives in a way that is broader, but less deep, less imbedded and less interdependent. We have rhizomorph roots spanning large areas but failing to establish depth in the soil and it is, after all, depth and stability of roots that enables health and heights of growth.

Community, cult, coercion and best intentions

O NE OF THE MAIN THINGS that puts people off exploring more communal patterns of living is that, for many of us, communes are synonymous with cults. There are actually quite specific markers that define a 'cult' but the ways we use the term, in quite a throwaway colloquial sense, are far broader than their boundaries. We talk about 'cult' brands, *The Rocky Horror Show* being a 'cult classic' and devotees of the 5:2 diet being part of a 'cult following'. Lumped into the term are ideas about obsession, fandom and group identity, mellowing the psychological definition into a pop culture adjective. One might describe their SoulCycle class or a railway enthusiasts' subreddit as 'a bit cult-y' and mean to convey exclusivity, belonging or niche interest rather than systematic psychological control. Co-living spaces and communes which have provided a breeding ground for a number of cults, are easily sucked into the word's orbit.

They're having a moment, cults. As part of the true crime wave that launched a thousand podcasts, there have been a string of programmes, films and series picking apart the conception, anatomy and downfall of the most bizarre and awful ones. It's not difficult to see why they make such compelling car-crash entertainment. The stories are absurd and so terrible that they leave you thinking, surely normal people can't have participated in that? And yet they do, in great numbers. Ian Haworth, an ex-cult member and cult expert I spoke with said that, as a conservative estimate, over 1,000 cults are currently operating in the UK and thousands more in the US. They can be split into three categories: religious or spiritual cults, ideological cults and therapy cults.

If you're thinking, but they could never recruit *me* because I'm too savvy, then you'd probably be wrong. Ian shares a theory of John G. Clark, Harvard Psychologist and world expert on cults, who suggested that rather than cults picking off the sick or vulnerable, being neuro-typical and mentally well actually makes you more susceptible to the psychological conditioning used by cult leaders because psychological conditioning is designed for use on the average mind (a small victory for us neuro-diverse folk).

In case cult-fascination has passed you by, I'll give you a flavour of a few that have hit the headlines.

OneTaste was founded in 2004. To an outsider, OneTaste was a US-based wellness start-up which promoted orgasmic meditation (OM) as a self-care and trauma healing practice. Participants in OneTaste's workshops took part in ritual cliteral stroking where either a partner or another workshop attendee would 'stroke' the women repetitively in order to achieve a meditative orgasmic state. They hoped to popularise OM so we would talk about it in the same breath as already established practices like yoga and meditation.

Ceremonies, conducted as part of their workshops, allegedly involved 'priests of orgasm' and included a ritual where a topless woman was stroked by seven men. Although this description for most readers would be enough to raise suspicion, OneTaste, and its founder Nicole Daedone, were actually seen as a legitimate movement, innovators in the growing 'sexual wellness' sector.

Daedone used the language of female empowerment and health to dress quite suspect practices in an acceptable cloak of wellbeing, healing and sexual empowerment. This platform allowed Nicole to be written about in *Vanity Fair*, appear on the cover of *The New York Times* Style section, give a popular TED Talk and feature on Gwyneth Paltrow's platform Goop. Behind the scenes, a BBC Radio series alleged, OneTaste employees – mostly former clients, who'd come in search of their full selves – got into debt paying for courses, were not properly paid and were coerced into sexual acts in OneTaste's residential OM houses. Former members describe Daedone as a 'messianic' character. OneTaste are now the subject of FBI inquiries over allegations of sex trafficking, prostitution and violation of labour laws.

OneTaste said 'any allegations of abusive practices are completely false'.

Ian told me that the kind of non-specific but warm and fluffy language I heard in OneTaste's media output is very typical of cults. Websites will talk about energy, love, empowerment, salvation and brotherhood but in terms that make it difficult to work out exactly what the structures are, and what is being promised. This linguistic overlap with the sometimes less-than-scientific wellness movement can make therapy cults harder to spot until you're inside them, perhaps easier to slip into for those who imagine cults as a religious problem.

Probably the most well-known cult-disaster is still the Jonestown massacre. Jim Jones's socialist community moved from San Francisco in the 1970s to establish the People's Temple Agricultural Project in Guyana, a utopian farming community more often known as Jonestown. The People's Temple had been operating in San Francisco for some time already and had even been involved in local politics. One former member reported being drawn to the community because they offered drug rehabilitation support to her family who were struggling with her teenage sister's substance abuse.

On the promise of establishing a Guyanan Utopia, free from inequality and to avoid increasing scrutiny from the San Franciscan media the People's Temple moved en masse from SF to a 3,000-acre plot in north Guyana, helped along in their migration by special dispensation from Guyana's socialist government.

On the surface the group seemed community-centred and ambitious. Numerous local officials praised the project. Jones's wife described the community as 'dedicated to live for socialism, total economic and racial and social equality'. Quite soon though, Jones's erratic control led to a deeply coercive environment. Jones demanded that members work six days a week from 6.30am to 6pm, followed by hours of rambling lectures about socialism, delivered by him over loudspeaker. TV was replaced by Soviet propaganda videos and any TV shown on the community's closed circuit system had to be accompanied by a Temple staff member who would help viewers come to the correct 'interpretation'. It was said that Jones studied Adolf Hitler's manipulation techniques in order to maintain control and was constantly paranoid about being attacked.

Following a visit from Californian congressman Leo Ryan in November 1978, which Jones feared would end in a negative report, Jones called a whole community meeting. An estimated 907 people died that night after they were convinced to drink fruit punched laced with cyanide in loyalty to Jones and the movement. The incident, which was the origin for the phrase 'they drank the Kool-Aid', became the world's most famous mass-suicide murder. One survivor reported that he believed they'd been given sedatives with lunch, which led the community to calmly accept the poison. Armed guards stood at the exits should they have decided not to.

The 'death tape', a forty-four-minute recording of the service, begins with Jones telling his followers, 'how very much I have loved you. How very much I have tried to give you the good life.'

Although religious and spiritual cults have different tools of persuasion, they actually don't look particularly different from ideological or therapy cults when it comes to methods of psychological conditioning and structures.

The 'Children of God' was founded in California by David Berg in the late 1960s. Though comprised of Huntington Beach hippies, with an anti-establishment bent, they started off with fairly orthodox evangelical beliefs, preaching abstinence and devotion to God. Like many other Christian groups, the Children of God used music to grow their following, filming music videos which took their message of exciting, young, anti-establishment Christianity to thousands.

By the 1970s, the cult claimed to have 10,000 members in 130 countries, many living communally in a former training ground near Dallas, Texas. Their way of life together was heavily shaped by the belief that a world-ending apocalypse and the return of Jesus was expected in 1993. Within their community traditional families were replaced by one large communal group where individual parents did not have autonomy over parenting. Because the world was soon to end, children were barely educated. Berg, also known as King David, or Mo, was mostly reclusive within the community but still dictated large and small aspects of life, from which jobs were allowed to how many sheets of toilet paper could be used per visit. He communicated the required beliefs and practices though his 'Mo letters'. He sent over 3,000 of these, which included changes in community beliefs, sermon-like admonishment and sometimes pornographic drawings.

An affair with his secretary and devoted follower Karen Zerby led a once-abstinent Berg to begin teaching polygamy and free love. In a 1980 Mo Letter entitled 'The Devil Hates Sex! – But God Loves It!' Berg declared that as God had invented sex for the benefit of humanity, they should enjoy it. His policy of sexual 'sharing' meant members could request sex from other members, including children. This extended to 'flirty fishing' where women were required to recruit new members through sexual activity.

Sylvia Padilla, a former member, shared in a 1994 documentary, 'I was convinced (sex) was like a duty. Sometimes you were revolted . . . but if you were asked and you refused you were going to be labelled selfish, unloving, uncaring and that you didn't really belong.'

There are thousands more similar examples.

Haworth also believes that any effective response to terrorism would acknowledge that terrorist groups are cults too. They follow the same patterns, grooming their recruits using similar techniques, promising community, enlightenment and belonging before taking control of their members' lives.

People don't choose to join cults. They present themselves to be loving, supportive communities that people want to join. In the same spirit with which we ask female assault victims what they were wearing, victim-blaming is rife within popular narratives around cults. We ask 'how could they have been so stupid? So blind?'

In fact, I can understand better than most why the idea of surrendering your personal goals for the sake of the shared rhythms and goals of a wider group could cause some red flags. For most of my primary school years, my family attended a church that has since been called a cult by the press and public.

I've rolled the word around my mouth, typed it out and deleted it, tried it out with my sisters and still it doesn't feel like it quite fits our experience, quite fits my assumption that they are something that happens to other people.

Coulsdon Christian Fellowship was a group I still have fond childhood memories of, though viewed now through a cracked lens. I helped to run the tuck-shop at the youth club selling astro belts and Freddos to other kids. For the millennium I choreographed a dance with my sisters at the church's New Year's

35

party accompanied by fluffy puppets we'd bought from the Gadget Shop. I cat-walked across the carpet-tiled hall in a paper and Sellotape reconstruction of the 'armour of God', including 'shoes of peace' and a 'belt of truth'. So good was the 'armour of God' activity I planned for the group that it won 'God-slot of the year' by popular vote.

As children we thought Howard Curtis, the church's leader, was a bit creepy. We made fun of his gruff booming voice, audible above the congregation during the hymns and I did sheep-like impressions of his singing with my two sisters baa-ing away to the classic tune 'These are the days of Elijah'.

Howard wore string vests, with the diamonds framing thick, black chest hairs and invited members of the youth group to 'special meetings' in his office. We opted out when our friends went in, rather than be confined to an unventilated room with his sweat-patched shirt. We only realised two decades later what we might have avoided.

He could be a stern character, quite demanding, but he also ran a chess club which helped children from underprivileged backgrounds to access chess training and competitions. As his lawyer stated at the trial, he was 'thought of highly' by many in the church and community. He had a grand vision to transform a former mental hospital and its large grounds on a hill nearby into a Christian mega-community and an aerial shot of the land was blown up and displayed on one wall of the church, a ten-foot image we'd look at as we prayed for his vision to become reality. Someone even claimed to have received a prophesy from God that we'd take ownership of the land and encouraged the congregation to financially support it. Money given to the church was talked about in terms of 'investment' from which congregants could expect both financial and spiritual return.

Even when we moved on, partly because of concerns around accountability, it wasn't prompted by scandal or upset.

In 2016, the church's leader Reverend Howard Curtis, was jailed for six years over eight charges including spanking naked church members for his own sexual pleasure. The judge summing up described him as controlling and bullying. Curtis allegedly claimed the spankings were a mental health treatment for trauma and would cure a 'a spirit of frigidity' improving the sex life of the victims. These crimes were committed as part of what he called 'Christian Domestic Discipline' and they stemmed from the belief that men should exercise spiritual authority in the home including physical discipline. I remember absorbing smatterings of this idea, that we shouldn't date until we intended to marry, and should find a man whose leadership we respected, but the presence of our matriarch mother who baulked at the idea of promising to 'obey' meant that the ideas didn't take hold in any permanent way. We were too busy eating Freddos and making up dance routines.

During the trial we asked my mum why she'd left the church, whether she'd known anything of what was going on. She hadn't, she told us, but recalled hearing Howard joke about how he could 'sleep with any of the women in the prayer group'. It had been a catalyst for us leaving. It wasn't the joke itself that had been the final straw, but the fact that when she'd asked him about it later, he'd denied ever saying it, and told her she'd misheard or made it up.

Either suggestion is absurd. My mum was autistic and had an extremely black and white view about truth telling. We never had Father Christmas in our household because she hadn't wanted to lie to us about his existence, and we knew where babies came from as soon as we'd asked in early childhood.

I'm still not sure whether 'cult' is the term that fits what transpired – you can have abusive leaders without having cults but I was reminded, whilst researching this chapter, of Howard's small bending of the truth to his will, and how it mirrored the way other cult leaders manipulated the truth. Leaders whose gaslighting opened the door for what followed.

If you want to check whether a group you're part of has cultish leanings then the best metric, counter-intuitively, isn't the group's beliefs. Groups whose worldview you find abhorrent are actually no more likely to be cults than ones that you subscribe to. Some of the biggest cults of the last century have been built around courses to 'improve your life', to appreciate every day and find greater happiness and success, sentiments that are unlikely to trigger any alarm bells.

Instead cults are defined by their practices, Ian tells me over Zoom. His work in the field over the last forty-three years has helped thousands of people escape coercion and understand how to help family members. Cults, he outlines, will have five trends.

First, and most importantly, they will use psychological methods to control members. The list of twenty-six methods he gives reminded me of the techniques that, in my previous job as a women's support worker, we helped women who were leaving coercive relationships to understand. They include 'love bombing', where members are pulled between being made to feel special and being subject to control, encouragement towards blind acceptance of confusing doctrine, removal of privacy, peer pressure, sleep deprivation caused, for example, by demanding late evening or early morning meetings, humiliation and isolation from friends and family.

Second, the group will take the form of an elitist totalitarian society. Elitist in the sense that they present themselves as the only group offering salvation, truth or happiness, and totalitarian in that you're unable to question these claims. The unique truth they're offering could take the form of a special connection with God, but it's just as likely to look like unlocking a practice that will lead to ultimate health and wellbeing, or political Utopia.

Next, the group will have an unaccountable leader. This leader is a special conduit to whatever unique benefit they've advertised. The leader is usually charismatic and might have special knowledge of a life-changing practice only available to you through paying for an expensive course, or they could claim to have special communication channels with God. In some cases the leader actually presents themselves *as* God.

Fourth, cults will believe that their end justifies the means. The Children of God's flirty fishing, garnering members through pimping out current ones, was justified because it brought people into the family, Daedone's sexual duties because they affirmed loyalty to the OneTaste philosophy.

Lastly, these groups will generate wealth that benefits the leader rather than members of society. Even in cults where squalid standards are described, cult leaders enjoyed a greater quality of life. Keith Raniere, founder of the wellness cult NXIVM, allegedly amassed hundreds of millions of dollars through selling life-improvement courses that would break down the self-esteem of its recruits and then be their source of affirmation. Members were branded with Raniere's initials whilst naked and tied at the wrists and ankles. Before their skin was marked they'd be asked to say: 'Please brand me. It would be an honour. An honour I want to wear for the rest of my life.'

Members of a group are not going to readily admit to being in a cult. They may not even consider themselves to be in one. Instead, the best approach is to ask practical questions. You need to know what's going to happen on a daily basis. What sort of diet is available? How much sleep do you get? What sort of relationships can you enter into? Who elects the leadership? What is the process for disagreement or complaint? If it's a religious group, is it associated with other groups of that faith or partnership projects? Is information restricted? Is it easy for friends and family outside to visit?

It might seem like a distraction to begin a book about finding healthy communities by delving into the world of unhealthy communities but actually the dividing line between the two is quite fragile. Communities can have deep problems without being cults, just like marriage can have deep problems without abuse or coercion.

Although cults are a specific category, behaviours that fall inside the definition of psychological coercion will have been experienced by all of us, whether that's in the context of a nuclear family, a workplace or a social group. The Cult Information Centre, founded by Ian Haworth, lists uncompromising rules, dress codes, peer pressure and a feeling of superiority created by finger pointing at the outside world's flaws as techniques used in coercive environments but, in reality, these are present in social clubs and sports clubs the country over without being dangerous. Cults represent a specific concentration of unhealthy community dynamic but they don't have a monopoly over dysfunction.

Whilst none of the groups I am visiting fit all the criteria for a cult, they will all be, in various ways, dysfunctional. Our attempt will be too, I expect.

It's also worth saying that these groups will be full of people whose views I disagree with. I realise this puts me on a bit of a tightrope in terms of tone. Popular wisdom can have us using disagreement primarily as a tool with which we communicate who *we* are, rather than accurately represent those we're disagreeing with.

I could brand these groups only by their flaws, by political, social and religious positions that differ from my own so that my condemnation would situate me on the right side of the cultural divides. I could reduce their rich cultures and lifestyles to a point of difference to make it clear where I stand. I think though, that I probably wouldn't learn much by going into communities with my judgement as a talisman.

You'll have to allow me a little grace on this one, I'm afraid. I'm not going to offer a scrutiny of the political, religious, economic or moral beliefs of the groups I visit, but rather look at the bones of their life together, both good and bad. I'm not looking for the perfect model for communal life which could be upscaled and rolled out countrywide, but rather want to learn from the flawed humans having a go.

Each of these groups will have former members who have been hurt by them, who have not felt included or valued or seen. The problem with Utopia is that its building blocks are flawed humans bringing their prejudices and failings along with their ideas and hopes. This isn't to minimise anyone's pain or disappointment. I've been in a place where I've invested a huge amount of hope and resource into something that's disappointed and it can be really painful.

It's vital to go in armed with knowledge about how community can become coercive but the truth is that no attempt to achieve Utopia will be perfect, and that sacrificing autonomy will always come with risk.

Throughout our community experience I am confronted with the reality that my own flaws are there to crash the utopian party. However perfect the vision of community we design is meant to be, I have no choice but to accompany myself into it along with my neurotic thoughts, self-doubts and judgemental opinions. There are times when I get so used to being needed that I depend on it, make it my own self-care. Communities are full of martyrs and idealists.

The larger the scope of your belief in the possibility of change, the wider the door is opened for disappointment to come through. As Lana Del Rey puts it, hope is a dangerous thing.

CHAPTER 3

Life at the Bruderhof

I T WAS A THROWAWAY LINE in a BBC 1 documentary, *Inside the Bruderhof*, that piqued my interest. I was half watching the TV and half browsing bathroom designs on Pinterest. Another tab was scanning flights to Marrakesh because an interior design Instagram influencer I liked had posted the perfect glazed tiles she'd bought in a Moroccan market.

One of the dads on the programme, who we would later meet, was busy feedings pigs with his family and talking about how the community helps them resist individualism. 'I don't want my children to grow up in a world where they're always thinking about themselves,' he said. 'I want my children to grow up thinking about other people. I don't feel the need to cram our children's lives with toys, they have so much more.'

I'd been on a bit of a consumerism binge since we moved into our own space. Having lived for five years in an environment with bunkbeds and practical furniture where my husband Sam and I had limited control, I now owned multiple vintage decanters and had recently spent £700 on an impractical velvet armchair. I deserve this, I'd thought, when I'd unwrapped it and positioned it next to the Ficus for a filtered photo. The world agreed with me in the medium of heart-eye emojis.

Like many of us, at the same time as I furnish and fund it, I'm frustrated by my own consumerist bent and wish I was satisfied with a minimalist lifestyle. I am very much a runner on the treadmill of capitalism, constantly consuming, not just material things, but achievements, experiences and accolades.

We were away recently with a friend Pat, who's in her sixties. We were sitting in her time-share in the Lake District, where she's been coming three times a year for thirty years, eating the same lunch of boiled eggs, sliced ham, salad and coleslaw she makes on every visit. 'Where would you go,' I asked Pat, 'if you could click your fingers now and be anywhere in the world, doing anything at all?'

She thought for a moment, looking out of the window at the drizzly view of Ambleside, its church tower and hilltops obscured by mist. 'Here at the time-share,' she replied.

I found her level of contentment shocking. The idea that the place she wanted to be most in the world was the chair she was sitting on stayed with me for days after. Not climbing in Machu Picchu, not eating fresh mozzarella at a Tuscan vineyard, not at the Albert Hall listening to Handel's *Messiah* but on a beige dining chair in a rainy English town serving us lunch.

What would life look like if I stopped listening to advertising premised on my dissatisfaction with life? How transformational would it be if I learnt to find contentment on the patch of earth I'm standing on? What would life, and global equality, look like if a posture of gratitude and sufficiency became instinct rather than constantly browsing for better experiences, professional progress and social growth?

Pat has captured something that, if universally adopted, would dismantle global capitalism: to be happy with just enough. Perhaps I would learn it too from the Bruderhof.

Before our visit I came across a Pathé short film about the Bruderhof made in 1959. An RP voiceover exclaims against a background of ruddy-cheeked children stacking turf: 'The twentieth century has been dubbed the "Aspirin age". An age of high pressure living with the majority of people under some kind of strain. Trying to keep up with the Joneses, trying to keep up with the hire-purchase payments, with the rent, the butcher, the baker, the milkman, the lot! So it's a happy change to see an industrious, cheerful community who have succeeded in eliminating practically all tensions of daily existence!'[1]

Though the video glosses over what was actually a turbulent and divided period of storming and reforming for the community,[2] the sentiment is only more relevant now we've swapped hire-purchase agreements for credit cards and milkman's milk for Netflix subscriptions.

Although the Bruderhof's Darvell site sits nestled within the ring of London's commuter belt, the conservative Christian community most exemplifies amongst those I'll visit how intentional communities have the capacity to separate themselves from cultural norms, to design and implement a new society in small scale.

In close adherence to a quite literal interpretation of the Bible, members of the Bruderhof renounce personal ownership, career ambition and even decisions about where they'll live. Included in their lifelong membership vow is a commitment to relocate to any of their twenty-nine global locations should the size and skills allocation of the community demand it. Along with the main communities there are outposts: the Bruderhof's members were at Calais distributing food in the 'Jungle' and in scrubs at New York's Coronavirus field hospitals.

It is the most enduring community I'll visit: the Bruderhof has existed in some form for over 100 years. They are resolutely pacifist and the two World Wars provided a catalyst for many early members to join as their groups become a haven for conscientious objectors.

Bruderhof members themselves spent much of their early period as refugees as they fled conscription and internment, first from Hitler's army, then from the British army and finally from conscription to Vietnam. One German member tells me over breakfast that when his father joined, he was living together with men who had fought in opposite trenches, having to learn to deny their own preferences in favour of those they'd once called enemies.

Their website's introductory pitch reads: 'Love your neighbor. Take care of each other. Share everything. We at the Bruderhof believe that another way of life is possible. We're not perfect people, but we're willing to venture everything to build a life where there are no rich or poor. Where everyone is cared for, everyone belongs, and everyone can contribute.'

Their vow of poverty means that none of the Bruderhof members have a bank account or salary. Before taking a membership vow you must give away everything you own, usually to family, charities, or to the community.

While I'm there I have tea with a Yorkshire couple, who had joined after they retired. They joke about the concern and confusion of the staff at the bank after they requested that their entire savings be emptied and the account closed. 'Were they of sound mind? The subject of some grand fraud?' Their family were also baffled at first as to why their parents would suddenly dispense with their hard-earned money and move far away from them. It was a good trade for the family though, the husband laughs, they got their inheritance early and they won't have to worry about looking after elderly parents or clearing a house. As with all older people, housing and care will be provided for them by the community.

The main source of income for the Darvell site is a large toy factory, Community Playthings, which mostly makes outdoor wooden toys for nurseries and schools. Last year the company had a £17 million turnover and almost £5 million profit. This money provides for many outside the community too: income inequality is not only eradicated within the community but also within the Bruderhof's global network of 3,000 members living in twenty-six locations. The residents encourage each other to live more simply so they can redistribute the wealth created by their business to the less well-resourced Paraguayan or Korean Bruderhof.

I'd spent the night before we arrived at the Bruderhof's Darvell community at a bottomless musical brunch in a London basement club. West End performers circled us belting ballads and swinging *Chicago*'s fish-net legs over our heads whilst we ate Japanese Bento boxes. Sashed hen dos fought for the attention of the prosecco servers that circled the tables trying to make the most of the 'bottomless' hour. I arrive at the 300-strong community in Robertsbridge, a Sussex commuter town, my boots still sticking with over-sweet wine. It is January, my first community visit, and I am in the throes of the first trimester of pregnancy. I'd spent the train journey alternately reading their guiding documents and retching into a paper bag.

We are picked up from the station in one of the community's cars, driven to the Bruderhof's nearby compound and shown to our accommodation. Within their electrical gates[3] is a village. Our flat, identical to those lived in by other couples, is in one of three large purpose-built blocks that join a factory, school, offices, farm and meeting hall to make up the site. There's also a grocery 'store', doctor's clinic, swimming lake, walking routes and biomass boiler that serves the community's energy needs.

Each of the new-build accommodation blocks, along with a repurposed manor, house identical micro-flats which branch off shared kitchens and bathrooms. Singles are attached to families and older people to those that provide support so, as well as being part of a wider community, members are part of smaller, family-like units.

Our host family, Deborah and Ray, are a couple about our age with two young children. They greet us with a finger-printed welcome sign made by their toddler and a food-laden table.

The first morning, we're up for a 6am breakfast after which we're given our first jobs for the day – on the production line in the toy workshop. Women start work an hour after the men to leave time for tasks in the home and school drop-off, which would usually get me on my feminist soap box but it's very difficult to protest when I'm left with an hour to drink tea and write after Sam goes off to work.

Outside in the corridor the women sing as they get on with the day's domestic tasks. Across the week we become quite familiar with the Bruderhof's repertoire of a cappella songs, a mish-mash of pan-European folk and sung graces. They span such topics as gratitude for our lunch to the migration of the musk ox. Had I encountered these pre-9am levels of bonhomie in the outside world, I would assume it was a preamble to whether I was happy with my current gas supplier or would I like to sponsor a stray Cypriot dog? Here, the geniality cannot help but rub away at my regularly worn cynicism. Although barely awake, I have admired frosted grass lawns, commented on the beautiful sunrise over a breakfast table and exclaimed aloud to myself how delicious my herbal tea is.

On first glance, as I start to absorb life at the 'Hof' (pronounced H-oh-f to rhyme with loaf, not H-off like the iceman or the actor), I'm drawn to the magic of the earth-mother aesthetics of the community. I love the way the cows are milked each morning for our cereal; the school where the year 8 children spend afternoons chopping wood for the boiler; babies in cloth nappies playing with wooden toys; the swimming lake where residents exercise; sourdough bread picked up from the community's bakery at dawn by children in pinafores streaming towards its warmth. In my free hour I wander down to the farm to scratch the ears of pigs and watch calves' breath mist into the cold air.

Ian, who works on the Bruderhof's magazine *The Plough*, tells me later over dinner that if I focus on those elements, I will miss the point. The media often tries to frame their life as a twee home-baked Utopia and ruddy rural cheer but, he reminds me, glosses over the radical adherence to the teachings of Jesus which is the central and only relevant value of their life together.

Mine is a common misinterpretation. The most upvoted comment on one of their YouTube videos of Laura, a young woman at their New York State community reads: 'I swear, this is Anne of Green Gables in real life.'

Ian makes sure I'm aware that the rose-tinted play-farm which I find so arresting, falsely centralises elements of peripheral importance and sanitises their radical Christianity into a rustic olde worlde Center Parcs that says very little about who they really are. I delete some paragraphs I wrote on the train.

When I get to the factory at 9am I'm introduced to two sisters in their fifties, Tikva and Channah, who will take on the role of my work aunties for the duration of our stay. Along with the long skirts they both wear headscarves, which in the last few years have become optional for women.

Channah gives me a pinny, sewn in another workshop on-site, and shows me how to screw planks from the wooden play-blocks together. Like all the work stations, mine has an adjustable work bench and tools suspended on retracting arms so they can be used with minimal physical strength. Across from me is an elderly man in a wheelchair doing the same job as me, along the bench is a woman in her eighties completing the next stage in our production line, and across the room is a young woman with cerebral palsy who, despite significant challenges around movement, with the help of her carer, plays a vital role sorting different sized rubber caps so they're ready for attaching to the cut edges of wood.

Channah tells me over our fresh mint tea and apples at 'morning snack' that she was book-keeper until this week and a classroom assistant before that. 'Is it not inefficient to just swap people round, after you've trained in a specialism?' I ask, gnawing at a lopsided apple that had been a supermarket reject from a nearby grower.

'Efficiency isn't our main goal,' she counters. 'Our main goal is to value people and do things well.'

For someone whose education and career has been built on a currency of competition, this is hard to get my head around, even though I am theoretically very critical of the capitalist framework which sponsors this view. In truth, I found the pace of things at the workshop a bit jarring. After my first hour-long shift I'd already worked out the best way to stack the wood in lines of three so I could maximise my output and felt a guilty pride when my pile of finished stock was larger than the elderly and disabled man opposite, who operated the drill with shaking hands.

In the outside world, our organisation is paid to take on staff with additional needs, to adapt our environment for them; here, their inclusion is automatic, not an afterthought but woven into the building blocks of the business and life together.

As no one receives a salary at the Bruderhof, and everyone gets the same accommodation and assets irrespective of input, productivity levels are not a metric of value in the workplace. There are different jobs, requiring different skills, but there are no gold stars for my well-ordered planks. Their website describes how jobs are organised: 'Each Bruderhof appoints brothers and sisters to be responsible for the various spiritual and practical aspects of the common life: pastoral leadership; stewardship of money and goods; education of children and youth; hospitality and outreach; and work departments such as farming, maintenance, kitchen, health care, and our workshops.'⁴ Although requiring additional responsibility and expertise, in theory, none of these positions entail better accommodation, higher rank or a nicer lifestyle.

Though not everyone I meet feels that socialism accurately represents how they operate, the Marxian maxim 'From each according to his ability, to each according to his need' is stamped through the Bruderhof's structures. Not just in the factory but across the site.

I help Channah clear the mugs from morning snack and she takes me through the bowels of the communal kitchen to return the milk bottles, bucket of apple cores and mugs to their relevant places. We walk through the industrial kitchens, abuzz with preparations for the community's lunch, made in vast floor-to-ceiling ovens, and cauldron-like stainless steel boiling pans. We travel down into the 'stores'. It's the room where members go to help themselves to shelves of food and collect the items they've ordered from the store manager. No one earns money, so of course, they can't shop for themselves either.

People are asked to consider carefully what they feel they need before submitting requests but for the most part items are bought as asked, allowing people to decide what feels important to them. Although the community is anti-smoking, one older man who takes comfort in the habit orders cigarettes every week and they are duly bought.

Shopping baskets labelled with people's surnames hold trainers, bottles of port and German beer, lightbulbs, new underwear and chocolates to be collected alongside the staples available on the shelves. Channah tells me that her husband loves to put requests into stores. She often stops to ask him whether he really needs what he has ordered. It sounds quite like me and my husband Sam, I tell her, when he's trying to order more model trains he doesn't need and we don't have space for.

Stacked up on the central table are three large hampers full of sweets, crisps, chocolates, cards and wrapped presents. 'Most guests wouldn't see those!' Channah tells me. These are birthday hampers ready to be distributed to residents who are celebrating that week. With 300 birthdays each year, these are a frequent sight. 'That's a whole job,' she continues, 'putting those together, working out what the person might really like on their birthday.'

As we make our way back to the workshop and begin work again, she tells me how her family came to the Bruderhof. Her father, Josef Ben Eliezer, a Jewish man, fled Hitler's Holocaust as a child, then was interned in a Russian Gulag where his mother died of starvation. His father sent him to find safety in Israel. Later he joined a Zionist army, fighting for the establishment of a Jewish state. Just a short time after being a victim of persecution, he found himself participating in violence and persecution to evict Arabs from their homes and towns in order to accommodate Jewish settlers. Horrified to have perpetuated the same violence that had held his family victim and disillusioned with faith and nationalism, he was in a dark place and searching for answers when he found the Bruderhof. Many years later, though Josef is no longer alive, his wife is still drinking tea in the workshop with his daughter, and the grandchildren he never met are at the school across the path.

After another hour and a half of work, lunch is served in the dining hall, as it is most days, where all 300 members gather to share bulletins, group singing and the day's main meal. The pre-food announcements include updates on current affairs, news of the marriages and deaths of former residents, and a notice about a community meeting that evening. This seems late notice for such a big meeting but as childcare is collective, and nobody has any other plans anyway (you can't go to the pub without any money), most of the community are free to attend. This is a world away from the months of WhatsApp messages and protracted social admin it takes me to organise a weekend away with four friends.

'They usually tell us on the day,' Channah explains. 'It can be a challenge for those among us who are particular about having our diaries organised in advance but it suits Alan!' She gestures to her husband who we've been sitting with for lunch. Though they're both older, they're newly-weds. They prefer a plant-based diet and their lunch comes in a separate Pyrex dish, one of a dozen which make their way around the room to the vegetarians, lactose intolerant and gluten free. I get one too, cooked to follow the pregnancy guidelines I sent over in advance and marked with my initials on the top. Two women who are celebrating their birthdays today wear flower garlands and are brought ice-cream sundaes.

Alan surprises me by taking a smartphone out of his pocket to check a news app. I'm already suffering withdrawal symptoms from my own which, with the exception of a quick email and social media triage during my domestic hour, I've left in our room.

Though the Bruderhof have Instagram and Twitter accounts, a popular YouTube channel and a website for their business, technology occupies a fairly limited role in their day-to-day world. I am keen to match them for the duration of our stay. Organising our many visits to different homes, we communicate at lunch or snack times. We knock on doors, rather than sending messages to confirm times and places. There is wifi but I find hardly anyone uses it. One of my interviewees tells me I can find her playing ball on the field between 8 and 10pm.

It feels like the early nineties again, a time I mostly spent standing outside Woolworths waiting to meet a friend at an appointed time. There is a projector for films but no one has a television and from what I can see, laptops are confined to the office rather than used after work. There's an internal library, and residents can order in books and newspapers through the 'store manager'.

Their insulation from the slipstream of popular culture means that references to Taylor Swift, *Ready, Steady, Cook*, Ant and Dec and Amazon Fresh at various times require explanation. At first, this blows my mind: 'You honestly have no idea who Taylor Swift is? Ant and Dec, you know, Ant, and Dec?' But after a few occasions of incredulity I feel like a disciple of capitalism lost in a foreign land and wonder if it's my version of normal that's slightly askew.

My screen-time goes from hours to minutes for the first time in years. It is a relief. It means I am more present and connected all week, fully immersed in life in the community and less plugged in to a thousand distractions. I'm shocked after we leave to find out that Boris Johnson's lockdown party admission, and all the commentary that accompanied it, had passed me by.

I wonder whether the internal focus leaves people feeling more cut off from the outside world? Whether it matters that

I have missed an announcement from the despatch box that ultimately won't impact my day-to-day existence in any tangible way? Or whether they're missing something by unplugging? A self-imposed censorship?

Later in the week Deb, who's a school teacher, asks me and Sam to share our experiences in her class. She emphasises how important it is for the kids to hear external voices as they discover their own way in the world, particularly as visitors have been sparse through lockdown and space for these outside influences has been slim. Some of the young people play in a village sports team where they have friendships outside the community but both primary and secondary schools are within the community.

In part, external culture is restricted to help maintain a unified whole and a distinctive Christian culture. This separation is not a by-product of their life together but part of how their unique life is sustained. Some aspects of culture filter down regardless. A number of the teens and young adults are wearing Nike or New Balance trainers they'd requested from the stores, twinned with practical jeans and ankle-length skirts. This concession to mainstream culture is rare enough to be remarkable though.

The library does not stock *Fifty Shades of Grey* or *Harry Potter*. Kanye does not play through the speakers or *Derry Girls* from the TVs. Beyond news sources there is limited engagement with current trends. They do not put on headphones to listen to Nirvana albums after teenage arguments. For better and worse, members do not have access to Instagram filters.

Teens growing up at the Darvell site will represent an increasingly small percentage of British teens not receiving sex education from internet porn. Nor do they watch programmes like *Sex and the City* or *Fleabag*, which might uncritically portray non-monogamy, casual sex or spectrums of sexuality and gender.

There is a phrase that often crops up on several Instagram accounts which I follow, aimed at broadening out the ways in which Black, LGBT, fat or disabled people are represented.[5] The phrase 'You cannot be what you do not see' accompanies unremarkable but oddly un-common content depicting Black dads and their babies, trans people in the media and disabled people in professional settings. There are bigger women in swimsuits and women with facial disfigurements giving make-up tutorials. The idea of these accounts is to rewrite the contrived norms we've absorbed our whole lives, to disrupt those shutter-stock images of middle-aged white men in boardrooms and blond-haired Madonna-and-child-esque images of ideal parenting that we've been given.

The types of role models available to those growing up at the Bruderhof are curated. The swirl of cultural norms available to the average British child, whether that's misogynistic porn, fast fashion and normalised war-play or healthy same-sex relationships, are edited down for those growing up at the Bruderhof. They cannot be what they do not see.

The Bruderhof believe that marriage was intended by God to be a lifelong commitment between a man and a woman, and it sees these unions as central to the community's structure. Their foundational documents state that God 'intended (marriage) – a relationship unlike any other – for the bearing and rearing of children'. There are a lot of children at the Bruderhof.

Their dating process, referred to as courting, is also very de-sexualised. After time in thought and prayer with parents and the community's pastors, would-be couples spend many months in private discernment and discussion, writing letters and walking along the path that circles their land. One newly-wed tells me that a kiss or even handholding would ideally not happen until couples had committed to get married. She feels this gave her and her new husband the chance to focus on what really mattered: whether they could disagree well, whether they wanted the same things from life, whether they had fun together and shared ideas about faith and the Bible.

Alongside a life-long and heterosexual view of marriage, gender roles within Bruderhof marriages are 'complementarian', a view which holds that men and women have 'different but complementary' roles. This, again, is from their foundational documents: 'The callings of man and woman in marriage are different, yet equal in worth. According to the New Testament, the husband is to be the head of the family, and the wife his helper. He must never dominate her, but should cherish and serve her in humility.'[6]

Whilst I can respect that a woman can be a feminist as well as a stay-at-home mum, or might want to observe life-long sexual chastity or wear a headscarf, I've seen the complementarian school of thought in my childhood church begin a very dark road. If the available scripts around sexuality and gender young people are exposed to are curated, are they really free to choose?

Footage and photos of the community often focus on these beliefs around gender, showing women in the kitchen and men on the farm, so I'm surprised on our visit to see the office and factory equally populated by women and men changing nappies and organising breakfasts. Contrary to my assumptions, the women I meet talk of feeling empowered, feminist even, and are fed up that the outside world makes assumptions about them being oppressed because of choices they've made. With so much help around them and a large group to share the domestic load, I've rarely seen motherhood so celebrated and supported.

In the end it is not specifically the gender politics that make me feel uncomfortable, as I anticipated, but rather the self-denial practised by everyone, regardless of gender, the giving up of control that membership entails. The meeting announced on our first night is a group study on obedience. Men and women pass around a microphone, sharing stories about when they've found it hard to sacrifice their will, but felt it necessary for the unity of the community. They've prayed for the strength to set their own preferences aside. Across the week there is talk of members choosing to give up academia, environmental activism, career ambitions, hopes of marriage, sexual preference, freedom to travel and autonomy over what they wear and read, all for the sake of their collective faith and individual purity. Without hierarchy or money involved and when membership is a choice, this obedience is not in the context of an obvious power dynamic that would make it abusive, but instead it is owed by everyone, to everyone. As someone who's expressed both their spirituality and activism in the form of resistance, of protest and reform, I struggle to get my head around it.

My husband talks to a worker in the factory who is considering joining the Bruderhof about whether he's ever wanted to let loose, head off to the pub or binge a Netflix series, just put the moderation and self-denial on hold for an evening and indulge his worst qualities. 'Do you ever just think "fuck it!"' Sam quite tactfully asks over packaging tape and manilla boxes.

Personally I couldn't and wouldn't conform to their scripts of gender, work, belief and lifestyle and yet, I can see a deep integrity in their self-denial too. In some ways, I envy the learnt selflessness of the community. 'It's easy to be against things,' a German man whose father had fought in Hitler's army shares tearfully over breakfast one morning. 'But what are you for?'

'Can you really feel free at the Bruderhof when so much is prescribed?' I ask Kaiya, a woman in her twenties. 'When you're even told what to wear?'

Kaiya is funny and irreverent. We'd met over red wine and crisps after an evening meeting and she'd told me about living in Peckham whilst she went to uni and going with her mates to Wetherspoons. When I interview her she describes finding her teenage identity in football and feminism.

'I'm not saying I love the long skirts,' she responds, laughing, 'I've just realised they don't really matter. Women are told what to wear and how to look everywhere, by their work, the beauty industry, media and fashion, clothing shops. Living here, I don't care about clothing. How I look isn't important, the pressure's off.'

'The thing is,' I reply to Kaiya, 'I completely agree with you that clothes aren't of fundamental importance but I couldn't bring myself to wear the skirt, even so.'

I would reflect on her words again the following week, preparing for a visit to the wellness-focused London community, Mason and Fifth. I'd spent the morning fretting about what to wear, borrowing from my sisters' wardrobes when I'd rejected the contents of my own. As much as I prized my freedom of appearance, some external control I had unconsciously subscribed to *was* setting an invisible standard, making me feel that my clothes were inadequate. In my freedom to choose I was still submitting to eternal control.

Conversation with Kaiya brings me to a much wider question around community living: How important is it for communities to have agreement and consensus? Or can a community can be as enduring as the Bruderhof with more diverse views, backgrounds and life experiences?

I should say that there's actually a wide diversity of views on many things at the Bruderhof. There are ardent Brexiteers and ardent remainers, would-be Trump supporters and passionate socialists. Their practices today are not fixed either. Headscarves were discussed, voted on and made optional. The new Korean Bruderhof chose not to wear the long European skirts in their context. They've done things differently before now, Ian tells me, and they will be different again in the future.

There is an agreement across the whole community, though, that these areas of difference play second fiddle to unity and should not get in the way of community cohesion. Individuals are entitled to whatever views they like, but self-regulate the importance of those views in favour of avoiding community disruption.

Alongside a decision towards unity over difference, there are lines in the sand where members must agree: marriage, pacifism, same-sex relationships, euthanasia, abortion and economic justice, for example. These outer edges exist in every group, whether they are explicit or not. Even the online community created by Queer House Party, an LGBTQ+ group whose USP is inclusivity, draws its own line; displayed behind the DJ is a banner that reads 'Fuck the Tories'.

The truth is, many of the communities I'll visit are a bit, well, samey. The environmental groups will tend to be middle-class, naturist groups quite white and middle-aged and religious groups quite politically homogeneous. Despite actively trying to connect across divides, our community was mostly marked by similarity too. Though our guests were asylum seekers, formerly homeless, queer and international, this diversity was never reflected proportionately in our permanent residents. The Bruderhof, too, regularly welcomes guests of all cultures and religions. There are visitors of all flavours but members are a consistent vanilla.

Like marriage, does it help to have things in common for long-term cohesion, or are communities much weaker for their homogeneity?

The question draws me to find out more about the Harlem Ashram, a community whose central tenet was unity across racial division. The power balance and different ideas about their vow of poverty meant their life together was productive but short-lived. Founded in the US in the early twentieth century, they used collective power to establish a community which embodied ideals they hoped to see played out globally, a pilot project for widespread social change. Their inter-racial community, inspired by the teachings of Gandhi, provided training in non-violent action to those wanting to challenge segregation. They 'helped

Southern African Americans migrating to the North find housing; investigated the use of violence by the police in strikes; created a credit union run by and for African Americans, Puerto Ricans and other minority persons; organised neighbours into a cooperative buying club; and conducted play activities for children on the streets of African American and Puerto Rican neighbourhoods.[7] Set in the context of the civil rights movement, their inter-racial community spanned extremely different views and life experiences. The ripples of their community were wide. One resident, Ruth Reynolds, became a leader of Puerto Rico's independence movement and another, James Farmer, led the 1961 Freedom Rides.

Pauli Murray was another former resident whose experience there helped shape her activism. The African American lawyer became a central figure in bringing together struggles for racial equality and women's liberation and is still celebrated today as a forerunner of intersectional feminism.

One comment wrote, 'The Harlem Ashram was short-lived, but it had a long afterlife . . . The life and afterlife of the Ashram represent a microcosm of 1940s Harlem: a city where African American, Caribbean, and South Asian populations, ideas, practices, and movements creatively converged in the 1940s, with effects that rippled irrepressibly outwards, across the United States, back to India, back to the Caribbean, and forward into the future.'[8]

The diversity that made the community so effective, also made it quite short-lived. There was disagreement about whether it was a 'definitely Christian ashram' or a broader fellowship and more fundamentally, despite being a group that championed racial equality, white men were over-represented in the governance, something that often happens in community development projects now. The community's vow of poverty, for example, borrowed from other monastic traditions, did not recognise that many African Americans had already come from a context of poverty and were trying to escape it. The impact of the Harlem Ashram was undeniable but its flame burned brightly and quickly. In truth, I've not come across similar diversity amongst the longer-established communities I've seen, communities which bring to mind the phrase 'birds of a feather, flock together'.

Is there less space for individuality in communal living? Or is a certain amount of self-denial part and parcel of living life together? Where is the right balance between being able to live out your unique identity and identifying as collective?

I ask Kaiya what she thinks, whether she's been able to champion individual identity within the collective. 'Do you feel you can really express yourself here?' I ask her. 'To be the person you are.'

I think of the startling uniformity of the place, linguistic, cultural and aesthetic markers that distinguish the community as you enter its gates. The long cotton skirts, the particular Bruderhof vernacular spoken in hybrid international accents with a smattering of US tics and fillers, the 1980s wooden furniture and mugs and crockery in utilitarian white, all repeated in uniform as though film set replicas.

She smiles. 'Do you know? Being myself is not something I worried about before moving to London and suddenly there was this huge emphasis on be yourself, express yourself, who *you* are, from advertising, from academia, from everywhere. I think people get so worried about expressing themselves that they don't just live. I found that the more you think about it, the more you get tied up in knots. I'm much happier when I'm taking care of others, thinking about other people. That *is* me expressing myself, that's when I'm really me. I don't feel I have to conform to any norm in how I act or who I am here. I think I'm expressing myself more now that I've got over trying to express myself? Does that sound weird?'

She tells me too about a role model she's found in a Bruderhof woman living at an outpost in Jordan working with Palestinian refugees, enabled to do so as a single woman because of the support of her community.

Kaiya finding her identity in a decentralisation of self is a challenge to a person who evidently values her own thoughts and opinions so highly she's writing a(nother) book of them.

Perhaps part of the truth is that those living at the Bruderhof have less of an illusion of freedom because they've made explicit the submission that is part of all of our lives. I willingly accept the external control of big tech, economic markets, the fashion and beauty industries and Big Pharma, for example, but they're packaged in a film of personalisation, marketed with the shine of individual choice that thinly disguises that we've all made the same individual choices and would struggle to choose otherwise.

Residents here cannot choose their food or clothes. Their choice of spouse is limited and always of the opposite sex. They cannot go to the cinema without asking or head into town for a coffee. They can't pursue a career in the music industry or paint their walls purple. However, they can disentangle themselves

65

from the invisible hand of market forces whose authority we sit under, if they're happy to surrender other parts of their lives.

They can ask themselves, if all jobs are paid equally, which job do I really want to do? They can have children without having to weigh up the childcare costs and recalculate mortgage contributions. They can opt out of social media platforms without sacrificing connection. They can live out their faith in a way that feels authentic. They can operate with an integrity to their principles that seems to me unreachable. I suppose it comes down to whether members here are truly free to choose, whether they've removed the other options themselves or had them taken away.

Our hosts Deb and Ray are keen to emphasise that even those who have grown up in the Bruderhof are encouraged to think very hard before committing to it life-long, to try other options first. 'It's a calling to live this way, and it involves sacrifice. If your reason for joining is that it's what you're used to, then that's not a good enough reason.'

One of Deb's roles as a teacher is to help young people think about what they want to do with their lives, whether that's inside the Bruderhof or not. Most members after school spend time at university, travelling or working away to explore other options before they consider membership. In order to be truly free to choose the life of the Bruderhof, you must be truly free to leave.

The community has certainly had its critics in this respect. Ramon Sender, a former member who left in 1959, with his wife and daughter still at the community, reported being allowed minimal contact with his family and not finding out about his daughter's death for some time after it happened. There are some troubling accounts in the early 2000s from former members who felt unprepared for the outside world; who, after being schooled in the Bruderhof's values, found it painful to find a life outside of them. One woman, speaking to the BBC under the pseudonym 'Samantha', reported struggling with depression and self-harm, feeling as though she must be evil because she didn't conform to the community's norms. Another, who left after growing up in the community, described a 'tremendous culture shock' in the outside world where he found himself floundering.

Since Sender's experience a 'resource office' has been set up by the Bruderhof which has distributed £1.5 million to former members to help them set up outside, as well as providing advice and practical support for those leaving. An Ofsted report from 2018 from the Bruderhof's Sussex school stated that 'leaders work hard to ensure that the school's unique setting does not restrict how well pupils are prepared for life in modern Britain'.

'To those who've been hurt by the Bruderhof, we can only say sorry,' one woman told me, reflecting on a period of fracture in the 1980s.

I ask Ian and his wife how matters around mental health breakdown in the community would be dealt with now. He tells me that they wouldn't hesitate to involve the police in response to accusations of abuse and that members are encouraged to seek external support from NHS mental health services when needed.

'Like everywhere, mental health has been an area that's grown for us. We've had to learn over the last few years how to better address it,' Ian says. As well as a qualified doctor, one of their young women is currently in London training as a mental health nurse to better meet the needs of the community.

It would be easy for me to dismiss the Bruderhof. I could categorise them as saints, as though their way of life is born from some unfathomably bestowed holy glow rather than the daily struggle of self-denial; that it is admirable but ultimately unavailable to us. Or I could zoom in on the ways in which their views differ from my own. I could list their flaws as though that would discount what their complete economic restructuring, hard-won integrity to live according to their beliefs, and radical departure from individualism have to teach us about living together well. The community allowed me neither of these spectating roles. They did not judge my own views or try to preach at me with theirs but rather lived out their beliefs in every meal and moment.

'I'm still not sure what to think,' I tell James Dennis afterwards. James has visited the Bruderhof as part of his coordinating work for Diggers and Dreamers. Despite never having had a faith himself and being part of environmentalist communities, he tells me that he thinks the Bruderhof might be the most successful intentional community he's ever visited. He describes walking back to his accommodation one night and seeing a group of children singing outside a lit window. When he asked what they were doing, they told him that one of the older members inside the room was close to death and the children had committed to sing a repertoire of her favourite songs until she left her body.

Those forgoing career choices, holding back political opinions to champion unity, putting aside climate concern, sexual attraction and preferred clothing choice for the sake of a collective community and their shared faith had so much to teach me about sacrifice.

'Why do we live like this? Because it gives us the best chance to address any social problem the world has to throw at them [the children],' one of the dads said to me. 'Try is an important word here,' he continued, 'because none of us is perfect, we're flawed people. I know that of course there's been loneliness or unfaithfulness in our communities. But living like this gives us a special chance to counter hatred, greed, war, infidelity, loneliness.'

I read from their website: 'Love of neighbour means that we keep an open door. The blessings of a life of brotherly and sisterly community are available to all people, rich or poor, skilled or unskilled, who are called to go this way of discipleship with us. Love of neighbour leads us to give up all private property, the root of so much injustice and violence.'

And yet, as I step on to the train back to London which gradually fills with squabbling school children, jostling commuters, school skirts rolled up and personalised with pin-badges, a cacophony of swearing and chewing, noise and cigarette smoke pulled into the momentum of the oncoming train, there is something of this dissonance that feels like home. Even if I could find a match for my worldviews in the Bruderhof and live there with integrity, my bubble from the outside would have to be more permeable. Perhaps I'd be the single sister in Jordan, the students in Calais, or in the Peckham house.

It reminded me of the lesson I taught to 13- and 14-year-olds at the school, sharing about REfUSE, the food project I help run in the North East: 'Our company works with Amazon to help redistribute their surplus food. They're a company that has made billionaires who fly to space, that has exploited its workers to get there and thrown away electronics containing minerals likely mined from very poor communities just to maintain the product's market value. You could say that by working with them we become part of that system, that we help that unjust system run. It's something I weigh up often.' I'd shared with them. 'When you leave here and decide what your futures hold, whether you'll stay or find a life outside, you're all going to have to make that decision for yourself, draw your own line. How much do you want to entangle yourself in a world that's murky and corrupt but try to live in it with compassion and equality, to be light in a world that can be dark and where do you draw a line and separate yourselves from it. To say "No, I cannot live in this unequal, violent world, and instead we'll build this new one from scratch and show others it can be done."'

Life at the Bruderhof is not a blueprint for the world, but I don't think it's trying to be. In the front of the book I read on my train journey there is a quote from first generation Quakers, written in the late seventeenth century. It reads: 'We do not want you to copy or imitate us. We want to be like a ship that has crossed the ocean, leaving a wake of foam, which soon fades away. We want you to follow the Spirit, which we have sought to follow, but which must be sought anew in every generation.'

I found it difficult to work out how I would implement the things I learnt at the Bruderhof back in my normal life, how I could use it to understand how we'd build our own community.

Their model is not one that could be transplanted into mainstream culture. The Bruderhof is able to exist *because* it exists apart from mainstream culture. As humbled as I was to see what their radical non-adherence to established value systems could looks like, I also knew that the rainbow of opinions, values, identities, beliefs and life experiences of modern Britain could not sit inside its bounds.

What it did teach me, though, is that we are not pawns on a chess board dictated by global systems, that we can in small ways and large, if it's really important to us, reject the version of value, good and family that we've been handed down. With enough people we can rewrite the value systems that govern us; in small ways we can choose to see as valuable what the world has framed as worthless.

At REfUSE, we have a cafe where people are able to 'pay what they decide'. It is a payment system that's not restricted to money – people can pay in time, skills and acts of kindness. This is a relatively small change, but it allows people to see the value in their time and generosity in a culture that may have told them that because they're not economically productive they're not valuable. It has radically changed the way people connect to each other in the space. Customers refer to the cafe's community as family, others credit being able to wash up in return for lunch with their growing self-esteem, connection to others or even addiction recovery. Other customers are happy to pay well over the odds for a sandwich because they recognise that what they're contributing is more valuable than food.

Of course then we leave through those doors and this sense of value-inversion does not translate into the houses and routines of that community, we aren't able to champion holistic economic equality. After a shared lunch there still remains, amongst the cafe's customers, huge income inequality. We do not reshape the framework, like the Bruderhof do, but within the broken framework we have, it is possible to champion a different way.

CHAPTER 4

Luxury co-living: Mason and Fifth and the Collective

MY FIRST TWO WEEKS VISITING communities in the South of England occupied the most opposing ends of communalism's spectrum. In contrast to the Bruderhof's co-living, which sought to create a set of norms that run contrary to mainstream economic and cultural systems and moral norms, the following week took me to visit company founders who have recognised a gap in the market for urban housing with wellness in-built.

These homes, pitched at mobile professionals, are designed to recognise the social needs of their tenants alongside the material needs and the movement is driven by real estate developers and co-living operators. Distancing themselves from the cultural fringes that that have occupied the co-living discussion over the last fifty years, these commercial developments re-market collectivism as a luxury project, pitching communally held assets as a tool for connection.

Making sharing aspirational rather than frugal is an about-turn for long-held views about luxury. Many of us have grown up seeing those who hold what most of us use as public services, privately, as having attained the ultimate signature of wealth. Luxury is chartering a private jet instead of using passenger planes, having a swimming pool at home rather than going to the leisure centre with the rest of us, employing a personal trainer instead of booking onto a HIIT class at the gym. For the wealthy, it's the logical conclusion of the move from public bread ovens to home appliances, building a world where everything you need is within your ownership and personal control. But these days, even the royal family are choosing to fly commercially. There is something about excessive private assets which has started to seem a little . . . crass.

With the climate implications of extreme levels of personal ownership and the disconnection to others that it implies, perhaps use of shared space could become the residential equivalent to private members' clubs. If time, sustainable living and wellbeing are the new luxuries and convenience and community interactions are a primary source of these, aspirational sharing is not such a leap.

In terms of investment, the idea is gaining traction. PMG, a housing developer in the US whose developments total over £6 billion, recently started a co-living department, X Social Communities.[1] Over the next five years, the company has 10,000 beds in development across American cities. It is the WeWork of bedspace, pitching flexibility, opt-out socialising, like-minded clientele and shared resources, including rooftop bars, gyms and saunas.[2]

In the UK, 'The Collective – *be more together*' is London's biggest co-living operator. Started in 2010, it also has sites in Berlin and New York. Their largest block in Canary Wharf describes itself as 'a haven of community and creativity'. At the time it was launched, it was the world's biggest co-living development featuring 705 luxury apartments. Their micro-flats are available for one-night stays as well as three-, six- and twelve-month memberships, with their flexibility marketed as a key part of their appeal for a nationally and globally mobile generation. A single monthly payment will cover council tax, energy bills, wifi and cleaning as well as rent to simplify its tenants' personal admin.

In September 2021, the Collective announced bankruptcy, following its failure to fill its City-based accommodation over the pandemic months and not having the income of fixed-term contracts to rely on. Many people wanted to leave cities in those months but inflexible rental contracts made that very difficult. The Collective's appeal had become its downfall.

Though still in the process of looking for a buyer, the building remains a home to its many residents. My request to look around yields a website link to a 360 virtual tour of the space which comes with the invitation: 'Take a look around and explore our new east London co-living space. Get your head down in the co-working space, work up a sweat in the gym, or unwind at the skyline spa and swimming pool. Why not check out the daily events, from breath work to business masterclasses. After that, retreat to your own beautifully designed studio and relax. This is home.'

The invitation was not literal, of course, but took me to photo and video content of the building.

The tower block includes a virtual reality golf simulator, a music venue, 'mindfulness zones', an aerial gymnastics room, gym and London's highest swimming pool. Your bedsheets are changed for you and socialising and wellness programmes are laid out in a programme which you can select from and feed into. Their life coach Raquel, they advertise, could help you set personal goals for 2022.

In the words of author and urban policy specialist Diana Lind writing about New York's co-living start-ups in her 2021 book *Brave New Home*, 'Wasn't co-living supposed to be a bit more kumbaya than this?'

Or perhaps, divorcing itself from the subcultures that bred communalism and allying itself with the market will be the only way to create connected housing in large scale across the world's cities?

In some ways, it does look like a wonderful place to live. The decor and facilities are far nicer than any of the flat-shares in estate agent windows on a similar budget, if you account for gym memberships, bills and paid cleaners. The trade-off is that the flats themselves are tiny. They offer a 'cosy' flat, measuring just 12 square metres for £1,439 per month, a 'comfy' one of 18–25 square metres at £1,798 and their 30-square-metre 'big' studios, starting at £2,294.

I take the DLR to the Isle of Dogs to get a sense of the space.

Canary Wharf is at the heart of London's financial district and its roads are walled in by phallic glass tower blocks. Although my GPS tells me I'm just by the river I spend 15 minutes trying to locate the Thames amongst the world's banks and branches of Pret so I can use it to orientate myself.

Until I see the sign through a window announcing it, and the ground-floor gym, The Collective is indistinguishable from the offices around it. A hip-looking young woman on reception is busy taking in a large number of packages, the Amazon logo smiling in duplicate up the side of the stacked tower of boxes. A blackboard opposite the entrance advertises circuit training, a New Year reflection on finding connection, film nights and meditation workshops. Though the ground floor cafe isn't open and doesn't look to have been for a while, people with laptops are dotted around low tables in the foyer.

The decor is fairly typical for an East London office-cum-gathering-space. White metro tiles join faux-industrial surfaces and ceilings of un-clad insulated tubes. These are offset by hanging plants and velvet seating in ubiquitous dusty pink. A lift takes you up to the private areas. Upstairs, the communal kitchen is vast. It offers twenty polished concrete counters, each with two electric hobs and access to an oven and sink. Next to the lines of counters are long shared tables and smaller round ones. The industrial surfaces and metal pendant lights which carry through from reception are offset here with tribal artefacts; there's a slightly incongruous spear, a wooden mask and some woven bowls breaking up the wipe-clean white.

The first floor also hosts multiple working, relaxing and social-ising areas where they've allowed a little more plastering, as well as dark green panelling, a library and more quilted velvet. The floors above are filled with studio flats and above those are the swimming pool and rooftop restaurant.

Down in the basement, there is a cinema, a gaming room, and a laundrette with walls of washers and dryers. They've gone for a more DIY effect here and the walls are covered with decals of handwritten gaming symbols and punny marker-pen guides on how to do your washing which edge into student-hall territory.

On first look, there's a lot to commend it. Despite its carpet boycott, set amongst the un-residential lines of the City of London it's clearly offering residents opportunities to find oasis and connection. I am left wondering why the management team aren't more interested in being written about. I leave my contact details with reception and am sent an additional link to the online tour the following day.

If The Collective's claims of providing a home are true, then they're a home with the bailiffs knocking. I wonder how it feels to live in a community whose endurance is dependent on finding a buyer before its assets are carved up and sold off by its lenders. The whole 'This. Is. Home, except better' branding feels quite over-marketed.

Does this awkward dynamic of commercialised cosy pre-date its economic collapse? If people felt a sense of belonging in the space, a real sense of home, would they have stayed in the pandemic?

My visit there doesn't reveal an awful lot but brings me to larger questions. What difference does it make to community building that, at its core, it's profit-driven? What does it mean for communalism that the co-living sector has marketed space sharing as aspirational? Does the re-branding of human connection as a luxury commodity mean that it's defeated its own point?

I meet with Penny Clark, founder of Conscious Coliving, a consultancy which supports co-living developers and operators to embed impact into their communities. She helps those housing developers pushing into the co-living sector to make sure that what they're building is embedded in engaged community and that the building blocks of connection don't get lost amongst the priorities of property development.

'So, in a sense,' she tells me, 'I think it depends from which end of the telescope, you look at it. Co-living might be really problematic or it might be an amazing solution. At the problematic end it's commodified community. It's taking something that people are doing anyway and turning it into a luxury product and delivering it to people. And then if we flip it around and look at it from the other end of the telescope, you might say, "Finally! Housing that acknowledges that we need social relationships, and that loneliness is a huge problem. Finally! Housing that makes sharing really aspirational to other people, that shows that we should value our experiences and our social connections over possessions and large amounts of private space." This could be a solution to climate crisis, to the housing crisis. It could help us to find infrastructures for people that mean they can live with a lower environmental impact. It could mean that they can live in the cities they work in rather than having to travel into the city from a suburb.'

Penny and I both admit a little guiltily that we have an uneasy relationship with intentional community networks. I tried to be vegan but found it too hard. I own a large number of reusable coffee cups but can never find the lids so end up getting the disposable ones and making sure they're out of shot in any photographs. The only company I successfully boycott is Parkingeye, who issued my husband a large fine in 2018 which he still believes was an astounding miscarriage of justice. Even then, I'll still use Parkingeye if he's not in the car with me. I lack the attention span for and interest in any mindfulness exercise that lasts over five minutes.

Throughout my visits this year I'll often feel a little fraudulent knowing those I'm meeting will likely assume that my years of experience imply a greater level of counter-cultural worthiness than is realistically the case.

'This is all very relatable,' Penny admits in response to my confessions. Although she's passionate about communalism and is in a discussion group about a developing community, her and her partner are yet to move in. She visited a number of eco-villages for PhD research around sustainability and was struck with how the planet needed our living environments to change. 'Those eco-villages were lovely, but not everyone is going to live in an eco-village,' she tells me. 'We need solutions that for a start are based in cities and that are a little bit less niche.'

Co-living, and its partnership with big business, offers an opportunity to scale those ideas.

'And, therein lies a big, big tension, right?' Penny shrugs. 'Because when you are a customer, that's inherently averse to being a community member. As a customer you expect to receive. As a community member, you give and you receive. Co-living is like communal living plus capitalism. It's communal living, plus investment and scaling. But scaling can make it very difficult to do something that's sensitive to place.'

She's become more cautious and sceptical but also feels convinced that with good standards of practice, working with co-living developers could change the face of housing so that it's possible to live more sustainable and connected lives in cities.

I'm so used to communal living being the preserve of utopian dreamers that I've previously overlooked more commercial models. Perhaps in my judgement of Canary Wharf's tall chrome banks, my definition of inclusivity is too narrow. If your time is very pressured, or you've been seconded to the City from another town or country, don't you deserve community too?

The currency of most communities is reciprocal contribution. Not having the time and energy to contribute would make the costs of reciprocity prohibitive. Commercial co-living has packaged up their solution to loneliness for single urban professionals and given it a brand makeover and a monetary tag, but perhaps in a world defined by production and consumption, those are the terms that will make connection accessible.

The Collective offer the benefits of community but has outsourced the responsibilities. It does result in a different end product though. If you're just buying connection, rather than also building it with your time and body, it is no wonder that over the course of the pandemic its residents hit unsubscribe. Financial commitment, which makes you a customer before you're a member, leaves you with an easy to reach 'opt out button', a shallower sense of belonging, perhaps?

I sit on a bench on the dockside to eat my lunchtime sandwich. The bench is an audio art installation so as I eat in the afternoon sun, a cockney voice tells me about what it was like to grow up on the Isle of Dogs. She re-lives catching eels with friends and having a network of family knitted across the houses which provided safety for children to play. It is stark that the only cockney voice I've heard on my trip to the Isle of Dogs is playing from a bench.

'People here are from every walk of life,' one resident at The Collective claims in a promotional video. Except that's not quite true. There are global accents but in the heart of East London, no local ones. This is not the fault of The Collective, but it does remind me that the ability of co-housing to provide a solution to London's housing crisis, which has led to an economic and cultural diaspora in London's East End, is not being borne out here. The same can be said for similar co-living projects across the world. In San Francisco, New York, Singapore and Berlin, the co-living sector is driven by the luxury market. Like The Collective these offer lifestyle options, private swimming pools and in-house wellness coaching.

In theory, minimising private assets and investing in communal ones could provide a solution to urban housing problems but not if the real estate developers currently funding these co-living start-ups continue to shape the sector. In order to maximise profits, they must market themselves as luxury products, building spas, bars and rooftop gardens in areas that have a high price tag. The Collective aren't trying to model a brave new world. They're not creating a more equal space where the value systems of modern Western living are displaced to make room for a better way of living. What they are doing is offering a more connected way to live for people living under those pressures.

I walk an hour across London to join co-living operator Mason and Fifth for the day.

In contrast to The Collective's financial straits, Mason and Fifth started over the lockdowns, took a fortnight to fill all of its rooms and have remained full with a waiting list of over a hundred in the eighteen months since. I want to know what made their fate different.

Firstly, their founder Ben Prevezer tells me, they're not real estate managers. They don't own their building which means the team didn't come from a starting point of trying to maximise the return on an asset. Instead they're a co-living operator. In fact, he doesn't particularly like this term either: 'I think co-living is quite a lazy description of the sector. It's coming off the back of co-working and the unicorn that is WeWork. Taking the co- and applying it to living doesn't do enough to explain what we're doing. I see what we're doing as the start of a real look at the all of the ways that we live and relate to cities.'

The distinction between real estate developers and co-living operators is important, Ben emphasises, because it leaves you with an opposite direction of flow. Your starting point is facilitating ways for people to find wellbeing and connection and from that place you find the physical space and finance to host the concept. They see their team as curators rather than landlords.

We get on to talking about The Collective and its troubles. 'Building community, there are some things we wouldn't compromise on. The problem with a 700-unit building is that you have to grab customers as they come because you need to get bums on seats. That's not a great way to build a community organically.'

Even in the bigger buildings they're looking at for future Mason and Fifth sites, the shared spaces would have a maximum number of apartments that they're linked to so that you'd never have over a hundred individuals sharing cooking and socialising space. He also would draw a line at offering one-night stays, meaning that the building doubles up as a hotel. It compromises the sense of belonging and ownership, he explains. And, twelve square metres, he thinks, is just not enough private space.

I'm visiting their Italian Building in Bermondsey. It contains twenty-eight studio apartments and a shared kitchen, lounge area and dining room, all open-plan in the building's basement alongside a separate shared laundry. The building is much smaller here, the communal space downstairs is 92 square metres but shared by far fewer people. Floor-to-ceiling linen curtains separate the space so it can be divided into four separate rooms or one.

It's tucked into a side street shared with a cafe and deli. The units cost around the same as The Collective at £1,800 a month, or slightly less if you're costing per square metre. Mason and Fifth also offers a programme of health, fitness, social and well-being activities. Alongside providing these in-house, members are taken on trips out of the city for outdoor swimming and countryside walks.

As I walk around the building Nick, the community manager, talks me through the design features. The furniture and furnishings at Mason and Fifth come from local makers in an effort to ground the building in its setting. Materials are organic and small details like use of colour, texture and lighting have been tailored to create spaces that are variously calming and energising. Outside each room is a box where phones can be stored so residents are able to maintain good 'sleep hygiene' and instil separation from technology.

The attention paid here to the effect of design factors on health reflects a live conversation that has significant overlap with the sector. As operators are re-designing housing from scratch, they're also thinking about how to design environments that can serve their inhabitants' health better, using 'evidence-based design proven to deliver wellbeing outcomes for end users'.[3] Co-living conferences run seminars on modular interiors, wellbeing centred building, technological integration and non-toxic materials.

'Historically, we've had to look after homes,' Ben tells me, 'but homes of the future should look after you.' Mason and Fifth is on its way to achieving gold WELL certification, a metric based on ten categories through which 'place' is experienced, including light, movement, materials, sound and nourishment.

This is from WELL: 'The role buildings can play in human health and wellbeing has never been more evident or more important. Thanks to an evolving evidence base, we understand more about the relationship between the physical environment and human health than ever before. We know how to create spaces that enhance – rather than hinder – health and wellbeing. We can measure – and then improve – the quality of our air, water and light. We can design environments that fuel our bodies, move us, keep us connected, inspire our best work and facilitate a good night's sleep.'

The business case for wellbeing is a big driver in the luxury co-living industry. According to these design approaches we can hack our homes to work better for us. It's an example of how individuals can achieve a greater quality of life through collaborating and outsourcing the management of their lived environments. Who has the time to understand how the subtleties of light and movement affect their mood? What behaviours are engineered by the flow of our spaces and how our bodies respond to various compositions of materials? By outsourcing the labour of understanding and implementing these principles to co-living operators, members at M&F may not even be aware of how their environment has been tuned to their wellbeing, but they still benefit from it.

It's the luxury co-living sector's alliance with tech and entrepreneurship that is bringing these focuses forward. It has in common with many start-ups an approach which seeks to reverse engineer the human experience, from nutritional choices and exercise to built design and shopping habits and use this understanding to create a product built around individual experience.

It's also an approach where the lived environment is entwined with technology. Like with many co-living start-ups, communication at M&F is done via an app. Residents can contribute to conversations, find out activities for the day, report problems and give feedback. This obsessive attention to theory and detail that Ben talks about can be immediately felt in the space. In contrast to the residents I introduced myself to in The Collective's foyer, everyone I meet wants to talk to me about life there once I explain my presence. Residents know one another. They also know Ben by name and Joe and Nick, the experience team who are on site every day.

I'm joining them for an energy healing session, one of the new activities scheduled on a weekday evening. Waiting on the mats for the burnt sage to circulate the room before the class starts, I'm surprised to meet a couple who live there together as well as women in their thirties and a recently divorced man in his forties. A few people help to push back coffee tables so we can make room for more mats.

I wondered, during my hour spent walking along the Thames tow path from Canary Wharf to Bermondsey, whether I'd feel the same cynicism towards Mason and Fifth that I had at The Collective, where in lieu of a housing revolution, I'd found property developers with a marketing strategy. The staff team at M&F includes an in-house 'feelings expert', which I struggle not to roll my eyes at. Although I can burn incense with the best of them, group energy healing is probably at the edge of my woo woo tolerance too.

Meeting the residents makes it hard to cling on to my scepticism. One woman shares that her mental health was at breaking point living alone in the pandemic and that moving to the Italian Building had marked a turning point. Another has just moved here from the US and has found in Mason and Fifth a solution to the loneliness of starting out in a new city.

It still is though, a way of living which enables residents to avoid 'adulting', the slightly awful newly christened verb of the millennial generation, shortlisted for the Oxford Dictionary's Word of the Year in 2016. 'Adulting' refers to the administrative burden required of adults, the bill-paying, house-insuring, handyman-recruiting and family politics. At Mason and Fifth, even emotional labour of having a shared kitchen is eased by washing-up being managed overall by the staff team.

I chat with a former resident a month or so later who stayed for just over six months. 'It wasn't fake, what you saw,' she tells me. 'It's a really lovely place to live. Everyone really is that nice, all the time. Of course they are. It's easy to be nice when you're rich and everything is being done for you.' She lives in a flat in the area now. It's harder work but she feels like she's living in the real world again.

'Isn't having so much done for you a bit infantilising? Does it make a difference that much of the hard work of community is given to you?' I ask Michael, a 41-year-old man who joins us for energy healing.

'It may well,' he responds. 'And there are people who live here but choose not to engage. Occasionally, I almost resent those people. It's as though they are here to consume the product of community, to have it as a lifestyle status of it but pick and choose whether to participate. It makes me think of those people who would really want to engage and participate but who are waiting for a bed space.'

Nick doesn't see it as a problem. He thinks that there are enough pressures on young professionals living in a city that handing over some life-admin to a staff team is a positive thing.

Ben tells me about another member who had struggled with life-long eczema, induced by unknown environmental factors and stress, who'd found relief from it for the first time at Mason and Fifth.

There's a lady in her fifties who works nomadically but keeps an apartment there so she has a base to come back to. You cannot escape that people here are paying for connection and the health that implies, but it seems they are getting what they're paying for.

'Having this instant community has made me love London,' one of the residents, Jenna, tells me. She moved here from Canada a year ago after seeing Mason and Fifth online. 'Friends of mine who've moved here have said, "London is busy, it's crowded, the weather's bad, it's hard to make friends." I just have not had those experiences.'

It seems hard to believe, not only that Jenna has found a positive living situation but that she's experienced the fundamental velocity and density of the city differently because of her housing. But that's what it feels like to her. Mason and Fifth has altered her relationship with the city.

'I don't know exactly how they've done it, but they've created such a good community,' Jenna goes on to say. 'It's nuts. I've never felt since coming here that I'm just consuming a product. The group chat on any given day will share professional information, or help with things. We cook together and people share their skills and hobbies.'

It's the vision that Ben shares when we have a coffee before the session, that remodelling housing would reshape cities and how we relate to them. It seems, though, incredible to see his very specifically drawn strategies borne out so concretely in someone's experience. How can Jenna not feel like a customer when she is paying for the service?

Ben tells me how he'd become fascinated by garden cities over the lockdowns. He's referring to a model of urban planning popularised at the beginning of the last century, when industrialisation was drawing more people into city living. Its architect, Ebenezer Howard, imagined 'slumless and smokeless' semi self-sufficient cities of 32,000 people in conjoined circles. They would be attached to other similar garden cities by road and rail, with a slightly larger central city. The developments would have the trappings of country life, waterfalls, reservoirs and farms but their concentration and connectedness would keep industry within reach. They were healthy, spacious and affordable but also gave good access to the city. The problem they were responding to, that cities are built as economic and industrial centres making them less ideal as a living environment, has been made more pertinent by our current urban housing crisis, vast inequalities and continuing air quality problems. Howard hoped that his model would do away with the poor living conditions suffered by the working classes, and create healthier living space for everyone. It is a sticking point.

'How diverse is the community here,' I ask Ben, 'around race, class, political views, income?'

He sighs. 'Racially, really diverse, people from all over the world live here. Income? Mostly middle class.'

The fees at Mason and Fifth would be prohibitive for me, so I can only assume that they'd be out of reach for most of the people that keep the space running, such as its decorators, cleaners and yoga teachers.

'It's something that we grapple with every day,' Ben says. 'How to provide genuinely affordable accommodation in a city. Particularly in London. Land in a city is expensive, building in a city is expensive, so what you're going to end up with is expensive. What we're trying to look at now is how we can create a model with greater optionality. How can we create buildings in the city, and further outside the city, which can be more affordable, but create connection between the two, rather than one less well off, one more well off. My goal is to create affordable living that is inclusive for everyone but this building is definitely not that.'

'What are the biggest barriers to this kind of housing becoming the norm and actually expanding models like this so they could include everyone?' I ask him.

'100%, planning law,' Ben responds.

I've heard this over and again in the co-living sector. Planning boards are renowned for blocking projects which would have provided large-scale affordable housing because they do not meet the criteria of minimum unit size or are a type of development which doesn't fit easily into a planning category.

The focus on density in planning legislation has not aged well into the cities of the present. It has left us with a planning process which is protracted. Permissions are withheld for developments which arguably better reflect the cities we live in and the people who want and need to live in them.

'The thing that always strikes me as bizarre,' Ben says, 'is that government puts priority in planning on one-bedroom flats. Why would you create that when you could make a model of housing that's more efficient, provides people with community and well-being, it seems so obvious to us.

'Part of the challenge is trying to explain what it is and what we're about, trying to get people to think wider than the models they're used to. We come up against problems with planning, again and again. The US is said to be bad, but I think it's far worse here. How many places have you been able to visit? In London? There's the Collective that went into administration, there's a couple of other people doing it quite small scale and there's us. London's a city that's crying out for this kind of accommodation, we've got a long waiting list, but projects like ours are few and far between.'

He got some bad news earlier that morning, he tells me. 'A partner we've been work with for 18 months pulled the plug because they can't get enough confidence around the planning. That would have been a 250-studio building, built from scratch to our specifications. It would have been the most amazing space. Because of the scale we could have made it more affordable. Honestly, that's the hardest thing.' He sounds exasperated.

'Everybody who comes to this building – investors, council officers – they say, we need some more of these, why aren't there more of these? Well, you tell me! We're working tirelessly. I've hired a head of real estate, a head of planning to take responsibility for the property side of it. We've created an idea. We've shown that it works. Our residents could go live anywhere else but they don't. Come to the building, interview every single one of the people that lives here.'

From the pilot of their twenty-eight-unit building, Ben believes he has created a solution that, scaled up, will build community cohesion, points of connection for whole areas. 'Town halls, religious spaces, our centres of gravity are gone,' he tells me. 'These buildings can become that. You have enough people that you can open up the assets to local communities. I've got this image in my head of kids and families gravitating towards that building to come and pick their vegetables, or listen to a talk. These buildings having the resources to become a meeting space.'

He's confident that the housing sector will have to recognise more communal models soon enough, to better reflect the areas we live in and how we live within them. 'This kind of living will become mainstream, and it will change the face of cities, but we're at a difficult point now where this doesn't exist so people need to be convinced, they need to be educated.'

Ben's thoughts are echoed across the co-living sector. Entrepreneurs talk about problems with planning and the challenges of being reluctantly allied with a real estate market where notions of home cannot be detached from priorities of investment. It's a market that has been slow to turn with the tide of human experience, whose stakeholders are so invested in the status quo that they're making it difficult for us to live in different ways within their boundary markers. Co-living could reform cities and the property market but its aims jostle against those of their shareholders.

Chris Bledsoe, founder of Ollie, a large co-living operator in the US, talks about how, during the building boom after the Second World War, 'homes became McMansions. Not that people needed all that space, but homes became a status symbol and also a piggy bank. A place to park wealth.' For so many people this tie between market forces and houses made the picket-fence version of home unachievable.

Home ownership stretching out of reach as house prices spiralled out of sync with earnings is one of the reasons that younger generations are struggling to put down roots. Can homes be affordable, green and interconnected if they're also someone's nest egg? If connection and time are the new luxuries and an investment model of housing is not accommodating these, perhaps this revising of how we see our homes and real estate in a wider sense is possible. What would co-living look like if we were able to divorce questions of how we wanted to live from the interests of the property market?

I leave Mason and Fifth convinced that it is allowing its residents to live in healthier and more connected way but wondering whether the property market, as it currently stands, will ever allow its model to be rolled out like Ben hopes. What would it look like if their standards to design mental, physical and environmental wellbeing into built environments could be implemented in our social housing sector? What if this way of life could be made accessible for those who need it the most? Ben is right, London is not yet the place to find models for affordable urban co-living. Neither are the dictates of property investment and development the best partner for community building. Perhaps innovation must be searched out in alternative financial models.

*

After two weeks of visits Sam and I drive back up the A1, the motorway spine which runs between London and the North of England where we live.

I feel like crawling into bed but instead we pack up our suitcases to move onto the community farm. It's my thirty-second birthday, three and a half years since we'd last lived with others and I'm nearing the end of my first trimester of pregnancy. Along with clothes and laptops we bring paintings by my mum to hang on the walls, the cereal canisters that fit perfectly into our kitchen alcove and our cat who loudly protests the move throughout the twenty-minute drive to rural County Durham. It is important, we'd decided, to make it feel like home.

We're not moving into a fully fledged community so much as deciding if we'd like to join the building process. It feels a

94

rather more daunting prospect than surveying an established community and deciding whether to join. We'd be committing to establishing an identity, building a set of principles and a financial structure, learning to work the land and designing the rhythms for a life together.

If anything, the confidence of the communities I'd been in contact with, whose identities were already set out in governing documents that decisions could be measured against, had made us feel slightly more amateur about the whole exercise. My years of wonderful chaos at Number 25 had not prepared me for the grown-up version of the idea, with the responsibilities of a family in tow.

We'd been linked up with the farm's current residents by mutual friends a few years previously as fellow communalists and we'd got to know each other over meals, distanced Covid socialising and prayer and meditation on Zoom. We had been, for a few months, in a tentative courting process, deliberating whether we'd decide to combine our living space, routines, parenting and possessions, and if so, how? And how much?

It had come to a point where we felt the discussions were better had in situ over a two-month trial.

It wouldn't be the first time we've put roots down on the farm. Over the Covid months, when our food project pivoted to meet the needs of emergency food provision, we'd built, next to the gate, a wooden stall which became a 'pay what you decide' food shop. Durham women's football team had raised the funds for the timber. The farm's residents, currently just one couple, have been running it weekly for over a year, planting their roots down into the soil through this sharing of food.

The farm's own first-year produce joined the intercepted surplus that could be bought from the stall. Although the rest of our Covid provision tailed off, the farm shop never did. The village is an under-serviced area and it was plugging a gap which we knew would not be otherwise filled. Those who used the shop began to help run it, and the Saturday stall was joined by chairs and tables where people sat and chatted and a few times shared pizzas cooked in a portable fire dome someone had made in the barn on site. Shoppers arrive on foot an hour before the stall opens to queue and watch the kids chase cockerels and take turns on the quad bike. Those that came asked for growing and cooking workshops and we are currently planning how they will run. Farm residents helped to set up a newly formed Residents' Association, which is organising its first litter pick.

Coming to the decision to up sticks and move in together feels like a proposal. Since the discussions about it started we'd been stepping around each other and our dreams of communal life, gently. Our discussions were peppered with caution: 'Of course there's no pressure at all', 'we're happy for you to say if we're not the right fit either' and 'let's just try it out and see how it goes'.

The farm itself is a beast of a property. The large house sits alongside a barn, wood-workshop and allotments and forest land. It is on the edge of a former colliery town so its front looks on to lines of miners' terraces but the woods and fields behind the house lead off into more forests and fields. Though they've repurposed the building for three couples or families, with an aim to grow to twelve, it is still conspicuously grand. Our flat, carved from two rooms and a landing on the second floor, comes with its own sauna. Given that we've lived without a bath for many years, it feels like an absurd by-product of a decision to live more simply – bloody nice though.

The village has its share of problems but like most places that endure a poor reputation, it's a narrative which glosses over an actually quite varied make-up of people and a strong and long-held sense of community that characterises the village. Neighbours know other neighbours and families might live across three houses in the same streets.

We will, though, be living in the tension of disparity. The two-bedroom terraced houses sold here this year started at £30,000. Like many large rural properties repurposed for communal use, the space we occupy is both grand and practical. A metal knight, previously installed on the gatepost, was dethroned by the farm's residents and now lies in the barn. A bizarre cathedral-style dog house now hosts tea-making facilities for the various projects which use the outdoor space. Whilst we Tetris rooms and corridors together into very small private living spaces and turned a cinema room into a shared office, we can easily seat eighteen for dinner.

Despite having friends in the village, my Southern upbringing suddenly seems much more significant than the years I've spent since in the next-door town running a food project. After our small brick semi in an expensive part of town where we'd comfortably occupied the spot as the scruffiest neighbours, we'd be newly taking an opposite role.

It's not a role I've yet settled into. I'd found myself defensively explaining our living situation to a college student I met on the bus who lived with an aunt and uncle in the terraces, who, having not seen me before, asked which road we were in. 'We actually live in a flat inside the main house . . . we're just renting,' I tell him, self-conscious.

It's a fairly low-risk trial. We'll be renting out our brick semi and putting the funds towards the mortgage interest here. And yet, we've become so absorbed by the question of us moving here that we've had to limit how often Sam and I discuss it, lest the decision take on giant circular proportions and we become twisted up in its pros and cons. The decision to move in is viewed by our families, at best, as eccentric.

We wrestle with ourselves over it. I'm quite convinced in theory that living communally is, in general, better for wellbeing and climate footprint, and would allow us to reduce our consumption, to pool resources to offer welcome more easily, but unpacking our bags into the wardrobe, setting our houseplants on its deep farm sills and informing my midwife we'd temporarily changed address made those beliefs feel less firm.

CHAPTER 5

Urban co-living
without the luxury

S BEN NOTED WHEN WE were talking about Mason
and Fifth, it matters who owns the building. The
demands of asset management and community building
can easily conflict. Certainly there is profit to be made in
providing housing that makes us healthier and happier, but it
will always be a luxury product unless we manage not to centre
their design on maximising financial return, to disentangle these
homes from the investment models which they rely on.

As a result, many of those seeking to create accessible urban
co-housing have, in some way, extracted themselves from the
pressures of the property market. This can play out both in the
private sector and with partially or fully state-sponsored models.

The former carve out affordability through private capital. This
might look like income-scaled mutual co-ownership models or
cooperatives, or otherwise acquiring the building in some kind
of extra-market way, by squatting or guardianship. The ones
compiling private capital but still prioritising affordability tend
to have a small-scale socialist bent. Affordability depends on
having some higher earners and some lower earners who each

agree to some sort of income-graded contribution scale. Former squats, or older cooperatives where the mortgage has already been paid, aren't required to service capital and so residents contribute far less than a local rent would be because it covers maintenance rather than interest on the property's capital value.

The latter rely on social funding. They might include state housing subsidies in the funding plans or run in partnership with charities. This kind of funding can cause problems in terms of creating mixed spaces as funding subsidies can take a quite targeted approach to distribution. A council might be given a budget to solve a problem around homelessness or elderly accommodation so it could be a longer route if you're proposing a mixed approach.

One marked difference between all these more affordable models and their commercial counterparts is that they tend to require a more DIY approach to the community's operation. Those added extras provided at luxury co-living spaces, such as oversight of bills, administration of washing-up and organisation of community activities, are a responsibility shared between the tenants instead of outsourced.

Mutual home ownership models *can* sound radical. The 'man's home as his castle' narratives are so ingrained in our assumptions around housing that buying membership in a cooperative feels far riskier than storing a set of deeds in the filing cabinet. If you're lucky enough to have saved very hard for a deposit, it could feel like a big sacrifice to add it to a communal pot instead. In fact, cooperative ownership is pretty common in other European countries – they're not considered risky or community-minded even. Mutual or cooperative housing in the UK accounts for just 0.6% of the housing market. In Sweden it's 18% and in Norway 15%.[1]

This doesn't always make cooperative models better managed of course – there are plenty of stories of badly managed co-ops – but grass-roots ownership has the potential, as a structure, to make housing cheaper, provide structures for connection and collaboration, and give tenants more power to shape their space.

To learn from our European counterparts I meet up with Iris Luden, a student and teacher in computer programming at the University of Amsterdam and Alexander Cronheim, who graduated a few years back and is still finding his way to what he'd like to do. They are part of the 'De Torteltuin' team, designing a soon-to-be-built cooperative block in Amsterdam. Their plans have been signed off by the city municipality and a few weeks after we meet they will formally receive the piece of land that will house their development.

The project started as a conversation amongst students who realised that the city they loved would not afford them housing after graduation. 'The seed which started everything,' Cronheim tells me, 'was the realisation of growing financial inequality. It was getting impossible to buy a house without a very high-profile job.'

Amsterdam's housing crisis is perhaps one of the most severe in Europe. As well as its growth as an economic and academic centre, which has drawn an international audience to its housing market, tourism has taken a huge amount of building stock out of permanent residential use. The canal rings that make up its city centre are lined on each side with static house boats, and squat wooden buildings on stalks which emerge from the water.

They're plumbed into the sewage network, we're told, and sell at a similar rate to the city's apartments: 'We need to put housing wherever we can.' Even these small plumbed moorings can retail for over a million euros.

Like much of Amsterdam, the piece of land that De Torteltuin will build on has literally been pulled out of the sea, a sandy pitch which has never before entered the housing market. In fact, because of the type of land agreement they've signed with the municipality, it will now never become the property of private individuals. Instead the cooperative will own the building and pay a low ground rent to the municipality.

The cooperation of the municipality is in contrast to London, where there's been a rash of quite controversial sales of formerly public land to private developers; Amsterdam has instead prioritised signing over its land to cooperative groups as part of the state's response to the city's housing crisis. As well as providing the land and support with the design and planning process, the municipality will be putting up the first two million euros for building in cash as a low-interest loan, and supporting them to secure the additional investment they'll need to build.

Amsterdam's housing problem is repeated across the world's cities. Between 2011 and 2019, some London boroughs saw rents rise by 42% and average wages by just 2% in the same period.[2] Craigslist and Gumtree are full of adverts for pull-out beds in lounges, and remodelled boiler cupboards costing hundreds of pounds each month on unofficial and unregulated lease agreements. Friends of mine working full time in good jobs have disrupted sleep in bedrooms they share with their children, or are clutching onto impermanent contracts, and they're the lucky ones. Data from the end of 2020 showed 10,510 households living in bed and breakfast accommodation. Council spending on temporary accommodation has risen 430% in the last decade to £142 million across a twelve-month period.[3] As the cost of living crisis tips more and more households over the threshold of affordability, this will only increase.

LILAC (Low Impact Living Affordable Community), based in Leeds, is the first community of its kind in the UK. They've used a DIY approach to development and management to try to address some of these problems. In models like theirs, no one is being paid to make your life more frictionless. There is no landlord sanctioning the use of Blu-tack and there are safeguards for those missing payments after job losses. There is collective responsibility for maintenance, permission to personalise your house and a sense that you need to draw on the skills within the community to create the spaces you want to live in.

One of the commitments to living at LILAC is that each member has to get involved in at least two of the 'task teams'. These include areas of oversight such as 'landscape', 'maintenance', 'finance', 'membership', 'learning' and 'food process'. They are referred to as 'spokes'. Each 'spoke' then meet as a 'hub' to make a little bicycle wheel of consensus governance, by which they'll make decisions that will impact the future direction of the community. (Their commitment to a jazzy communal lexicon is every bit as strong as in commercial co-living spaces with their place-makers and #Gather circles.)

Theirs is an example of affordability achieved through the sharing of assets between members rather than state subsidies. Members don't own their properties, but all the properties are owned by the society, which members have a stake in. In order to buy these equity shares each household contributes 35% of their income. As well as the society's mortgage, this money goes towards maintenance, bills and improvements. The mortgage contributions become equity shares which members can withdraw at a later date. If all the equity for your property is acquired, then your contribution drops to 10%.

Rather than being tied to the property market, the value of these equity shares is linked to average earnings in the surrounding area, meaning they'll remain affordable in perpetuity. The model encompasses a wide range of incomes. The founding members include academics and writers. The site's tour guide works freelance, earning less than £15,000 a year.[4]

As one LILAC member says, a postman can come and live here, and in twenty years when property prices have continued to grow out of sync with wages, a postman can come and live here.[5] Those earning more are getting something for their money too – a more diverse and more equal home.

LILAC's 1.5 acre site consists of twenty houses, ranging from one- to four-bedroom units. Like Mason and Fifth they spent time working out how to draw the resources and skills they needed from the local area, situating the building in its location through design. Members involved in setting up the cooperative society helped to build the straw bale walls themselves and were collectively involved in the design. They are extremely passionate about straw. There are photos of the community surrounded by straw and a little window in one of the walls where you can see into its straw-y innards. You'll not get through a day's visit to LILAC without some discussion on its insulating merits.

As well as being available locally and non-toxic, this straw insulation is part of what makes these properties meet the Passive House building standard, which makes it a 'low impact' development. Passive design principles, originating in Austria, can reduce the need for central heating by 90% through relying on blocking heat-exits and bridges, using orientation to make the most of the sun's natural energy and having a heat recovery system. The LILAC houses are also built with solar panels so energy bills are extremely low.

Alongside the houses, there is a communal block that contains a laundry room, a communal kitchen where they eat together, a shared meeting-space-cum-playroom and a shared office. There are also four shared guest rooms, which strikes me as a brilliant idea. How many millions of UK houses have a room reserved for a guest which remains empty 90% of the time? What if everyone could just have a share in their street's communal guest room instead? How much more space would be freed up and money would be saved?

The buildings, though in a built-up city, are cocooned in green space. There's a large decking which sits over a pond. In the warmer weather the community share coffee breaks and their evening meals together there. Up from the pond is an allotment area tended by most of the residents that provides vegetables for the twice-weekly communal meal. They have shared tools and a community tool shed, so no one household will own a drill that will be used for its ten-minute average.

Along with these internal points of collaboration, there are multiple points of integration with the community surrounding it. Though I wouldn't go so far as to claim that they've created a third space for the local area, which would slot neatly into the role of the community centres we've lost, they do provide a few touch-points and a certain bulk of enthusiasm which can galvanise community action in the wider area.

The community host a food cooperative, which is available for non-members, making organic food affordable for people in the surrounding area through bulk buying. LILAC also run wider community events including folk nights, film screenings, discussion nights and a swap shop. They host community association meetings, and even a polling station. It's important to those that live there, one member shares, that it's a stimulating place to live.

The methods that underlie LILAC have a lot in common with the commercial co-living sector. Like many of the more convenience-driven businesses, tech is embedded in their structure. They've created software to run their financial systems and equity allocation.

Also in common with the more commercial co-living sector, there's a sense in which they've 'hacked' the designs and assumptions which govern our living, taken them apart, looked at the data and put them back together in a different way. It's an approach which starts from the point of view of the end user and works back to design, rather than adopting conventional design strategies and retrofitting them to the needs of the members.

Celia Ashman, one of the community's founders, talks about this process of rejecting traditional housebuilding practices that were inadequate for community building, like having provision for two-car parking as standard with each house and holding household privacy as a priority. Their end goal was to live with reduced car reliance, so why build it in? They didn't all need large private entertaining spaces, so why not dispense with them? They didn't value distinct boundaries of ownership and wanted to provide wider community space, so why design in large fences to boundary the land?

Going against the grain of conventional building assumptions, as with every project I've come across, made the project harder to push through planning processes as it didn't fit the assumptions planning boards usually work with. The designs were sent back from the planners with comments about inadequate parking for the number of houses and required a little back and forth to push through.

It's interesting looking at how models that started from a point of community needs and based the design on those, such as Mason and Fifth, compare with communities that retrofitted a building to adapt to the needs of the community. I felt quite jealous looking at how easy this design process made their life together once it was built.

In our own community journey this has been one of the biggest challenges, adapting physical space designed with nuclear families in mind to suit our needs. We've spent the last hundred years building homes which centre around the nuclear family. Often older houses, which might have provided for several generations in previous years, have subsequently been carved up into flats for individual families, with additional kitchens and bathrooms built into each unit.

The farm we're living at would have certainly housed multiple generations as well as workers but has been renovated into a family home with wide spaces and very few doors. Almost the entire communal area is open-plan, leaving your Zoom meeting, or crying baby to echo around the whole house.

The process of returning to a communal space has been a little ad hoc. Our lounge area has been created from a landing by blocking off a door and adding another that goes straight into the hallway instead. It can't fit a whole sofa or TV as well as two bedrooms so if we want to spend time privately we sit in bed to watch TV like students. We've managed to carve out a room for one baby in what will be our lounge until she needs it, but if another came along I'm not sure where we'd put them. It is a case of behaviour shaping design, and in turn design shaping behaviour. Even if we want to change the way we live to be incidentally more connected, those behaviours are now embedded into the foundations of our three-bed houses and difficult to change.

The new-build estates which have grown up in great patches across the UK hugely reflect these design priorities. Each has a small garden fenced off by six-foot-high divides and a strip of decorative, but ultimately under-used, front garden. This grid of green which runs in lines alongside ribbons of brick is often accompanied by very little communal space. A publicly accessible play area, which would have provided much better use than a thousand parallel postage stamp lawns and decorative front beds, is rarely prioritised in these new developments. They're built around a priority of ownership and privacy, regardless of whether they serve our desired end use.

Paul Chatterton, one of the founder members of LILAC,[6] talks about the way we design our living spaces being part of a much wider conversation. Like many others, he cites turbulence as the Petri dish in which their community conversations started. Their ideas were set in the context of three major upheavals: the 2008 financial crash, the Cop 15 meeting in Copenhagen which brought devastating environmental concerns to the surface, and riots around the UK born of deep societal divisions and inequality. The question they were asking themselves when they were drawing out the space, wider than just 'how should we live?' was 'how do you respond at a community level to these national and global crises?'

How do we build local economic resilience? How do we make environmentally sustainable accommodation? How can our environment create positive community? How can this be made accessible for people with different incomes and circumstances? How do we create a step change in how our places are built and allow communities and neighbourhoods to thrive within cities?

The space reminded me a little of the concentric circles of Howard's garden cities in micro, an attempt to carve out healthy, affordable spaces that could accommodate working-class families, enabling them to live adjacent to industrialised cities and, crucially, work.

LILAC are a midpoint between the developer-driven city co-housing sector and the kumbaya self-build straw huts. Their community relies on financial tech and robust legal agreements, including written policies on tech, parking and meals, but also on shared parenting, inclusivity and organic vegetables.

REfUSE's co-director Nikki and I, often joke that the growth and development of our food project has turned us from hippies into hippies with ten-year financial plans, scaled-up hippies. We are grubby activists with suits, a board of advisors, safeguarding policies and annual accounts. Sometimes I miss the days when we were climbing over fences and hoisting each other wheelbarrow-style into wheelie bins to audit the contents and find usable food, but in order to achieve sustainability, and establish our collection programme and warehouse which processes 13 tonnes a month, we needed to engage with investors, local and national government and corporate food suppliers.

LILAC's journey is similar, embedding co-production and accessibility into a project which, although just a drop in the property market ocean, has become a serious blueprint for equal housing. Usually with community living projects, a few unhappy former members are par for the course, but the only negative review I can find is a three-star google review left by a disgruntled delivery driver who couldn't find his intended recipient.

It probably won't surprise you to hear that turnover of the houses is rare. In their first decade only two properties have come up and there was stiff competition between those wanting to move in. Choosing between the applicants, one member revealed, felt like a difficult process.

So if the mutual co-ownership model is such an improvement on the status quo, why aren't we all doing it? Because honestly, no one I know has the time and energy spare to make it happen. Sure, living in a development like LILAC could enable health, financial freedom, a stimulating and fairer environment, but just hearing about the ten-year journey that preceded it is exhausting.

For many forming LILAC, it was a part-time job. That is perhaps why, for all their income diversity, cooperatives like LILAC still feel quite middle class. They're not always accessible for those who are time-poor. Don't get me wrong, LILAC has a broader income diversity than almost any community I've seen. In terms of income, belief and sexuality, relationship status and age their community spans a spectrum. But the learning team at LILAC are very aware that their community lacks the ethnic diversity of neighbouring Kirkstall. It's one of the topics they cover with those coming to tour the community. Just one of the twenty households comes from the global non-white majority. There's also a heavy presence of white-collar jobs, even amongst those on low incomes. There are freelance artists and creatives stitching together pieces of work into a salary but no supermarket shelf-stackers. There are nurses, but no carers. Whilst a postman *could* live there, there aren't actually any postmen living there.

One of the barriers here is that membership at LILAC does require an income of some sort. At present, there isn't provision in their set-up which would make the lease agreements compatible with rent paid by housing benefit, although, in many cases, the state contribution would exceed that of the lowest accepted household income. They could reform this to enable social tenants but the reality is that I doubt it would do much to change the make-up. The question that LILAC are circling around though, is much bigger than their own financial legislation: how do we make the communal living conversation less culturally middle-class?

It's what we're asking too. The reduced financial contribution of shared living is going to allow us the greater financial freedom but do we really need it? We were already on the property ladder – albeit in the North East of England. We're the winners of the housing market rather than its victims.

Places like LILAC rely on the dogged hard work of a collection of individuals who relentlessly swim upstream against the currents of planning, construction and investment norms. Amongst their founders are academics and experts in urban housing and planning, those who had the energy and vision to push it to completion over the course of almost a decade.

It's a classic catch 22. Those straining at the edges of work, parenting, health and care roles are unlikely to have the wiggle room in their energy to build a housing model from scratch. Like systems of financial capital which keep those on low incomes spending more for the basics, those who are time-poor are kept under the control of the profit-driven private rental market because they do not have the ready time-capital to spend ten years redesigning it.

LILAC have been reflecting on how they could actively promote the concept of co-living among ethnic minority and working-class groups the next time a household becomes available. It'll be easier now that the community is established, of course, but by that point, the cultural imprint of the group is firmly in place, the community has been shaped along the lines of those who had the time and energy to give to it. It's a problem that affects so many cooperatively owned spaces.

When I was in Stuttgart, I visited the most wonderful mutually owned, collaboratively built block, based at the former Olga Hospital. The flats squared off a green space which provided an oasis in the middle of one of the most populated parts of Germany. The bottom units had been let to a cafe and pharmacy. They'd not all been built that way, some plots in the development were built with private investment, and another had been developed by the state's social housing provider. On paper, and in walking through its leafy enclaves, it was every bit the future of green and equal housing. The cooperative block had put their weight behind a bid to host a state-sponsored community centre there, with an on-site social worker. Their community services were incredible.

'Look around you though,' the social worker told me, across a flower-topped table in the community centre. She was gesturing to the empty room. 'This is such a well-resourced centre. My job is unlike any of my colleagues', I get to do proactive work, run really positive things. My colleagues who are social workers in poorer towns nearby would love to have even half of this.' Instead they're in a sixties building, fielding drug problems and child removals, she told me.

Even in the social housing block, most of the tenants were quite middle-class working families. The migrant and refugee families who did make it there had wonderful resources, drop-in counselling sessions, free speech therapy and parenting support but there weren't too many.

'It's amazing that the organising group could fight for these spaces in their community,' the newly appointed social worker explained, 'but none of them are here using them. I've only met a few tenants from those cooperative blocks. This centre would be much more use in towns where people might not have the capacity, the networks and vocabulary to campaign for them.'

The group at De Torteltuin talked about this phenomenon in terms of 'intellectual capital'.

'We can hold a lot,' Iris told me. 'We have the time, we have knowledge of how bureaucratic things work, we know how to communicate well with the municipality.'

They sent invitations to eighty-eight different groups advertising for involvement, targeting those who might be vulnerable to the housing market, those on low incomes and refugee groups. 'It's been hard though,' Iris continued, 'because no matter how many groups we went to, the people applying to be involved looked and sounded just like us.'

They had made some progress, involving a group of three refugees in the design group, with a few more hoping to join. She was very aware that if the group wasn't more inclusive at this design stage, then it would be difficult later on for it to be truly diverse. If a place is built and shaped by people who mostly don't look and sound like you and who have different ideas and priorities to yours, will it ever feel like your space?

Before it's embedded into normal housing practice, trying to co-create these new standards will always be exhausting and always favour the empowered. LILAC have done a lot to include those from every ethnic group, income scale and class and yet the terms of the exercise have made this pretty difficult. You can't build these spaces without having significant non-financial resources, a vocabulary around community development and a network which would enable you to know the route there.

*

Running against the grain, when the grain is as firmly marked as it is, has its own challenges. Any project which seeks to create a different financial system also still sits in tension with the economy they exist in. Divorcing yourself from the dictates of the property markets does, in reality, have its downsides. Namely, that when you move in you've extracted yourself from the property market that won't be as easy to re-join.

If property prices continue to rise disproportionately to average earnings those wanting to leave would, in real terms, get fewer bricks for their pound on exit than any they came in with. If you sold your house and put the equity into LILAC when you joined, you might be buying a smaller house on exit. If you've saved your pounds over many years and life already feels precarious, I can understand this would feel a shade too risky.

Co-housing models which rely on state funding and charity or housing association partners rather than grass-roots activism, whilst they come with their own problems and are famously slow, can require less of an energy outlay for those that will live there.

ShareNYC was a project proposed by the New York City department of housing and development. The project announced in 2019 three winners of a challenge put out to developers to create truly affordable communal housing in New York. It's a city that faces a very similar property market to those I've described in Amsterdam and London, beset by widespread gentrification and some of the most expensive cost per square foot rates in the world.

Louise Carroll, one of the department's commissioners for ShareNYC commented: 'New York is one of the most culturally rich cities in the world, and our housing stock should reflect that diversity. With ShareNYC we're blending affordability with flexibility for a wide range of New Yorkers as we explore this new model.'

The statement reminded me of the cockney accent speaking to me from its East London bench and the unique cultural importance of East London, its lively docks and history of trade, craftsmanship, and music. Its pie shops, jellied eels and Pearly Kings and Queens whose buttons I remember jangling down the high street in my childhood visits twenty years ago. Like New York, the cultural richness of East London was not visible on the Isle of Dogs.

It's the story of every global city defined by its role as a financial centre. Brooklyn's boundary-breaking Black music scene repackaged as novelty in hipster bars serving $15 cocktails, the Amsterdam squats my artist mum lived in, in the eighties, replaced by Airbnbs, Los Angeles's struggling actors and beat poets pushed out by property tycoons, leaving the city with the largest unsheltered homeless population in the US. New York's ballroom scene and queer houses fetishized in TV series but replaced with those who can afford NYC's extortionate rents.

Communities of colour and marginalised groups are the first to go, their contribution to the industry and cultural richness of these cities not reflected in the space they're allowed to take up. Can a design project like ShareNYC help cities like New York maintain their cultural richness? Can it change the identity of our cities and how we relate to the diverse groups within them? Can it help us keep the world's biggest cities inclusive and alive?

The project has managed to overcome some of the most common barriers co-housing projects find. Because local authority departments are driving the proposals, allowances have been made to make it possible for these designs to get around zoning legislation, building smaller and more densely packed private spaces, and larger shared facilities. The developers and investors are working in partnership with charities and co-living operators

116

so buildings will include additions like support and coaching alongside social spaces.

The chosen proposals are a mixed bag of post-shelter accommodation, serving previously homeless populations, and more mixed developments which include a smaller proportion of market-rate housing. I spoke to one of the architects for Ascendant's thirty-six-unit development, which won one of the city's three commissions. It's still in the pre-development stage. The building will be managed in partnership with The Ali Forney Center, a charity which serves New York's young LGBTQ+ population.

With a higher prevalence of family rejection – 90% of those the AFC work with cite homophobia as the cause of family breakdown – LGBTQ+ people account for a staggering 50% of those homeless in New York. New York's queer history is so embedded into its cultural identity, from *Will & Grace* to the drag balls depicted in *Paris Is Burning*. It's part of what makes New York so unique, that it is home to a thousand colours. And yet, this cultural diversity is sharply reflected in doorways and under the city's bridges.

New York's boarding houses, or residential hotels, used to be infamous places where criminality, necessity and eccentricity met. You might have heard them called flop-houses. They weren't always safe and good quality housing, Chris Cirillo, the architect from Ascendant's team told me, but they filled a vital role for low-cost housing which hasn't then been replaced. Those on temporary contracts, between houses, whose financial credentials wouldn't support a tenancy or who didn't have a deposit, would have options. Now that option is more likely to look like homelessness or living out of a car. These hotels come under a housing category called SROs, or single-room occupancies. That they haven't been replaced, Cirillo told me, reflects both the economics of gentrification and an urban bias and underlying racism that exists across the US. Areas were re-zoned to prevent SROs being built because people didn't want that kind of accommodation and the inhabitants that would depend on it on their streets, bringing down the value of their properties. SROs were quietly legislated out.

New York's housing crisis has prompted these decisions to be re-evaluated, an approach coming straight from the mayor and the state's own housing and planning board who commissioned ShareNYC. The building that Ascendant are proposing to turn into low-cost shared accommodation was recently re-zoned to allow them to build more units on the land, making their development possible. These units are not temporary accommodation, like many similar projects but designed to allow LGBTQ+ young people at risk of homelessness to build home and independence in a supported context. The base of the building will include support workers from the AFC to help ease the process.

The eight-floor building will house four units per floor. Whilst bedrooms are private, bathrooms are shared. Each floor is paired with an adjacent one to share a large living room, workspace and kitchen set out across the two floors. The nature of the funding means that all tenants will fit their target audience, those approximately 18–25, at risk of homelessness and LGBTQ+. Projects in partnership with the state tend to have these kind of constraints which make designing mixed housing more difficult.

The thirty-two-unit project has been meticulously designed to meet the requirements of a group in desperate need of housing. The picture painted by their blueprints and artist's impressions of the space shows housing that will no doubt increase the health, wellbeing and positive outcomes of those that will eventually live there. Three years since they won the commission, though, they're just tendering for a construction firm.

It has been a slow process. 'We need these units yesterday,' Cirillo told me. There have been a number of pilot projects like theirs but the process is still too constrained to scale up. In fact, though the ShareNYC projects were given the green flag in 2019, none have announced the first foundations being laid. Compared to the immediacy of the profit-driven markets and more informal arrangements, these state developments are sluggish, bound up in red tape.

Can non-luxury commercial shared housing plug the gap between the sluggish progress of state developments and the unaffordable time-costs of cooperative living? PadSplit is a start-up that claims to be doing just that. They occupy an interesting crossover space between the co-living sector and the informal housing that dominates cities. Their model for SROs has been drawn on top of already available private assets rather than looking to build or renovate from scratch. Retrofitting of existing housing stock has cut out the middleman of planning, building and financing. If we simply look at the numbers of people they're housing affordably in the world's most expensive cities, then they're one of the most successful co-living operators globally.

Unlike other co-living operators – Common, Ollie, The Collective and Mason and Fifth – PadSplit's approach includes an Airbnb-type model. More than an operator, it's a platform, an app which oversees the marketing and operations of private property retrofitted into affordable co-living spaces. Their model will be used in more formal projects too, alongside Common and The AFC, they're the third operations partners for ShareNYC, partnering on a project that will be built in Cypress Hill. Smaller, privately owned properties, marketed on a large scale are the model's bread and butter.

The way it works is that property owners will renovate their houses, splitting them up into a larger number of rooms. PadSplit then uses their platform to market, sell and provide an operating system for the spaces. Their prices are well below market rent.

They are treading a fine line. It's an approach which allows landlords to make units increasingly smaller and less adequately served in the name of affordable development. Cirillo told me about some of the creative techniques he'd seen used to get around zoning laws: curtains separating off rooms and even sleeping pods placed in a communal area so that more people can be fitted in without the walls that would designate them as additional rooms and make them illegal.

Zoning laws may be inadequate for the cities we now have, but there is no desire to bring back the poor-quality flop-houses they legislated out. As Penny Clark, the co-living consultant, said, talking about her experience of the sector, 'Done really badly, it becomes a way for companies to shove people into smaller and smaller rooms, have a communal lounge and give them pizza once a week as a freebie on a Friday then slap the word community on the website.'

PadSplit certainly hasn't been immune to this type of criticism. Kathleen SayVon, a fifty-nine-year-old woman living in Georgia found her PadSplit house listed for $130 a week including utilities, a figure which amounts to just 40% of the average monthly rental prices for one-bedroom flats in the area. However, SayVon told the *New Republic* in 2021 that the property she lives in was badly kept and they were issued unexpected additional fees, such as a $35 housing application fee. Worse, the flexible arrangements allowed for housing instability. Evictions upon non-payment of rent were informal, allegedly marked by a change of locks and an email at short notice. Instead of formal leases tenants have 'member agreements', leaving tenants in a grey legal area and giving them less recourse to challenge these evictions. PadSplit isn't their landlord. They're just a middleman who operate the buildings. The language here is key. The PadSplit website talks about members and housemates, but not tenants. The bill is payment of 'dues' not 'rent'. 'PadMates' are encouraged to communicate through an app where they 'shout out' good housemate behaviour and 'call out' messiness or milk theft. Should these platforms not solve your shared living issues you can report those you live with via a rules violation page where you can also file video or audio evidence of the behaviour to the support team.

Rebecca Burns, the *New Republic* journalist investigating the claims, spoke to senior Atlanta attorney Margaret Kinnear: 'We've had calls of either, "We're going to put you out after Friday" or, "We're moving you to another location, and you have no choice in the matter,"' Kinnear reported.

PadSplit are currently the subject of multiple litigation cases from former tenants for damage of property and unfair eviction.

Despite these complaints it is, in one sense, still easy to understand why the PadSplit model holds appeal. Listening to their founder Atticus LeBlanc talk about PadSplit providing alternatives for people living in their car, or without any heating, it's obvious that their model is needed. Their tenants have an average $25,000 salary per year. Members' ages range from nineteen to ninety-three. He rightly points out that in a sector directed at young professionals they are a very different model and their housing really is affordable. He talks about structural inequality, admitting 'these folks don't have any other options'. They don't have the same churn as the luxury co-living sector because people haven't got alternatives to go on to. For LeBlanc that lack of choice isn't a negative – PadSplit is filling a gap, not creating an ideal.

In reality, what they're doing is making informal housing arrangements, which are incredibly common in cities like New York, a little more visible. Of course it's not ideal, but it hasn't *created* precarious housing, it puts some organising systems and transparency around a type of housing that's already the norm.

LeBlanc talks about using the private sector to circumvent the slow-to-progress social housing. They aren't waiting for governments to wake up to the housing crisis, and are trying to solve it now with the resources they already have. 'We can make affordable housing possible, by also making it profitable,' he told the Millionacres investment and real estate podcast. The ShareNYC project is taking years to house the number of people that PadSplit can in a month by utilising spare space.

LeBlanc, in trying to swerve the clunky demands of large property developments and retrofit existing investments instead, has leant into the control of market demand. In some cases this has led to a focus on necessity at the cost of dignity. The fact is that the market isn't a good control mechanism if we're looking to achieve fair housing provision but it does provide a way to achieve the volume of housing we need with speed. As cities continue to grow, I suspect that all these models of co-living will become more common. Some will be built beautifully by individuals who come together, investing their time and energy to imagine a brand-new system; others will start life as policy documents sponsored by planning departments to legislate against homelessness, and others still will patch together what we've got into an imperfect solution that was needed yesterday, playing Tetris with private assets to make sharing profitable and possible.

CHAPTER 6

Hippy communities, now and then: rural, intergenerational, sustainable

O LD HALL FARM BEGAN LIFE as a classic 1970s hippy commune, and in some ways, it still carries much of the same spirit.

It was birthed in a tumultuous decade: mining strikes, widespread droughts, sexual, racial and feminist revolutions. By 1970 the Soviet Union had drawn equal to the US in the nuclear arms race, bringing mutually assured destruction into the realms of viable threat. Protests against the Vietnam war and campaigns for nuclear disarmament were entwined with the hippy subculture which had migrated from the US to the UK in the late sixties, joining forces at points with the early environmental movement. Together, they emphasised the relationship of people with planet, and brought into question the norms of nationalism that the Cold War had marked out.

It was the decade of anti-establishment music, LSD, the first VCR recorders and Findus crispy pancakes. Joni Mitchell was lamenting a paradise paved and replaced with a parking lot, and asking farmers to put away the DDT, the pesticide responsible for damaging populations of fish-eating birds. Dean Acheson, a former US Secretary of State told an audience in the sixties that Britain had 'lost an empire' but 'not yet found a role'.[1] The ensuing tussle for the cultural heart of Britain was played out over the next decade in pop culture and political ideology. Coming off the sixties, collectivism was at its height, the top rate of income tax was 83%. The trades unions were powerful and dominated British industry. But in a surprise 1970 victory, the Labour majority government was replaced by a Conservative one led by Edward Heath.

Against this soundtrack of Joni's 'Big Yellow Taxi' and industrial picket lines, the founding members of Old Hall were part of a new wave of environmental socialism. The original residents started to gather when a group of three families had a dinner-table conversation about whether they should find a large house and all move in together, grow their own food and share resources. It's the kind of conversation I have with my sisters and friends often, imagining different wings for each of us and an outdoor cinema in the summer, but without any real plans to book a removal van.

When the nearby friary came up for sale, giving their dreams some bricks and mortar within which to take their shape, momentum gathered. They put an advert in *The Guardian* in February 1974 which read: 'Ecological Living, Setting up community Suffolk. Very large house, 50 acres, beautiful setting, Mainly middle-class socialist. Few more participants required, with capital.' The group gained enough interest that, after a false start and a failed buyer, there were enough people to go ahead with a collective purchase for £75,000. The new housemates consisted of twenty adults and fourteen children.

Jill, who moved in in the seventies and is now in her eighties, describes the place as having been rooted in flower power. Communes like Old Hall, whose relationship with the land finds its origins in the geopolitics of 1970s Britain, even after fifty years of resident turnover, need to be understood in the context of their beginnings. Although they're one of the most enduring and largest, the community at Old Hall were not unique. Communalism in Britain and the US was thriving. They were one of a number of agri-socialist communes that sprang up in the period, establishing small-scale utopian projects which provided a home for political, environmental and cultural priorities.

Set against a backdrop of Constable's Suffolk agricultural landscapes, Old Hall is now home to forty adults and twelve children. The friary is a vast building, with a spinal stone corridor running through the middle, giving access to its 120 rooms. At one end is a large chapel. It's used for parties now, and one surface is still crowded with empty drinks bottles from a birthday ceilidh a few days before I arrive. Outside its entrance are rails of fancy dress, a packed-away pantomime stage and large tubs full of roller blades which the children use to skate circuits around the chapel's smooth stone floor. A statue of the Virgin Mary wears strings of necklaces and holds a glitter ball in her outstretched hand.

At the other end of the building is a large bright hall, used for yoga and occasional co-working, along with a library and lounge. A communal kitchen and dining room in the middle provide the heartbeat of the place. At any time of day there are bread-bakers and tea drinkers, people washing up, making children's packed lunches or checking the rotas to add themselves to free cooking slots. Crops to be sown and newly arrived lambs are announced in chalk on various blackboards which line the kitchen walls. It's simultaneously grand and shabby. A mezzanine dining room with ornate oak panelling is joined by mismatched chairs and 1990s carpet tiles. The corridors of the stately home are bare stone and bathroom floors are covered by practical lino and attended by laminated instructions about wet floors and temperature controls. My room has a metal bunkbed. 'Let me find you a towel that's not too rough,' my host offers, leafing through the selection in the airing cupboard.

The account of their early days, compiled from the memories of Old Hall's residents for a book, *The Patchwork History of a Community Growing Up*,[2] are beautifully relatable to my own experience of setting up an unconventional home with friends, gathering scraps of skills and experience and pasting them together with hope and enthusiasm. Mal who, with her husband, was tasked with dividing the original friary into fourteen private units and other shared space wrote: 'As Kev and I are both poncey artist types and not hot on maths, you can see that it was a brave – very seventies – decision to give us the job. We were both available on the spot rather than over-qualified but also, at that time, in our elated group, we all had the confidence to try anything.' Rather than just looking at unit size, they added nice views and good sunlight into the valuations and gave additional space to those whose windows faced a hedge.

Almost fifty years later, those units divided up by Mal and Kev still host a number of the original members, with several more buried in a forest-side graveyard on site. They've been joined in the time since by those also seeking a life more communal and more connected to the soil underneath them.

I'm picked up from the train station on foot by Sophie and her daughter Julia who is ten. They moved into the community when Julia was a toddler so she's grown up around its communal kitchen, a group of pre-teen girls providing live-in friends. The mother-daughter pair had lived in quite a conventional house before then but had moved halfway across the country to be a part of Old Hall and have Julia grow up there.

The walk back takes us through three miles of flat agricultural land punctuated by wide low rivers. Sophie and Julia point out their favourite spots for swimming and riverbank shingle beaches where you can dry off, an arc of trees providing a changing room. Julia shows me where she likes to play by a river's dam. As we near the farm Sophie guides me through the shape of the land. A paddock where bullocks are separated off, fields which are grazed by their sheep and left fallow in alternate years, a path around the perimeter where the cows are led to pastures new.

Their original fifty acres has grown now to seventy as farmland has been added to its edges. Along with sheep, pigs and milking cows, there are abundant vegetable crops. Potatoes are chitting in an outdoor store, growing purpled roots before they're planted. They're dug in at intervals so residents can start harvesting them in the spring and enjoy a year-round crop. Brassica seedings are sprouting by the greenhouse and raspberry bushes are being thinned off so that come summer there are walkways between the thorny bushes wide enough to move between the rows of berries. The spare clumps of root and raspberry twig are gathered into recycled food packaging to be sold to passers-by at the gate. The field has been kept manageable over the late summer and early spring by green manure, thick Phacelia whose roots have fixed nitrogen in the earth and whose presence, like residents at a Guardianship, has prevented unwanted squatters coming to the patch whilst its violet flowers have provided bee and insect habitats. I'm told about Old Hall's approach of working in partnership with the land's natural resources and instincts rather than attempting to master it with machinery and chemicals. It's what you'd call permaculture.

Although the community are also reliant on some gas and oil, particularly when their biomass boiler is on the blink as it is during my visit, much of their energy is provided by natural resources too. The biomass boiler is fuelled by fallen and coppiced trees, their wood seasoning in barns. Warmth is drawn from deep underneath the turf by a ground source heat pump. A field of solar panels interspersed by the fruit beds and compost heaps provides electricity in the summer months.

Though much about the place and its inhabitants has changed since it formed in the 1970s, their interdependent relationship with the land has not. The year is still marked by its seasons here, and they still ask what the land might need from them, as well as what they might need from the land. It strikes me as quite slow at first, inefficient even, all the pulling of weeds on our hands and knees, leaning across cardboard walkways so that our footprints do not spoil the soil with their heavy impressions. But several days later, once my thumbs are too rough with dirt and trowel calluses to operate my iPhone's fingerprint ID, I recognise the therapy in it. There was a pleasure in the small ways in which I started to understand from Sophie how the comfrey enriches the compost, the un-dug soil sequesters carbon and companion plants give crops protection from weeds, drying sun and battering winds.

The tearing away of people from the land we occupy and the industrialisation of our food systems that the early environmental movement fought against is now complete. Many of us admire the natural world but occupy a spectator role towards it, taking walks across the countryside but failing to recognise our dependency on the soil. There are no spots on our supermarket apples. Despite the fact that Scottish peatlands sequester more carbon per square metre than the Amazon rainforest, we continue to merrily dig their stores for suburban rose bushes.[3]

Largely we are cut off from the cycles and systems that create the food that we eat. Massive bio-diversity loss, exploitation of the planet's resources, destructive gas pipe-lines, water and mineral conflicts, and deforestation to make way for palm crops and soya cattle feed are the fault of a system where we are at a distance from the processes by which our plates are filled, possessions are produced and energy is mined. Our food system alone is responsible for 30% of global greenhouse gases and we throw away a third of what is produced. At Old Hall, their critical mass and shared space allows the residents to live in communion with the land. They can milk by hand in a bucket and shape cheese in the dairy, because they have enough people to commit to a twice daily milking schedule. Like other communities, they're able to redefine what is of value within their enclave.

If it sounds like they have created Utopia, then it is one punctuated by weekly meetings, break-out groups, inter-community politics and governance structures. Although members here have been drawn together by a life lived in partnership with the land, and the opportunity to live in ways which serve the planet, there is no guiding book, no shared set of principles that unite the octogenarian farmer, woollen-socked middle-class mum, pre-teen girls and Nepalese beautician into a consensus about how those green ambitions should be spelt out.

They live closely together but do not follow the same religion, hold the same politics or sign up to the same worldviews. 'We're twenty groups with twenty different ideas about how to live,' someone tells me over lunch when I enquire as to how the community dealt with Covid. 'The community is just a microcosm of the world outside.'

There are unresolved discussions about what money should be spent on, how children should be brought up and what food should be eaten. There are vegans in the community whose resources contribute to cattle rearing, and childless singles whose dining room is scattered with Duplo. The various perspectives and priorities rub up against each other as they share space.

Life here is marked by a surprising lack of consensus. Although the Bruderhof practised some of the same ways of living, following the rhythms of the land, their external measure of control provided by a religious manifesto gave these practices some uniformity. If not consensus as such, then an agreed submission of self-will.

Here, life together trundles along without this agreed set of principles or sense of external control. It makes for a more inclusive but rather hotch-potch approach, both ideologically and aesthetically. The physical space is imprinted with the personalities, skills and preferences of those who've given their time to it, some enduringly and others stamping their personalities on the land before they leave it. Formerly, resident Swedes built a sauna, a thatcher thatched some houses which are now leaning a little in his absence and starting to bald, and a collaborative approach to building an outside toilet on the allotment led to a building whose top doesn't quite match its bottom. It looks like a tiled mushroom.

The food we eat each night is a reflection of its chef. My first night we have cheesy pasta, baked beans and boiled cabbage and my second a tapas of garlic sautéed broccoli, turmeric rice, gingery wilted spinach, spaghetti with vegan vegetable sauce, and toasted cashews. Even the farming, which ties them all firmly to the soil, is met by multiple different approaches. There are staunch no-diggers who want to leave nettles and grass to mingle with the crops, the traditional farmers who want to rotovate the soil, self-sufficiency enthusiasts planting beans and pulses, and vegans who, left to their own devices, would put the cows out to pasture and focus on oat milk production. The different techniques are marked in a patchwork blanket laid across the squares of land.

'Not everyone stays,' one of their longer-standing members Fabio, a Colombian man, tells me. 'They like the idea of Utopia, but it doesn't turn out how they thought it would.' Members are happily unguarded about this lack of cohesion, telling me about conflicts around potential members, disability care, parenting, balance of work, private education and feminism.

Last year a polite note was posted on the hallway board telling 'gentlemen members' that perhaps the live-in female volunteers might find compliments inappropriate. It caused uproar amongst the gentlemen members over whether they were the unofficial target for their innocently meant remarks. These dialogues surround both large and small decisions, and frameworks for dealing with conflict have been developed.

During my visit a disagreement about whether to keep, sell or throw away a legless pool table, which has leaned against a chapel wall for a number of years, was playing out around kitchen conversations, noticeboard contributions and their Friday community meetings. I was part of three separate mealtime discussions on the topic and found a note pinned onto the hallway noticeboard and signed by several members, pleading against its journey to the skip and citing it as a community asset. Someone had added a pencil comment to the printed A4 asking 'Does anyone know where the legs are?'

Potential new members are also a hot topic as their request to join has to be agreed upon by existing residents. I meet a German woman whilst I'm there who is visiting as a 'pot member' hoping to be accepted. A few times I am greeted in the dining hall by the enquiry, 'Now, are you the pot member or the writer?'

The woman was conscious that she had to get around and meet all the residents so that they had a reference point for when her application came. Not everyone is accepted. If there are concerns that a potential member would be disruptive to the community's harmony, they are turned down, regardless of their potential financial contribution. Decisions are relational rather than following a set of criteria. The community is a sensitive balance, and adding new people to the mix, who would share the decision-making power equally, is not taken lightly.

The conversation topics have changed in shape since Old Hall's conception, but the same items still crop up in quite similar ways they would in a four-person household. After the first three months of the community in 1974 a list was compiled to discuss the finer points of a communal food budget. 'Vices' for consideration were as follows: *Cigarettes £140, Ribena £30, Crisps £2, Shoe laces £2, Ryvita £8, Vim and Bleach £3 and Fish Fingers, £10.*

Working these things out with fifty people is undoubtedly energy intensive and for many of us, the last thing we want to be doing after a busy day. 'You ought to have been here when crunchy nut cornflakes was the big topic,' Naomi, who's recently joined, tells me laughing, before adding, 'I think we're too tolerant. If there's one person who doesn't agree, they should just lump it.'

At Old Hall, decision making is built around a consensus model rather than a democratic one. Jill tells me about a harmony group, set up during some intra-community fractions, whose purpose is maintaining peace amid disagreement. Someone actually being asked to leave is rare and only comes after a series of mediations and group meetings, a process set out in writing for the community to follow.

'You can't be a grudge holder if you live here,' Maya, a young mum, tells me. 'Those meetings can get quite heated. I just go in and say it how it is but then you have to wake up the next day and think, great, it's another day. It's wonderful living here, but it comes at a cost.'

The governance that would, in other more top-down models be provided by a leadership role, in a non-hierarchical consensus model is given its mandate by mutual consent. Under this system, community members are equal decision makers and effort must be made to 'listen to and accommodate divergent opinions' rather than over-ruling them by majority. This is what Naomi meant by frustrating levels of tolerance.

Conflict is a common feature of community life. Wider issues around conflict resolution and governance come up at every place I visit, and often at our own. Their pool-table-gate reminded me of our charger-gate when people were driven to tears after a disagreement over borrowed phone chargers and the boundaries of private property. Cars were fair game but after that day phone chargers were not.

Dialogue amid difference is not always something we're good at, whether that's between neighbours, friends, families or in the workplace. Disagreement is often played out through passive aggressive Post-it notes in the office kitchen, silent resentment and water-cooler back-biting. Really finding consensus across disagreement is a fine art.

The communities of similarity created by single-person or family households, and opt-in socialising, allow us to distance ourselves from those we might disagree with. We do not have to argue the point, but neither are we forced to understand it, creating a culture which feels fractured and those we disagree with seem 'other', opposite us, rather than next to us.

People call this dynamic the 'culture wars', or 'identity politics', both of which have become quite unhelpful terms wrapped in layers of commentary and co-opted by either side of a divide. The art of sitting with difference is a model for dialogue that requires both parties to be on board. However, if we can truly seek to understand those whose views we disagree with, and make all parties feel heard, it would radically change how we relate to one another and I believe would bring progress in the face of racial, generational, economic and gender inequality.

In expanding our primary social unit to encompass people of different generations, perspectives, races, classes, neuro-diversities, family set-ups, gender identities and sexual orientations, we are forced to look sideways, and outside of our own views. This is taken to pretty extreme levels by the physical sharing of space.

Dialogues that would usually be confined to an individual or possibly a romantic partner are split open and exposed to a greater number of views. What should you be spending your savings on? Should you prioritise improving a shabbily decorated lounge or spend the savings on new energy storage technology? How messy are you prepared for your house to be? Does it matter if one person puts more effort into domestic tasks than another? Should you be ordering from Amazon? What are the criteria for new people? How do we make people feel more included? How can we invite greater economic diversity?

On the noticeboard next to the signed letter about the pool table there is a list of those who'd been voted into 'convenor' and 'officer' roles and so are responsible for drawing together, medi-ating and minuting meetings on their given topic. There are twenty-five different positions including social convenor, health and safety monitor, friary funds auditor, treasurer, recycling convenor and youth convenor. Their time-intensive system is the opposite to the PadSplit 'callout' app function. The process of leaving Old Hall is complicated compared with the ease of a

PadSplit reshuffle, and their drawn-out processes of consensus decision-making and compromise reflect that they're in it for better or worse and should find ways to come through difficult decisions with both parties still feeling like they belong in the community, that they have been heard. Esther Perel, the well-known relationship therapist, calls this willingness to take in what the other person has said 'fierce intimacy'. The opposite posture of disagreement is contempt, when in disagreeing with someone we see the other person as lesser, focusing on their identity rather than their ideas and creating a culture of dialogue marked by defensiveness on both sides.

If we want stronger communities, residentially or non-residentially, then the fierce intimacy of hearing those we disagree with is the approach we'll need to take, not opting out but creating mutually agreed structures within which we can disagree well.

The diversity of perspective at Old Hall, though difficult at times, is also the thing I found so arresting about their community. Beyond the similarities of a middle-class socialist majority and available capital, there are many other ways in which they are a pick 'n' mix of identities. They're fairly racially diverse compared to their surrounding rural area, with around 15% non-white. They've come from a variety of backgrounds and experiences, parents are dual and single, folks are straight and queer, and their age span reaches from three to over ninety, meaning that life together is defined by it being deeply intergenerational.

Jo, whose daffodil-covered grave Sophie pointed out to me on my way in, was one of the founding members who died at the farm the previous year, aged 100. They are expecting a new baby to be born this summer from a family who are yet to move in. The over-seventies are living a very different life here than they would in an age-homogeneous care home. And for the young families too this dynamic is transformational.

It's funny how remarkable this seems to me when inter-generational living has been the norm for thousands of years and still is in much of the world. Care homes and single-generational housing are the more recent development. In the US in the mid-nineteenth century 70% of over-sixty-fives were living with children or children-in-law.[4] This didn't always corre-late with poverty, as many of us might assume. In fact, in the nineteenth and early twentieth centuries, the poor were less likely to be in multi-generational households as additional extended family members added to the stability of richer households, holding their wealth collectively and keeping inheritors close.[5] Similar data is true if we look at intergenerational living in Victorian England where household sizes included live-in help and commonly two or three generations, both by choice and necessity.

The popularity of intergenerational living is rising again, to levels much more similar to Victorian England than 1990s Britain.[6] This trend correlates with the CEO-to-worker pay ratio widening to Victorian levels and a bulbous property market; however, intergenerational communities have been associated with greater wellbeing, too. Having additional people to share the time-costs of running a house and parenting can take the pressure off both parties at a time when most families need both parents to work, as well as providing a wider social network.

Rather than being a model of housing which favours elderly relatives who are avoiding isolation as one might assume, living intergenerationally has been proven to benefit the wellbeing of all parties. The stereotype of loneliness as an affliction of the elderly is simply untrue. Parents with children under the age of five are more likely to feel lonely and isolated than the over-seventies.

We are all familiar with the phrase 'it takes a village to raise a child' and yet so often parents, and particularly mothers of young children, are home alone scanning Mumsnet for advice, watching *Cocomelon* reruns or else having to pay £10 an hour for the 'opt-in' social interactions of a baby sensory class or a toddler group. Our soon-to-arrive baby is one of the reasons that we've been drawn back to communal living now, the farm providing the lure of that village within which we'll raise our child. Parenting in a collective has many of the same benefits as living in a collective. Resources are more easily shared, meaning that we don't all need to own the same set of toys, books and bottles. Opinions and experience are more diverse, meaning that expertise and reassurance is more readily at hand. Childcare responsibilities are shared with a wider group so time resources can be pooled more naturally. In multiple-family set-ups children can play with each other, removing the onus on parents to constantly arrange entertainment.

I chat over dinner with Helen, a mum who lives there with her four-year-old son Ollie. She has recently started back at work as a palliative care doctor and tells me that she can't think of another way that returning would have been possible. Two other members at Old Hall cover the school pick-ups on the days she works, bringing Ollie back to the farm and looking after him until Helen returns.

I build sandcastles in the garden with Ollie whilst we chat about his favourite games and places to play. 'Do you want to know who my first and second best friends at Old Hall are?' he asks me, then announces proudly, 'My second best friend is Richard.'

'Richard the farmer, who we had dinner with last night?' I ask, thinking perhaps he's got the wrong name. The Richard I'd met was one of the founder members and is now quite an old man. I'd found him a stern, silent presence. A few minutes later he comes ambling across the garden from the milk shed; the little boy jumps up from the sandpit and points, 'That's him, my second best friend.' (His mum still occupies the top spot.)

I sit with Jill on low stools in the milking shed whilst we talk, the rhythmic spray of milk on plastic bucket providing a soundtrack. She brought up her children here in the seventies. Her daughter, now with her own teen children, still visits Old Hall most days during my stay. Jill describes joining the community in 1976 with four children in tow. She came, in part, because she needed to get out of a difficult living situation she was in and said she found security and support for them all here, alongside a simpler life. There were always people about to watch over them and plenty of land where they could play outside.

Like the children at the Bruderhof who had grown up around a large number of adults, Old Hall's kids are articulate and thoughtful. They mingle amongst the members over dinner, sitting with different parents and play in each other's units after school. There are tantrums, of course, but alongside a lot of play and creativity. There is a sandpit, climbing frame, tree houses, trampolines, bikes, cats and guests and other children constantly available.

Julia, who picked me up from the station with her mum, has arranged my room for me, adding fresh flowers and a water jug and creating a reading nook. 'Maybe I'll be an interior designer?' she says, as they show me my room. She adopts the role of host and refills the flower arrangements, straightens my unmade bed and refills my water jug for me during the stay. 'What books do you like to read?' she asks over dinner. She and her friend, who also lives at the farm, perform dance routines in the kitchen whilst we bake a cake together, squabbling over which of their routines are the best to show me.

In addition to these benefits, though, many of the parents I speak to talk about parenting in a communal setting as their biggest conflict area. Decisions about parenting are inevitably intertwined with the other family units making the same decisions within the shared space. Should children have to eat what the adults have cooked or will you allow them some frozen fish fingers and peas? How much technology is allowed? How much supervision do children need?

It makes parenting infinitely more complex if families you live alongside come down on different sides of these decisions. Can your children, eating kale soup, share a dinner table with the kids from the next unit who are allowed turkey dinosaurs? Is there a standard level of expected chores children have to do?

'We help each other out informally,' one of the mums tells me, 'but I wouldn't really call it co-parenting. Kids playing together takes a lot of pressure off individual parents and you know other people will help you out but we have such different ideas around parenting that it would be impossible to really co-parent.' Some families are more liberal, some are relaxed. There's an inherent vulnerability which comes with your child having their worst tantrum to an audience of forty-eight.

Being part of a conventional family unit living with the wider chosen family of a residential community also brings the additional challenge of sustaining familial identity within a corporate one. Maya, who runs a beauty business on site and cooks weekly Nepalese feasts, tells me about the difficulties of balancing the needs of her family alongside those of a bigger group. Old Hall is set up as one household. Individuals aren't really supposed to have kitchens, although there are some small stoves and microwaves in the flats. Maya talks about carving out boundaries around her family time to make sure she prioritises her growing daughters, amid the swirl of demands that can easily engulf her time. Sometimes she takes plates of food from the dining hall to eat together in their unit, or cooks a one-pot dish on a small electric hob in their flat. I see other families doing this too, collecting a stack of filled plates and balancing them up winding stairs so that their family can eat the meal together.

'They must feel like they're your priority, that you're available to listen to them,' Maya emphasises. I can understand her concerns. Amid the cacophony of voices, in a space like Old Hall where kitchen and bathrooms are communal, it must be difficult to put boundaries in place so that your time and energy are available for family, particularly when other members may not have families of their own. The juggle of this identity as both collective household and individual family, even in the small daily rhythms, seems tough. I know our family will have to navigate it too.

Wider than the tension between family unit and collective is the tension between the collective and the world outside of it. Discussions about the outer edges of communities and decisions about where the lines of duty should be drawn crop up at almost every community I visit. The Bruderhof have sharp boundaries around family time but experience a tension between personal and collective identity. The naturist community I'll go to on my final visit draw a line between welcome and safety. Ben at Mason and Fifth toys with how their buildings can be accessible and positive spaces for local neighbours but in the end, its doors remain closed as they prioritise giving their residents positive spaces to live. In less extreme ways, Sam and I will have to work out how and when to prioritise our marriage and new baby over the de facto social swirl that is our shared space.

It is a set-up which, for families, holding together a unit within a unit, requires intentional effort and stubborn adherence to boundaries. But one which, watching the children move confidently around the space, feeling at home with a wider group of people who are young and old, white and brown, disabled, and non-disabled, seems worth the effort.

The older generation are more diverse than the younger ones. As discussions around parenting reflect life in the outside world, so, in some ways, do their financial arrangements also mirror the problems we can see in global property markets, with younger people struggling to get on the ladder without help.

Most people I speak to express misgivings about the economic arrangement drawn up by the founding members but also can't think of one that would work better. As in the original *Guardian* advert, those buying into Old Hall must have ready cash. The building is still split up into units but now, after almost fifty years of amendments and additions, the units have been further divided. You might own three-twelfths, half, or even eight-thirtieths of a unit. This then corresponds to the original proportions worked out by Mal and Kev, but is tied to the value of the average surrounding property market. When you buy your section, it's called loan stock. In purchasing your half unit, you're buying a twenty-fourth of the total loan stock of Suffolk One Housing Association. A unit which was £10,000 in 1974 is now over £300,000. A flat for one to three people would be around £100,000.

The scale isn't totally linked to market indexes. I pop in to see one resident, Sue, who lives in the old Mother Superior's quarters and uses a wheelchair. It's a warm, wide space with a lounge, kitchenette and large fireplace. Sue is a master seamstress and the corniced walls hang with elaborate embroidered pieces of art. 'How many units is Sue's flat?' I ask later, trying to get my head around how space correlates with loan-stock value. 'Still half a unit' comes the reply, 'but Sue needs wider spaces to move around.'

In this way units are also allocated according to the needs of families. It seems quite a fluid process, like most things, being hashed out at community meetings. The loan stock does not work the same way as a mortgage would. There is a fund that can lend money for those wanting to buy, given in legacy by a founding member who had died, but it's capped at a small proportion of the unit.

Banks will not give a loan against a share in a community space that can't be repossessed should the borrower default, so those joining need to put up the whole amount, or at least most of it. New buyers also need to wait until loan stock is available. You can only buy it from those who have it to sell. Likewise if you want to move out, you have to wait until someone new wants to buy your loan stock. For one couple I speak to, this meant two years of visits before someone was leaving and wanting to sell their loan stock. For others, after a relationship breakup, for example, it might leave you waiting to get your capital back some time after you've decided to move out.

The model doesn't have affordability woven in like LILAC does, and would be a barrier to many wanting to move there, but it's easy to understand its appeal too. External funding from mortgages would put them at risk of repossession, a fate that has befallen a number of similar communities. Its financial structure is one of the reasons why Old Hall still exists, unlike many similar 1970s communes. In other models, a generous philanthropist covering the cost, or subsidising other members, introduces a difficult power dynamic. I was told about another group which established themselves on land on the invitation of an aristocrat environmentalist, planting and building on the land before being turfed out a few years later when he decided to go and live at an ashram instead. Having loan stock that is linked to earnings, like at LILAC, would be a leveller, but could make moving out of Old Hall difficult. Those wanting to leave would find their real-time property cash has lost value compared to the market and not be able to afford the kind of house they'd likely have sold to buy the loan stock, leaving people reluctant to contribute capital to a project when they know it would depreciate, or else, make people feel trapped there by a lack of housing options available on exit.

All of this leaves the property allocation of Old Hall as a microcosm of the world outside too. My grandma lives quite modestly in the house she's lived in for sixty years, now alongside bankers and property tycoons as the area has become unaffordable for any of the younger family. Likewise, at Old Hall older members are more economically diverse than younger ones. There are occupational therapists, a doctor, a writer.

'This doesn't always play out in terms of privilege,' one resident tells me, whilst I'm digging in rows of chitted potatoes ready for an early harvest. The cash investment alongside a therapeutic rural setting, and low ongoing costs means many of the residents have come to the farm after some sort of upheaval. One member pays the fees here with PIP after being registered disabled, another with compensation from an incident, a third with inherited cash after the early death of a parent. 'People often come after a tragic event and being able to live here is the silver lining.'

Once people are at the farm, living costs are extremely low because they're being shared by so many people. There's one payment for maintenance, council tax and energy bills of £75 a month per household and another £60 will cover all your food for the month. If you're able to stump up the lump sum to purchase loan stock, these are living costs which could bring a huge amount of financial freedom. Although I'm sure they exist, I don't meet a single person living there who is working a full-time job. Instead people drop down to part-time hours, freeing up time to spend on the land and with children, taking the foot off the accelerator. It's an attractive set-up, a life where the day-to-day pressures of work–life balance are released by low costs of living, where those living there can step off the treadmill and smell the roses. It's the reason that those weeds can be hand-pulled and cows hand-milked.

*

The intergenerational relationships I see at Old Hall send me in search of projects which have recognised the mutual benefit of intergenerational connection in more conventional contexts, that have sustained vertically connected communities in more urban settings, both residential and non-residential. In many Western contexts, where interconnected generations are the exception rather than the rule, displaced by our lifestyle norms, there are those bucking the trend, engineering the conditions to facilitate them.

The most well-known of these movements celebrating intergenerational connection can be found in Germany's Mehrgenerationenhäuser. Mostly they run community centres that pepper the country where crèches, kindergartens and play groups run alongside groups for the over-fifty-fives. In Stuttgart West, in the south of Germany, I visit one of the first residential Mehrgenerationenhäuser which provides retirement housing also.

The building, which runs the length of a whole block and is three storeys high, has a publicly accessible ground floor. The foyer is parked wheel to wheel with a line of prams and mobility aids. The top floor is split into twenty double flats housing twenty-three residents, between the ages of sixty-five and ninety, and the middle is a state-run kindergarten.

The bottom floor is more like a traditional Mehrgenerationen-haus, a series of meeting spaces where all these groups can converge. Whilst I visit there is a baby yoga class taking place, a group for parents and a subsidised lunch being served in the garden. The twenty tables are mostly full; taken up by the upstairs residents, baby class attendees and local families who come to use the sandpit and playpark. The cooks have made extra for the Ukrainian families that come for lunch twice a week as part of their work to integrate them into local family support systems. As we eat our chickpea curry, there is a stalemate in the walkway between an elderly lady with a walking frame and a tricycling toddler.

We have lunch with Ulrika, who doesn't live on site but comes as part of a befriending scheme for incoming refugees. She is in her seventies and both her children have grown up and moved on to different cities, where her grandchildren are growing up. 'There's something for everyone here,' she tells me. 'Whether you want to garden, volunteer with refugees, cook together or help with children.'

She befriended a young Gambian man there when she first started volunteering; he's now got a flat and a job, but still keeps in touch as a friend. 'I've thought before that I'd like to live here in my later years,' she says. 'You have your own apartment, but you can also come together with people.'

Other people that live outside the centre come along to activities. Pinned to the walls of the cafe are posters recruiting volunteers; 'Are you an older person who likes to read with children?' One asks. And another: 'Would you like to come and share music with the kindergarten?' Along with these groups the centre runs intergenerational theatre and yoga. There are groups for single parents and support spaces for parents of disabled children. Does it feel chaotic to live with such a thoroughfare, I wonder.

I put the question to one of the residents I meet in the lunch queue. She's in her eighties and leans against her walker as she orders food. 'It's wonderful. Just wonderful,' she tells me in response. She doesn't have time to say much else, as she's rushing off to meet some lunch companions.

The flats they live in are around forty-five square metres and cost between 600 and 800 euros a month, inclusive of bills and activities. Some of the residents pay the sum privately and others are helped by the state. It functions like sheltered accommodation with nine-to-five support but residents can arrange care privately and many stay until the end of their lives.

Jonas, who is in his thirties with floppy hair, oversees the housing upstairs. He tells me that many residents shared with him how lonely they had been before coming to live there. Incomers often had had no connection to neighbours, felt isolated and didn't have relatives nearby. He believes their wellbeing has been vastly improved by their intergenerational model.

Back in the UK I speak with Tom Randle, an architect with Levitt Bernstein working on a similar project, one of the first of its kind in the UK. The co-housing block he's helped to design will be shared by the over-fifty-fives and students from one of London's biggest universities. The space will be designed to embed intergenerational connections into the day-to-day lives of students and older people. In parallel to fostering a mixed community, they hope the project will help provide affordable housing for students who may otherwise find city-centre living inaccessible.

Melfield Gardens, which has recently received planning permission, is to be built a short train ride from the city centre. The building will house thirty-four older residents and eight students in a combination of differently purposed co-living spaces. Along with these there will be communal areas used by both groups, a shared post room, laundry facilities and green space. In the gardens there is a store that will house bikes and mobility buggies.

Planning departments and funders like to work in easy-to-understand 'types', Randle tells me. They're used to seeing applications which tick the boxes for 'elderly housing', 'affordable family housing', or 'student accommodation', which trigger straightforward planning precedents and funding streams. This mixed student space and sheltered accommodation, which, like LILAC, is also built to Passive House standard, does not fit within any standard box.

The student spaces will be mostly aimed at post-graduates and in exchange for subsidised rent they will agree to be 'good neighbours'. What this looks like in three dimensions is yet to emerge. Rather than concrete time obligations, which would give shape to their 'good neighbour' clause, the student tenants hope that natural friendships will frame the relationships.

'What if they then just take the reduced rent and don't do anything?' I ask Randle.

'It'll be based on trust. We hope those who've been drawn to live at an intergenerational project will want to build community,' comes the reply. Structured meeting points between the two groups will be provided by monthly meetings.

The consultations with older residents and university students are ongoing and will continue to be as the first residents move in. A photograph from the consultation shows a grey-haired man in a beige jacket taking a guided tour of the facilities via a virtual reality headset.

Projects like these, of course, come with as much risk as reward. Intergenerational divides which crop up at the Christmas dinner tables are far less weighty if you can all go home at the end of the day and laugh about funny old grandad/the youth of today.

*

My week at Old Hall, adapting to their pace and value system, was so enjoyable. I ate beautiful organic food, spent time on the land, connected with other people and was welcomed around their dining tables. Even knowing about the challenges, disagreements, clunky economics and endless meetings, the care and connection to each other, the planet and the health of individuals and their community was such a contrast to the lives that most of us live, that it felt like an oasis. Life at Old Hall is incomparable to the time and connection-poor rhythms that govern the lives of most of my millennial professional friends.

But in that positive community exists a tension, felt in so many utopian movements, that in concentrating your energy in creating a better world in small scale, you merely live alongside a broken system insulated by your improved version. Which is the most effective way to live a good life?

I found myself in discussions with various residents during the week about whether energy would be more effectively spent buying a plough, sacrificing the soil quality and campaigning against the tyranny of industrial meat production? Is the loudness of tying oneself to proposed fracking sites and risking arrest more effective than the quiet commitment to a patch of earth? There is an awareness there that in opting out of these systems the residents of Old Hall are not reforming them, only providing a living model of another option that wouldn't be available to most people.

Almost every member I speak to in every community is grappling with where to place the boundary line between inside and out. The line between family and residential community, and the line between this community and the world beyond it. A protective moat, which prioritises safety within its bounds, can feel like it's missing the point, building a wall around paradise. An open border to their life together, though, can leave those shouldering its operations burnt out as you increase the numbers that draw from the space but who aren't responsible for it. Community necessitates strong bonds between a group, the flip side of which is exclusion. This is necessary for positive group formation – there are maximum healthy group sizes, questions of responsibility and safety requirements. So how do communities juggle their roles as social clubs and hosts? How do you decide how permeable the line around our interdependent social groups needs to be, how blurred the relationship between inside and out and where the duty of care ends? When do we let someone eat at our table and when are they allowed to rearrange the furniture? Are we still living well if we're creating a fairer space which isn't available to all?

Looking back on the community I was part of in my twenties, the place where we drew this boundary between internal well-being and external impact, or rather didn't draw it, was one of the things that made our community feel unsustainable as our lives gained the additional responsibilities of commitment to partners, children and parent-care.

The door was almost always open. People could stop in for a meal, those who were homeless came to use the washing machine, we took people straight from park benches and allowed student graduates to live rent-free at our cost, when we didn't really need to, just because they asked. We perpetually said yes. I owned almost nothing that others were not welcome to use, including my time and energy. The only space I held as private was the 90cm width of mattress on my top bunk.

Other housemates were better at putting in boundaries but I hadn't learnt that yet. I was hyper-aware of my own privilege compared with those that came through the doors and a bit of a martyr. I felt a real urgency about the scale of inequality and impending climate crisis. I was at a stage in my life when I had energy to spare and enjoyed being at the centre of the swirl. I took unhealthy pleasure in the exhaustion of it, in the total absorption of being needed. It took me a long time to learn that I was allowed boundaries too.

There were points when the right thing would have been to say no to the person in need and prioritise our own needs, shut the door against the demands of the outside world and look after each other. I talk about this tension over cups of tea and trowels with the Old Hall residents. The tension of looking after families, of managing the constant pitter patter of community care and of asking whether they're doing enough, whether living in such a principled way is adequate action for a burning planet, whether it's inclusive enough or green enough or making wide enough ripples to the outside world.

A partial resolution to this tension is found by opening Old Hall's doors to strangers for seven months of the year. Guests, often coming from the WorldWide Opportunities on Organic Farms (WWOOF) scheme, are housed and fed in exchange for work on the farm. They are taught to till, prune, plant and harvest, and like me will learn how the soil can produce its own nutrients, the cows tend their own young and the land provide almost everything we need if we seek to understand it.

As we pulled weeds from the patch intended for oats, Sophie told me that when the instability of food systems became reality in the first months of Covid, one of her first thoughts was that if they disintegrated further then Old Hall would have to take on some responsibility for sharing its resources with the wider community, that in the face of a food crisis, they would have to realise their role as a local resource. She talked about wanting to make sure that their community shares its learning with others and doesn't become an eco-refuge for those lucky enough to have the capital. I'm not sure she realised quite how well they're already doing this. How easy it is to be over-critical of our own efforts, to believe the grass of positive impact is greener on the other side.

I also look at those highlighting racial inequality outside police stations, living a zero-plastic life and doing breath work with their children, and feel that my own shabby efforts to live in kind or green ways look disappointing in comparison. Even at Old Hall I thought guiltily of the plastic box of M&S tropical fruit salad and disposable cups that accompanied my journey over.

Us trying to cover every base makes me wonder, is the intentional community conversation, and wider discussions about activism, too caught up in its own perfection? In our search to live in better ways are we set to become those worthy activist stereotypes who I avoid at weddings because they make you feel guilty about cheese and plane travel? Is my compare and contrast exercise of shared houses putting too much pressure on our homes to be ticking every box, being affordable, connected, diverse, altruistic and welcoming? Why am I trying to make a project of my housing, give it a selection of external outcomes? Does it just need to provide a kind, connected oasis from the pressures of life, allowing those living at these projects greater wellbeing and capacity to be able to do what makes them and those around them thrive.

Perhaps that's why the question of whether we want to move into the farm feels like a mountain to climb. I'm not considering whether we want to live with others, which would be a much easier decision, but rather whether we want to turn our home into a project.

It's a thought that brings me to look at those who have instilled the positives of intergenerational community, shared resources and connection to the land around us into their lives in smaller ways, woven into the living structures we already have, creating these points of meeting with people and planet in cities. Making projects accessible to multiple homes rather than turning our homes into projects. Perhaps it's OK for our food project to house our activism and our home, the more private and slower plod of daily commitment to the ground under our feet.

CHAPTER 7

Residential drug rehab: designing in vulnerability in a community of necessity

W E'RE ON THE COUNTY DURHAM coast, a series
of towns built around former mining collieries dotted
along the North Sea's shoreline. It's breathtakingly
beautiful, an expanse of beaches scaled by cliffs and punctuated
by stone stacks and exposed reef-limestone caves. Sea glass and
rounded bricks intersperse the shingle in evidence of the coast's
former industries. Glass-hunters sieve through the stones in search
of the transparent, coloured rocks to be made into jewellery.

East Durham is the home-turf of Billy Elliot and the towns
are still structured around those iconic lines of caterpillar brick
terraces. Since the 1980s the towns that line the sea have been
unevenly gentrified so that preserved former wagon ways and
kitschy boutiques sit alongside employability centres and empty
shops. The chippies and village boxing gyms have been joined
by ice cream parlours and tapas bars. The coastal towns oscillate
along the deprivation index in negative correlation with food
festivals and beach-front developments.

It's also my home-turf, one of my favourite places in the world. It's just a twenty-minute drive from where we're living at the community farm. Its stones are the ones I imagine during my sleep meditation podcast when the slow, even voice tells me to picture where I'm most at peace.

We come here often for sea-front dinners and to swim in the cold North Sea at Seaham, Blackhall, Easington and my favourite, Crimdon beach, joining groups of women tailed by neon safety buoys.

The town I'm heading to has not one, but two, large residential rehabs where people come to live together so they can work through drug and alcohol recovery. I'm not staying with the groups but joining them for a series of mornings, afternoons and evenings to get a sense of how their life lived together looks. I'm brought into 'the fellowship' by Jimmy and Col, who I've known for a number of years through volunteering together at community projects.

The fellowship refers to the collective of groups that follow the twelve-step recovery programme, better known by its composite parts: Narcotics Anonymous, Alcoholics Anonymous, Gamblers Anonymous, Sex Addicts Anonymous or any other. More important than the object of addiction is acknowledging the unrelenting grip of the disease and taking steps towards freedom from it. I've known these institutions as the background hum to Jimmy and Col's lives, as well as many of the people I've met over the years at our community project. Although addiction has been a regular feature of my life, supporting women in prison and after release, I've never had a reason to go along to an NA or AA meeting before. It's run for addicts and by addicts so even those whose lives have been quite affected by addiction may well not really understand how these spaces operate.

For me, NA or AA was short-hand for a church hall with laminated A4 signs that these friends would congregate in on Thursday evenings. I understood it as some kind of recovery social club.

After meeting London's co-livers a few weeks before, for whom a prerequisite to joining is some degree of success, Jimmy and Col would be introducing me to those united residentially by failure. In a world where we allegedly judge a person's trust-worthiness and credibility within seven seconds of meeting them and cast people out of the realms of acceptability for a single mis-informed tweet, it is rare to find a community where joining is premised on admitting your flaws.

Communities of addicts meet in village halls and church basements around the world and in almost every town in the UK but it's not rare for the early stages of recovery to take place in a residential house. These two are made up of multiple house shares joined to two central activity hubs. The first is a men's organisation and the second mixed. The residents of both collect in the fellowship's central meetings, joining those living externally or in 'moving on' properties to make up a large local recovery community.

Jimmy, a Glaswegian former resident, brings me into the men's centre to meet the residents and to attend the first of a series of meetings I'll go to over the following four weeks. It has the markings of a council building; non-slip flooring, padded office chairs and a metal tea urn which is in constant use throughout

161

the day making strong coffees and tea with three sugars. There are fire-exit signs and the wipe-clean cladding of a statutory service. By the building's entrance is an office where staff can be heard dealing with the administration carnage which comes after someone has withdrawn from the tsunami of active addiction and is required to look back on the chaos which litters the beach behind them. One person is on the phone to Citizens Advice, another is counselling on methadone prescriptions and a third is wrestling with TalkTalk over the bill of a resident's former house which had been collecting debt in their absence.

The period of time when someone is in the throes of addiction and life is crashing down around them is referred to as 'the madness'. 'It reminded me of being out in the madness . . .' someone will say, explaining how they felt visiting old friends. Or 'When I think of the kind of things I did when I was in the madness, I can't believe it was me.' Some before and after photos are pinned up in the hallway, mugshots with eyes half focused and ashen skin twinned with smiling, clean-shaven men. On each wall is a poster carrying a motivational quote or a point of explanation, taken from the twelve steps: One day at a time. We do recover. The only way to fail is to quit.

Jimmy had rung me the night before my visit to fill me in on the some of the fellowship's idiosyncratic conventions as I would if I were taking a friend to a Buddhist meditation or a life drawing class. 'When people speak they begin by admitting they're an addict, so if you're not an addict, it's best not to speak in the "sharing back" part. And at the end, when the pot comes round, you wouldn't put money in the pot as a visitor. It's very important that the groups are self-supporting.'

This emphasis on accepting responsibility for your own recovery, whether that's covering the room hire between attendees, or not passing blame for your behaviour, comes up numerous times over the weeks. The language of self-awareness and personal inventory that I would otherwise associate with quite therapised millennial women comparing Enneagrams is common parlance here.

The meeting at the hub is a mixture of those living in the rehab's accommodation and those in drug recovery communities in the local area. The attendees might have been clean and sober for a decade or a matter of hours. These meetings are part of an extremely scheduled life. Particularly when you first come into the centre your days are governed by timed meals, one-to-one sessions, medical appointments, group sharing, recovery workshops. There's an emphasis on discipline and schedule and their life together is formed from mandatory blocks of activity in working hours and voluntary ones at evenings and weekends. I ask Sean, who's been at the centre for four months, to tell me what he thinks it's important for me to know about their life together. 'It's about structure,' he replies. 'We need structure. We need love and care, of course, but the environment makes a massive difference. One bad egg can set off a domino effect and it's about having structure and discipline.'

The day might begin with a meeting looking into the causes of addiction, followed by counselling sessions, a group sharing time, communal lunch, a game or two of pool, exercise, communal washing-up, volunteering time and a workshop on healthy coping mechanisms. Almost every evening there will be a group meeting in the local area too, where you might hear from another recovering addict or share your own story so instead of spending the evenings in the house-blocks, many head back out to these.

As well as the regime, this structured environment is exemplified through the twelve steps which govern life here, offering a route out of addiction. Understanding how their life together is scaffolded by these steps is essential to looking at how these residential communities are built and sustained.

The first three steps are about admitting you have a problem and that you cannot solve it alone, but must turn to a higher power outside yourself. Some people at the fellowship use God, Allah, Buddha, the Universe or energy, and others the power of community or relatives they've lost. The substance of your higher power doesn't matter in itself, just that you turn your will over to 'God, as you understand them', rather than trusting in your own devices.

In Russell Brand's more digestible retelling of the steps, from his book *Recovery*,[1] which follows his process of his recovery from multiple addictions, these first three involve admitting 'I am fucked.' And then accepting: 'I'm not, on my own, going to un-fuck myself.' They mean accepting help.

'Step four,' Brand then says, 'is when it gets a bit fucking admin heavy. Grievances and resentments. Inventory of your wrongs, I wrote down things within me that made me feel ashamed and separate from the world forever . . . I could never be accepted. I could never be good enough.'

At the two centres, this is a big moment for people. They write down their whole life story. Parts where they've been hurt and parts where they've hurt others. They tell the whole story of themselves to this group. Step five is to be completely honest with someone trustworthy about who you are and how badly you've messed up.

From here, it involves asking for help from your higher power to rectify these patterns of behaviour, making amends for the wrongs, whenever possible and beneficial, continuing this process of self-evaluation daily and then reaching out to other addicts to share your recovery. Going through these steps is called 'step-work' and it plays out through meditation, mentoring relationships, written self-exploration, and regular group attendance. They aren't linear. You don't graduate from the steps and then leave them behind, rather they become a way of life, constantly deferring to a power outside your own, regularly journaling your weak points, understanding your patterns of behaviour and maintaining recovery through supporting others towards it. Some of those I meet in the meetings have been clean for years. Even some of the staff who have been sober for decades come along to the meeting with those whose sobriety could be measured in hours.

The first, all-male group I attend with Jimmy consists of around twenty-five men, sitting in a large circle at the centre. I should say that the descriptions of meetings from here onwards are anonymised and spliced together from six separate meetings, both in East Durham and elsewhere. NA and AA meetings are extremely vulnerable spaces and it's important that everything that's said inside the meetings remains private. It also reflects that they're quite cookie-cutter, the framework on which these gatherings hang make them uniform.

The meetings begin by someone reading out a statement which lists its purpose and the rules that govern it. These statements actually take a while to get through but here's a concise version.

NA is a non-profit fellowship, or society of men and women, for whom drugs had become a major problem. We are recovering addicts who meet regularly to help each other stay clean . . . There is only one requirement for membership . . . the desire to stop using . . . Anyone may join, regardless of age, race, sexual identity, creed, religion, or lack of religion. We're not interested in what or how much you used or who your connections are. What you have done in the past. How much or how little you have, but only in what you want to do about your problem, and how we can help. The newcomer is the most important person at any meeting, because we can only keep what we have by giving it away.

This statement is then joined by several others, read by different members of the group listing beliefs, the details of the twelve-step programme and the guidelines for participation. This happens at every meeting so some parts people know by rote. They are the notices that we have to get through before the meeting can properly start and are recited in speedy monotone.

One of the men then gives out tokens which symbolise the number of days someone has gone without using drugs or drinking alcohol. 'Any one-years?' he asks, pulling out a box of coloured keyrings. He runs down the scale. 'Six months? Three months?' A man raises his hand and is given his token along with applause from the rest of the group. The same happens for a thirty-day token, earning the man congratulations. Finally, the one-day token is announced. A man sitting by the door quietly nods and the room erupts in cheers and whoops. Those around him get up and slap him on the back. 'Amazing you've come along today mate.' They invite him to stay for lunch, and to come along to other meetings throughout the week. Seeing him take

166

the token and accept the group's invitation to join, just one day since his last heroin injection, is so dignifying, so affecting that I have to swallow tears.

The group continues with a guest sharing their story over twenty minutes. It's a journey of addiction in its most stripped back, bruising, raw form followed by those around the room taking turns to reflect back their own experiences, sharing in the darkness of addiction admissions about lost jobs, stolen money, neglected children and dishonesty. They air out loud fears and insecurities, selfishness and grief. I think of the things that occupy my night-time thoughts, but that I rarely have the courage to formulate and articulate.

Everything about the constructed community is designed and intentional. These descriptions would be recognisable to members of the fellowship in Derby or Delhi, Manhattan or Manchester. Its unvarying patterns provide a framework within which honesty and vulnerability are unavoidably the terms of engagement. Alongside the familiarity with self-exploration, there are conventions of speech which are extremely particular to the fellowship, a recovery vernacular which marks out those who have been part of these communities.

The most well-known part of this linguistic DNA, which has appeared in a thousand films scripts, is the addiction statement. Even those giving administrative details will precede the announcement with it. 'Hi, My name is Mike, I'm an addict. This meeting will last until 8pm with a ten-minute break at half seven.'

For those of us who've heard these words primarily as a pop culture reference or character device in a TV script, their meaning may be diluted. What I come to realise over the weeks is that this statement is at the heart of the fellowship's running. It is a personal articulation of the first step, the statement which admits you to the community.

Step One: We admit we are powerless over alcohol/drugs – that our lives have become unmanageable. It's so embedded into the meetings that it's like a vocal tic, repeated hundreds of times across the day by everyone in attendance. Step one is the opposite to the humble-bragging LinkedIn profile, the MBE placed casually in your email signature, to the 'by-lines in *The Guardian*, *The Sunday Times* . . .' that I tuck into my own two-line bio. It is Russell Brand's 'I am fucked' on repeat.

Rehabilitation communities do not allow for members to brand themselves in the way we do outside. It doesn't matter what you 'do', whether you're a banker with a high-functioning cocaine addiction or a homeless alcoholic, you arrive as equal – and equally powerless. Entering into the community is dependent on this admission of failure and powerlessness.

'Addiction,' Col tells me, 'doesn't discriminate, whether your family's got money or not, whether you've grown up on a poor council estate. An addict is a man or a woman whose life is controlled by drugs or alcohol. You take it, you take more and eventually, you have no control and start to do anything to get it. That's it. Then you reap the consequences. So you'll get a lot of different circumstances and lifestyles here, hotshot lawyers with loads of money. You get people with nothing, people who are beggars on the streets. You get people that've had professional careers and lost them.'

Sean, who'd been living at the centre for four months, told me that he'd been a support worker for those in drug recovery until the previous year and was a poster boy for successful abstinence. He hadn't realised how bad his drinking and use of crack had got again until he was furloughed over the Covid lockdowns and suddenly there was no structure to mask his using, no nine to five which tempered it. He spoke about the humility of coming into a building he'd taken his clients to for many years and admitting that he needed help too. Details of wealth, connections and status become irrelevant once superseded by the collective admission to powerlessness condensed down to 'I am an addict'.

It is perhaps this naked vulnerability, this mandatory stripping away of pride and self-sufficiency on entry, that makes these communities of sober alcoholics and clean addicts some of the most powerful examples of interdependent connection I've come across over a decade of community work. There are few things that bond people together so quickly as the courage of exposed fragility. I've found so many times that my crumpled, sobbing, cat-haired, pyjama-clad self, or someone else's, has ushered in closeness in a way that meticulously curated hosting never would. It is permission giving, allowing others to let their guards down too. And yet, it's a trap I so often fall into, even in my search for community, covering hurt, denying needs and wanting to be seen as the resilient one in order to be liked or accepted. My instinctive reaction to feeling socially or professionally insecure is to re-fortify the defences I have built around my inadequacies. To bandage the wounds of others in public and lick my own behind closed doors.

'Me, I'm so full of fear,' Sean tells me over sausage casserole after the meeting. 'You are too, Mike,' he says, gesturing to the man across the table who was there for the first week. 'Completely full of fear.'

'No I'm not!' the man replies.

'Bullshit,' Sean responds. 'You're almost as full of fear as me.' They carry on eating lunch, as though the terror that they are newly aware of after emerging from the fog of addiction is as normal a conversation topic as football or weekend plans.

'How do you do it?' I ask Col. How do you get twenty blokes to sit in a circle and talk about their biggest fears more fluently than my therapised female friends in their twenties? Like most of the men here, the version of masculinity Col inherited was not one of group sharing, feelings rounds, and admissions of fear. The geographical context is important here. The closed mines, which still leave their mark on landscapes and lungs, are impressed on cultural identity too. The ruthless stripping of jobs and community assets engineered by Thatcher's government have meant that the emphasis on pride, regional strength and masculine stoicism in the face of suffering became a way to resist. People are used to working hard, putting on a brave face for the sake of others and not making a fuss. Grayson Perry chose the area as the backdrop for his documentary series on masculinity, *All Man*, for this reason, spending time with one of the county's many boxing clubs and embroidering a mining banner with local colliery banner groups.

Col is tall, broad and muscular with tattooed scenes running from his shoulders down to his wrists. His facial hair is sharply angled around his jaw and he's smartly dressed in box-fresh trainers. His criminal record, he tells me, is 'longer than that door'. He is one of the most emotionally intelligent people I know; perceptive, extremely kind and very self-aware. His own journey with addiction started with cannabis use at fifteen and steadily declined into twenty years of selling and taking class A drugs and living in and out of prisons. 'I'd not been conditioned to think like that from being a child,' he tells me, reflecting on vulnerability within the recovery community. 'I wasn't brought up in a household that was functional, and loving and caring. There was a lot of domestic violence. And I was terrified of my dad. I wasn't taught to go, "I'm scared of this" or "I'm struggling". No one I knew was talking like that. But coming here I started to learn by watching others do it and seeing the benefit of it. If I hadn't ended up in treatment I'd never have been able to. A lot of people died before they even had a chance. I'm lucky, I'm still alive myself.'

I'm reminded in every meeting of those who aren't there, whose recovery journeys ended at a wake. 'We have to do it. It's that simple,' another man tells me over a cup of tea. 'I ended up crying to a whole room of people today. I hated it, really hated it. But I want to stay clean and if you stop sharing your shit, you're in the danger zone.'

Brené Brown writes and talks extensively about how vulnerability is the foundation for connection, that it is utterly necessary in order to feel fully loved and fully belonging. Connection is why we're here, she writes, it gives purpose and meaning to our lives.[2] 'Shame is really easily understood as the fear of disconnection.'[3]

What we mean by shame, according to Brown, is that we're scared that if people really knew us, how uninteresting and neurotic we are, how cruel and self-centred, how weak, self-hating and undignified, they would think us not good enough for connection. Not worthy of belonging. And yet, what is in evidence in those meetings is not shame. Even in the darkest, most revealing moments where individuals take responsibility for causing unimaginable harm to their children and families, where people share the depths they went to in order to buy drugs or alcohol, the room responds in unison: thanks for sharing. In a safe environment, that vulnerability is the weapon with which we can counter shame.

Karen Slater, a regular at recovery meetings around the North East, wrote about her experience of addiction and recovery in her book *My Journey Through Hell*.[4] She talks about the power in that moment of sharing. Once she's told her story with her head held high, people can no longer say behind her back, 'She did this?' 'She did that.' 'Have you heard what she's like?' In telling her story out loud, even in its thinnest parts, she's owning her flaws, presenting her whole self to the world and pronouncing: 'I am still lovable, I still belong, with every scar and failure.' No one can control her narrative and shame her with it.

Brown says that allowing ourselves to be really seen like this is the only way to really feel belonging within our communities. 'You either walk inside your story and own it or you stand outside your story and hustle for your worthiness.' The only difference, Brown continues, between those of us who have a strong sense of love and belonging, and those that don't, is that the former group believe that they're worthy of it. They are able to tell the story of who they are with their whole heart. They find connection by having the courage to be imperfect in company.

Recovery communities are premised on that courage to be

imperfect because they have to be. They are designed in such a way that vulnerability isn't just the route to connection, but the route to admission. Everyone in the room needs to be on board for it to work and so they set these expectations into the concrete of their interactions.

After a few meetings of identikit organisational statements, I found myself losing focus at points, thinking, 'Yeah, yeah, we've heard this, can we get to the sharing part now.' Sometimes the structures which govern the fellowship's culture of vulnerability are so prescribed that moments of connection felt contrived.

Pick a word out of the jar and reflect on what it means to you.

Take a token to mark your point on the journey.

Now do a written inventory of your life, including every hurt and every wrong.

Now share it.

This person is going to be your sponsor, a relationship which entails that they help you through these twelve prescribed steps.

When you've got to the twelfth step – share it.

But this intentional emotional admin is what keeps the show on the road.

Addiction reveals in solid form the disconnection that is the opposite of vulnerability. The extremity of addiction, whose effects are felt in every facet of life and which ripple out to family and friends around us, demand an extremity in the approach to countering it. The community's scheduled and intransigent pursuit of positive connection must be as all-consuming and far-reaching as the addiction had become. Because of this, recovery communities provide an example to us all of how we can embed the practice of mutual vulnerability into our inter-actions – in less rigid ways, sure, but just as intentionally. If we learnt from their absolute insistence on honesty, the radical self-examination, their commitment not to judge those who come through the doors, then we could enable radical connection in our residential and non-residential communities too.

For those sitting in circles of chairs, inclusion in a positive supportive community isn't an optional extra that will improve their wellbeing, it is the life raft that will prevent relapse and even death. Their connection is designed to displace other connections. Recovery communities pull their members out of the grip of another community that had formed around dysfunc-tion and facilitated it, a community that had enabled individuals to stay in destructive spirals, that had colluded with decisions that harmed them and the people around them.

For most people joining the fellowship, recovery entails the breaking off of relationships that have been part of their previous life. Col tells me that trying to maintain relationships with alcoholics or drug users is a rite of passage for someone in recovery. 'You think, I've got myself together now, I'm in a strong place, I can still spend time with those people without using drugs again. It's a fool's game,' he tells me, 'because inev-itably, if you sit in a barber's, you'll end up getting a haircut.' Though it might feel quite laboured at times, the inflexibility

of the programme forces healthy communication, good boundaries and radical acceptance of personal responsibility. In its
best iterations, those that make up the fellowship create a
community that is as enabling, encouraging and mutually
vulnerable as their previous communities were enabling and
encouraging in the destruction of the things they loved. It's
always OK not to be OK.

What's interesting is that this rigidity doesn't come at the
expense of open boundaries. I think of those communities I've
met across the weeks that built a distinct culture but are then
required to protect it in some way, to fortify this safety around
its outer edges. In several of the meetings I go along to people
admit to using drugs before coming. Very few people stay clean
and sober at the first attempt to do so. The meetings are full of
those who left with a three-year token and came back to collect
a one-day one.

Despite all the feelings circles, those houses are extremely
challenging places to live. Everyone coming into the building
carries with them the underlying reasons for their addiction, and
the trauma, relationship breakdown, violence and criminality that
comes with it. Most of those in the room will have victims
standing behind them and have been victims themselves whilst
using. Recovery communities have not only to create a safe
holding space, but also to carry this dysfunction within its framework. Life there is chaotic and can be fraught.

Col told me about the disruption it brings to the community
when someone who has been a part of their homes, life and
recovery slips away, or even dies. The houses where they live are
'very tough' places to live. Col tells me, 'You've got different

ages, groups, egos, different levels of trauma and abuse and lifestyles and circumstances and all of that. All these guys are in here for different reasons. Maybe he's trying to get back with a girlfriend or trying to get the kids back, maybe someone's doing it for themselves. Then they're put in houses together and have got to get on. Can you imagine? At the end of the day, you can only do your own recovery in your own life and your own conduct.'

'There's connection,' Sean tells me, 'but there's not always friendship'. He doesn't imagine the people he's met here to be lifelong friends.

Again, their structure, and a vast amount of patience, is the way they erect boundaries to keep those in the community safe but also to keep the door open, to not build a version of community that is dependent on erecting fences around recovery. One of these boundaries is that, for the residential settings, one relapse can mean that you cannot return to the house for a month. The meetings themselves do not have any requirements around sobriety but the houses have strict codes and people being banned for short or long periods is a regular occurrence. I hear people pleading that their slip-up be overlooked being required to leave anyway. It can seem harsh.

The stakes are high. If people can make it through, then these small intense communities are able to provide a bridge to wider community and inclusion in society. 'You get that connection, you build that hope, you build that strength,' Sean explains. 'You talk about digging deep in here and it's that. Digging deep into your soul and trying to forgive myself, trying to re-join society. It's hard because we don't love ourselves. We get told that we're a waste of space, that we're scum, smack heads, crack heads, all of that, but we're all human beings.'

'I used to walk the long way so I didn't have to make eye contact,' one lady shares in recognition. 'Now when I walk past someone, I look them in the eye and say good morning.'

'I pulled my hood over, never looked up when I walked,' a middle-aged man replies.

Angela, who runs the mixed centre, shares that almost every week she goes to buy flowers and gives them out to a stranger. 'When you're an addict you're scum. The worst of the worst,' she tells us. 'Because of your own actions and because of how society sees you you're barred from society, barred from community.' She's been clean for many years now. 'I've spent long enough looking at the ground and I'm not doing it now. I look up now.' There's a nod of recognition around the room.

In the same spirit of repairing relationships with the wider community, volunteering is an important part of recovery. It's the outworking of both making amends and giving back what's been learnt. It's the scheduled re-joining of wider communities. That's how I know so many people in recovery; they are the engine of community cafes, charity shops and drug support services. Admittedly, taking the relapses into account, addicts have been some of our most challenging volunteers but they have also been our most valuable ones, working out their steps at the washing-up bowl.

The admission to this community is a gateway to becoming part of society. That's why people work so hard at it, why they are vulnerable, admit to strangers their worst moments and most abhorrent thoughts in a room where others will reply 'me too', why they fix the outer edges of their lives into the fellowship's scaffolding. Those connections are paving stones not just to community but to society.

This about-turn in how someone sees themselves and is seen by the world around them reminded me of a friend of mine, Dave, who's the caretaker at our cafe and community project. He came to us on mandatory community service and over the last year he's withdrawn not only from the heroin that he'd taken for twenty years but also the methadone that replaced it. He falls firmly in the category of our most valued volunteers.

There was a fight in the street near our project one day. An older man with learning difficulties had started a conversation with a group of teenage girls on the bus. One of their fathers had misunderstood his intentions and had followed him, spoiling for a fight. Dave whisked the man away to safety whilst I talked the girl's father down. After the interaction Dave was shaking. 'That left me fucking wounded,' he told me later. 'My whole life I'd been Dave, the guy who'd do someone in for you. Who could make a petrol bomb or look after your stolen goods. I've always been good for it. And here, I'm suddenly Dave, the guy who'll look after the lad in trouble and walk away from a fight.'

It wasn't just my instincts that had shocked him, that my assumption had been that the man was most safe in his care, but that he'd come to see himself that way too, that his reaction had changed radically from the outside in. 'I fucking wept when I got home,' he told me the following week. Recovery communities are not meant to be a finite replacement of your community, to provide a complete social world for you. They are intense and specific support networks which provides the access code for wider flourishing, which help you completely alter your patterns of communication and in doing so change your relationship with the world outside.

Step twelve makes clear: Giving it away is the only way you can keep it. Sharing the fruits of sobriety is the only mechanism by which your own achievements are able to persist.

Russell Brand again: 'The twelfth step is where we unpick the great problem of our age, self-centredness, narcissism, obsession with self. I start to look beyond self-centredness, knowing that it'll always be there but not having it as my coordinate. My guiding start becomes "are you being kind to anyone". Pause for a moment to think, have you done anything for anyone other than yourself all day. If the answer is no, that's a weird thing for a social animal.'

Step twelve is why they do not wall off their sobriety to newcomers, even those with shaking hands, quick tempers and one-day tokens who might destabilise the community. Instead, they have sharp boundaries for what they expect of those there and clear rules for engagement. They understand that self-flourishing will only persist in so far as it's passed on to others, that in order to thrive we must give to others the conditions that they need to thrive. This is a huge challenge to those of us juggling with creating positive living environments which promote well-being, give solutions to the housing and cost of living crisis, that provide environmentally sustainable living and kind, supportive connection. Can we really keep these things if we create borders around them barring further access? If we build our communities as enclaves? Which boundaries are necessary for safe, flourishing communities and which ones could be their undoing?

Jimmy and Col have no reason now to stay within those communities in their move-on properties. They've both been clean and sober for a number of years. Col is dating a police-woman. Jimmy is one of the most well-liked and respected men I know. Both could easily leave the mess and dysfunction behind and build nice new lives at a distance that would not be stained by those years of addiction. They would not have to deal with their own experiences mirrored in those coming in, in the chaos of relapse and dysfunction of randomly grouped people healing from trauma in asymmetric parallel. They wouldn't have to tell anyone about their addictions. They don't, though. They give hours and hours of their time, at no cost to these groups. They know a condition of their wellbeing is enabling others to have the same.

Though these recovery communities are the most particular of any I'll visit, and the framework of their life together is unlikely to be one we'll replicate, I come away from my days on the coast having learnt so much about the mechanics of building healthy communities, and asking much wider questions about shaping a better world. The honesty of those meetings made me reflect on the dysfunction that most of us allow in our lives, relationships and community. Outside the extremes of addiction we dismiss toxic relationships, moral superiority, judgemental gossip, co-dependence, classist and racist standards, and poor boundaries with silly memes. Sending a pint-size glass of pinot captioned 'haha, wine mum lyf' is easier than saying 'parenting can be really lonely'.

What if those whose lives we live adjacent to, whose pavements we share and voices we can hear through the walls were really telling us what is going on for them? What if we took the example of these recovery communities and had the courage to say it first? To be those people within our local communities who set the agenda on vulnerability.

What kind of communities could we create if we allowed the ubiquity of human frailty to disrupt the power dynamics of inequality? If hotshot lawyers had the humility to be taught by homeless men? What if firm boundaries around our own health and wellbeing allowed us to say 'no' more often and more effectively? What if we understood that privilege, fortune, wellbeing and connection are best served by sharing them?

CHAPTER 8

L'Arche Edinburgh and building community with learning disabled adults

I DID WONDER ABOUT INCLUDING L'ARCHE communities here at all.

They operate a model for residential community where those with and without learning disabilities build a home together, as friends and equals. The movement, started in the sixties, is global; there are 156 L'Arche houses in 38 countries.

In 2020 an internal investigation revealed L'Arche's most prominent founder, the almost-sainted Jean Vanier (literally: there were rumours the Pope would give the man a sainthood) used his spiritual authority to abuse a number of non-disabled women. He coerced the victims, including a nun, to silence by suggesting that the sexual encounters were in some way divinely ordained.

Kirsty, who oversees L'Arche's four Edinburgh houses, described the revelation in terms of grief, a loss which shook the foundations of the movement. Particularly for older community members Vanier had been a figurehead of a fight for personal and structural justice and the recognition of human rights for all. He was admired world-wide for his championing of the voices of minorities, and yet, used that admiration to coerce young women into unwanted sexual relationships. They brought in councillors and psychologists to help the communities process the news. Some members left.

L'Arche is, though, made up of tens of thousands of people. None of them have the global platform that Vanier did, they did not hold the pen or have the ear of the Pope, but they remain radically living out principles of equality in the currency of the everyday. It's them I visited and whose journeys I'm writing about, those living in quiet, committed ways against the grain of culture and society.

This rupture in its history means that L'Arche does not fit easily into the narrative we'd like to assign it. There are no heroes and villains. Instead there is the uncomfortable grey space, there is commitment twinned with disappointment. I felt it was important to include L'Arche because real life, and the added intensity of communal living even more so, demands shades of grey. Each time there is some fallen public activist or disgraced movement, there are behind hundreds of individuals whose worlds have been shattered too but who persist.

We've been at the farm embarking on our two-month experiment for a fortnight when I travel a few hours north to spend a long weekend with two L'Arche houses. The housemates are a 50–50 split of 'core members' who have profound learning difficulties and 'live-ins' who don't. Additionally, there are 'live-out' assistants, friends, volunteers, artists, former L'Archers and their families and pets who orbit the houses, making up its daily rhythms and interactions.

When someone signs up as a live-in for a twelve-month minimum, they agree to work more-or-less a full-time role in the house, helping to cook meals, care for the core members and create a positive home environment with those they live with. In return they receive their transport, food, lodging and a small stipend.

It attracts a very global make-up. Housemates travel from all over the world to be part of L'Arche houses in different countries. Despite changes to immigration conditions and the challenges of Brexit, which have made it more difficult for people to come, the housemates I meet at St Oswald's are Ghanaian, German and Spanish.

There are waiting lists to become a core member at L'Arche and those applying have a broad range of learning difficulties. Some live semi-independently and require little in the way of physical support and others have limited movement and severe cognitive impairments which mean they would be unable to complete tasks such as washing, or walking to the shop without constant accompaniment. Many have limited or no ability to communicate verbally.

Conversation, though, is not in short supply. At St Oswald's, I meet Clive who is able to use just a handful of words but communicates with Hannah and Hugh, a live-in and an assistant who are showing me round, through sound, body language and gesture. Hannah throws a tea towel over each of our heads in turn whilst Clive rocks with laughter at the sensation, at the sight of us disappearing under gingham.

It's not necessarily my comfort zone. After a decade in community work I can confidently attend to a heroin overdose or

185

deescalate a conflict but at St Oswald's I find myself awkward and floundering, a spectator. The focus of some task or other would have provided an anchor for these interactions but in being a home rather than an activity centre, these relationships are not governed by the comfortable dynamic of service user and support worker, structured around a set of expectations. They are built instead from the looser, less prescribed equality of friendship.

'Did you have experience working with learning disabled adults before coming to L'Arche?' I ask Hannah and Hugh, whose interactions seem to me completely natural.

'None.' They both tell me.

'If anything,' Hugh adds, 'it was almost like I was put off by the disability aspect. I was drawn to L'Arche but wondering whether there was a way I could get involved without actually doing the care role.'

Hannah nods. 'I liked the idea of going out with people, supporting them, but the actual care side sort of scared me. I was 18 at the point I joined.'

Hannah and Hugh came to St Oswald's from quite different sets of experiences. Hugh is in his late forties, has a masters in translation and had spent a number of years working in the field before feeling drawn to give up that work and become an assistant at St Oswald's. He has a wife and two kids. Hannah came over from Germany on a year out after graduating. In her second year now, she had decided to stay at L'Arche and then in Edinburgh longer term. She is bold, and describes herself as feminist and part of the LGBTQ+ community.

St Oswald's, where they both work, is unique, even amongst the L'Arche model. It's more of a hybrid between a traditional

L'Arche house and a care home, designed for core members who have significant physical health disabilities additionally or are receiving end-of-life care. The residents may have complex needs or a terminal diagnoses.

The house was originally set up in response to the needs of a core member who had developed dementia, Kirsty explains to me. It was difficult to find care which would recognise the challenges of the condition along with those that come with his learning difficulty and limited ability to communicate verbally. This means that their community has been a space both for care, and for death and dying. On the wall are photos and crafted tributes to two former core members they'd lost in the previous year.

I'd made the trip up to L'Arche with my friend Fran, who works supporting adults with learning difficulties and autism to volunteer at REfUSE's community cafe. Before coming to us she had spent six months as a live-out assistant at St Oswald's. As soon as we arrive, one of the residents who she'd become quite close to during her time there wheels his chair over to her seat until he is right up next to her. 'James Bond,' he says, sharing a private joke to show he remembers her.

Other than being mostly set out over one floor, and having mobility aids fixed to chairs and stairs, the house looks like any other. It has a large lounge and dining room, a garden with vegetable beds, a sunroom, and a kitchen where morning teas are being made and drunk. Clive likes to help make the tea, throwing the top of the teapot on the floor and laughing at its clang on the ground. 'Sure, it would be easier just to do it myself,' Hugh tells me, 'but if we can do it together, it gives him more autonomy, and it's more fun for us both.'

That L'Arche provides a home rather than just a service permeates every part of it, the design of the building, the making of tea, the interactions between people, the collective decision-making process, the language. Being a communal home rather than a care-service means there is no staff room, no packed lunches and no separate lounge so that the assistants can get together at the end of the day and debrief. We all eat lunch together, a vegan lasagne which allows everyone to share the same meal. Before any of the live-ins begin eating they reach first for the plates of the core members and chop the food into small pieces which can be eaten with a spoon. Then everyone starts together.

In contrast, Fran went on to work in a conventional care home after she'd left L'Arche and found it jarring that staff at the new place issued an early lunch for the residents so they could then eat in a separate room without being disturbed by them.

This sense of cohesive home across huge health disparity is the most compelling part about L'Arche but it also threw up the most challenges over the Covid lockdowns. Assistants, whose homes and workplaces were one and the same, felt like outside of their bedroom doors, they were constantly needed.

'Right at the beginning of COVID I literally thought that by the end of April, half the people we supported would be dead,' Kirsty tells me, reflecting on the fear of the early pandemic, particularly for disabled communities. 'And, the conversation was – would we have enough food for people? We had to just go to normal supermarkets, we're not set up with big care-home caterers because we're not care homes. So, you know, the assistants were going to the supermarket and getting four tins of tomatoes, and having to do that every day in order to feed people.'

'There was quite a high rate of burnout during that time,' Kirsty continues. 'They couldn't even leave their own home, and go anywhere, so you lived where you worked. You can't really get away from your work and you can't really get away from yourself.'

It was the same dynamic that many of us faced in working from home or having care roles from which the usual respite was unavailable. Our houses that are usually fluid places with people going out to work, school and for social occasions became a one-pot dish of rest, work, parenting and leisure. It was a time without relief when the stale air cycled around the same four walls. For those living at L'Arche, where care responsibilities are woven into the facts of living, this dynamic was intensified and the impact it had on the mental health of their community was significant.

This uneasy boundary between self-care and the ever-present needs of others reminds me so much of my own challenges in our first community. Like Fran, and the others, mine ended in burnout too. 'Over Covid, it just didn't work,' Fran tells me.

The PR of diversity and inclusion doesn't give much space to the reality that connection across difference can be draining and costly. Ask any Black person working in a white majority environment who is faced with the added emotional tax of people's assumptions, any manager who commits to covering employees' mental health days, any friendship group negotiating economic disparity. It can be easier to just . . . not.

We separate ourselves into groups of similarity because, in the short term, it makes life easier. We create structures around inclusion and social care, outsource it to statuary services, charities and helplines rather than supporting one another because the work of care can take more from us than we have available to give. Challenging these often quite clinical structures that hold us in power dynamics with others may be dignifying and empowering, but if it demands more from each party than they have available, then it's ultimately not sustainable.

Many involved in L'Arche though, *have* been sustaining community there for years. There are L'Arche families who have been living in and out of the communities their whole lives. Who've had children within its folds and whose children have become live-ins after them. Kirsty has, herself, been there for thirty years. So what's the magic formula? Are they all just better people than me?

The cast of characters who circulate L'Arche do not speak about charity, they do not see themselves as there to give, a posture which would eventually leave them empty. Instead, I hear many stories about a more mutual, deeply held sense of belonging.

I ask Kirsty why she's stayed for so long when there are better paid roles, where less would be demanded of her. 'I keep coming back because of Marcus,' she says in response. She is referring to one of their core members who has been with L'Arche for years.

Marcus's communication tool is to find a point of connection with a person and then return to it each time they meet, a marker of familiarity, a shared interest or activity. For Kirsty, whose dad died around the same time as Marcus's mum, their shared grief is their ongoing point of connection. Although, on paper,

Marcus's communication is hampered by his disabilities, each time they see one another he initiates a moment when he asks, 'Did you know my mum died?' and then gives her space to share about her own bereavement. Many years after the bereavement, this recognition of its enormity by a friend is rare and precious.

Anna, who manages St Oswald's, tells me how being at L'Arche, with its culture of radical acceptance, provided a supportive context for her to come out as asexual. One of the core members from a previous project, in seeing her preparations for her first Pride gestured to her that he was gay, something he'd not found the courage to do in other settings. The two of them made rainbow flags together for her to take.

Hugh tells me that L'Arche allows him to experience a broader conception of masculinity. He'd always felt that he didn't fit the scripts that he'd been given. An old Harrovian, Durham University alumnus, father of two and professional translator, his gentle, kind qualities had always made him a black sheep amongst bullish white ones. He writes beautiful, vulnerable poetry, speaks in a reticent, sing-song tone and thinks for a long time before speaking, assembling the words correctly in his head before delivering them. At L'Arche, what it is to be a man is stretched out to cover a broad range of human masculinity. One can be a man and require your food cutting up into small pieces to eat from a plastic spoon. One can be a man and require help to wash and toilet. One can be a man and be physically vulnerable, and emotional, enjoying arts and crafts, or the sensation of a tea towel over skin. This culture radically reframes, in micro, the boundary lines of masculinity, for Hugh as much as for the core members. It meant that he could find a community of acceptance too.

Hugh wrote this, reflecting on his time at L'Arche:

People Like Me
A poem for J, who died at St Oswald's last year
(For J, 1957–2021).

> I know
> What it's like
> To not
> Fit in.
>
> How could I
> Fit in
> When I wasn't like
> Other people?
>
> Now I fit in.
> Not because
> I've found people
> like me,
>
> But because
> I've found people
> Who don't care
> That I'm not
> Like them.

Hannah's stories about belonging here are similar. She came over from Germany at eighteen and describes the members at

St Oswald's as her first flatmates. Her time here has been marked by some of the most harrowing experiences of her life. Two of the core members who she'd become extremely close to died during her first year. It was during the Covid lockdowns and she recounts working nineteen hours straight, holding Maggie's hand so she'd not be alone when she died. She describes them gathering around the bed of another core member Sue, singing 'You are my sunshine' as she drifted away. Unable to go out and let off steam because of the demands of the lockdowns she tells me the year had a negative impact on her mental health. And yet she also says that she used to tell Maggie: 'You're the best first flatmate I ever had.'

'I moved straight from home here,' she explains. 'So I lived with four disabled people and four people from all over the world. When I moved here I basically lost all of my friends back home because of some stuff that happened. And I was so sad. Sometimes I have really bad days, really bad mental health. And I think, "Oh, I don't have any friends. I'm so lost in this world." And I'll just come in and Clive will look straight at me and say, "Oh, my pal".'

'They're not just friends,' she finishes. 'They're amazing friends. They're such good friends.'

To my shame, I expected the live-ins and assistants to be a cast of worthy do-gooders whose life here is an act of charity. It's a much smaller life than I could imagine living, much more restricted and domestic, surely an act of self-denial? Instead, I meet people whose friendships with learning disabled adults, and the value-shift that enables, had allowed them freedom in their own identities; Anna finding a safe context to explore her queer self comfortably; Hannah finding community and friendship again, where even in the pain of death and its following grief she was able to get to know herself and grow into the adult she now is; Hugh being released to see a whole possible spectrum of masculinity; and Kirsty to acknowledge her own loss.

Reframing what is of value changes the terms of engagement for everyone, challenging norms of masculinity, capitalism and friendship.

Hugh tells me that one of his jobs is to take Clive out on rides in the van. 'Basically,' he relays, 'all he's interested in is going over speed bumps. It's literally his best thing. He also quite likes going on roundabouts, so we find a route with the most speed bumps and roundabouts and just drive around.'

'So you don't go anywhere?' I ask.

'No. You don't really go anywhere. I mean, I go somewhere kind of, just to give us a bit of a focus and so we can stop for snack. Then we come back via as many speed bumps and round-abouts as we can. I used to think "he needs to go somewhere new to experience something or see something different." But literally, after a couple of years, I'm realising that was my idea. Now we go to a place where there are thirty speed bumps in a row. So yes, it feels nice that now we know what we like, what works for us. It's his favourite thing.'

Whilst modernity encourages us to optimise our time, to bio-hack our productivity, life at L'Arche can see inefficiency as more dignifying. The teapot lid thrown on the floor and the drive to nowhere are as valid as the quickly ticked off tea round and the fixed destination.

It was, for me, a powerful illustration of diversity and inclusion. Not some act of charity or a PR exercise but a change in dynamic which will give every member the conditions to flourish. If we were all able to include disabled members at the heart of our communities, designing spaces, frameworks and terms of participation in such a way that they are not disadvantaged by access, it would bring radical changes for every member of those communities. It would disrupt the notion that our value is linked to our productivity. It would challenge social systems which are built on exclusivity. What would that look like in our workplaces? Local communities? At other intentional communities like the farm?

This diverse culture has helped contribute to a wider change in the narrative around disability. Just as Harlem Ashram was a catalyst for wider changes in civil rights, and LILAC has provided a national challenge to the problems of property market gentrification, the way of life in L'Arche communities has permeated the wider culture.

In the early years, Kirsty tells me, the core members would arrive from asylums: 'Forty/forty-five years ago if you had a learning disability, you were put away in a big institution. And so the first generation of people that were welcomed into L'Arche communities in the UK mainly came from those big institutions with no family, or very little family involvement. They were quite institutionalised. One woman that I supported in London, literally carried her life around in carrier bags, because in the institution, you just put on the clothes, which came out of the cupboard, whether they were yours or not. You didn't have anything which was yours. Because you lived in a big dormitory there was no privacy.

'So that was very much the starting point into which we were just offering a home with more of a family feel to it, deliberately smaller with four or five people supported to live there rather than huge places with hundreds of people.'

Many people in that first generation were not used to having choices, being recognised as individuals or even seen as human. This extreme power dynamic which faced early communities and still faces all communities made up of those who are a mix of race, disability, class, age and communication skills makes me reflect on a much larger question: how do you truly create space for those who have traditionally been disempowered to be community leaders and decision makers within our communities? International live-ins often speak multiple language and the core members might just have a handful of words or communicate through expression, body language or sound. In these circum-stances, it can be a damn sight easier to make the decision about what's best for someone on their behalf.

It reminded me of life in our first community, where we sometimes had at the table those who were fleeing violence or had been homeless. Our longest guest Tom, who stayed for five months, forced to the surface questions about governance which we had not had to consider before, discussions about how our life together could be shaped by everyone who was part of it. Coming straight from street-homelessness at nineteen, he brought with him some of the trappings of his normality. A magpie chick found in a garden nest became resident under his bed, fed on a diet of minced worms, and an air-rifle was brought into our pacifist house. He killed and skinned a pregnant squirrel after a discussion on free-range meat. We had to find the balance between letting him fully express the person that he was and the needs and preferences of others that lived there, to balance everyone's opinions and personalities. We had to acknowledge not just how much he had to learn about living in a stable environment but how much more he had to teach us about not having had one. The air-rifle was kept in storage for the duration of his stay and together we built Bobby the magpie an outdoor home he moved into when his feathers came in. Usually a vegetarian, I helped Tom to slow cook the squirrel and form the meat into nuggets that we served to our friends.

Kirsty talks about the processes, developed over many years to empower core members to make decisions about how their homes feel and operate. They facilitate feedback sessions which help people use images and sounds to express how they feel about life there, having check-ins where time is taken to discern what someone's preference is.

Collaborative shaping of environments is the longer route. It would have been quicker and tidier to assume a parental role to Tom, issuing a set of rules on his arrival, but which would have stunted him and not recognised how much he had to bring. This communal working-out of boundaries, sometimes with those for whom the learnt skill of deliberative debate has not been made available, involves thinking beyond discussion as the only tool for consensual decision-making.

Like us, L'Arche are still learning. Fran tells me about a moment when she was working at St Oswald's. She was administering a syringe of medicine to one of the core members. One of the live-ins turned to her and asked, 'Does he prefer his medicine in a syringe. Is that the most dignified way we can do it?'

'She was right,' Fran reflects. 'I'd never asked him whether he wants to use a spoon or not. I'd just copied what I'd seen everyone else do. And it *is* a bit invasive, getting things shoved in your mouth, when he can't control the speed that it goes out.'

The care sector, which is chronically underfunded and time-starved, does not tend to operate on a collaborative power dynamic, they do not have time to. The assumption that you'd syringe medication would be completely normal. Building a home, rather than efficiently administering care, involves unpicking these learnt assumptions around disability.

Sexuality too has been an area for growth and learning. 'Thirty years ago, that wasn't even a conversation we were having,' Kirsty tells me. 'But part of recognising the whole person, and acknowledging individual rights, involves facilitating people's journey of discovering their sexuality.' She describes a core member in one of the London houses who would occasionally put films with sex scenes on her iPad in the communal lounge, inadvertently playing moans at top volume to those who shared the room. As her communication was limited it wasn't clear whether those scenes were chosen specifically or merely the result of a random combination of pressed buttons but none-theless it was decided that the live-ins should treat her watching as a positive and healthy exploration and suggest she watch the remainder of the show with headphones or in the privacy of her room.

Their insistence on giving space for the tentative, or perhaps even coincidental, exploration of sexuality by their core members made me reflect again on the experience around disability I'd seen at the Bruderhof. Barriers to inclusion in their communal life had been designed out but, as with all members, their communal life involved denying parts of themselves which transgressed the agreed system of belief. In prioritising unity, members were unable to bring their whole selves to the table.

L'Arche's slow work of redefining what is valued in their communities demonstrates, in a very particular and extreme way, the power that communities have to turn popular thought on its head, and design an internal culture which runs parallel to mainstream society, and yet sends ripples out into it.

Their life together has re-assigned great value to a group who are so often marginalised. They've endeavoured to level the playing field so that those with learning difficulties are brought out of society's negative equity, not despite their learning difficulties but because of them and the unique gifts that come with them.

There is a scheme which runs in our local area where businesses are paid to take on adults with learning difficulties as interns. It's actually a wonderful scheme, and it's brought kind and capable young adults to our community project. It's not an unusual programme – it's a model happening up and down the country – but it made me stop and think. Are we designating the time of our learning disabled neighbours so low that they're in negative equity, that we're paid to take them on?

The narrative at L'Arche is that assistants without learning disabilities have as much to gain from their learning disabled counterparts as they have to give them. This kind of idea appears as a slightly self-satisfied statement across activism. For me, it conjures up a TV presenter visiting an orphanage giving a slightly contrived speech to camera about how little Timmy has 'taught them so much'. The mutuality of the community here, though, does not feel inauthentic. It is threaded through the stories I'm told in ways large and small.

Of course, that mutuality tipped during the pandemic where the intense L'Arche homes became their residents' whole worlds, preventing outings, art classes, trips over the speed bumps and respite and relaxation with those outside of the bubble. The burnouts and mental health declines of live-ins during the pandemic showed what it can look like when community demands from you more than you have to give. It showed the value and necessity of the wider community within which the houses are held.

Now that the world has opened back up, the boundaries at L'Arche are once again becoming more permeable. The large cast of extras who circulate the core communities, who'd been assistants once, who'd married and had families within L'Arche, who'd worked, left and come back, are now able once again to be a part of life there. Across the weekend these extras take core members for lunches out and visit for cups of tea.

On my last day I join an art club at the central meeting space where members from each of the houses can meet and mingle. They show me pieces – drawings and paintings – they'd made together for Grayson Perry's art club. The art was to be sent to the L'Arche community in Ukraine, who they've been meeting with on Zoom since the start of the conflict to share prayers and encouragements.

We are a mixed bag at the art class. Some L'Arche semi-independent members attend, along with a German Franciscan friar, and Polish and Spanish former live-ins. Some colour patterns on paper, others draw across Ukrainian flag templates in A4 and others still paint rounded stones someone has collected on a beach trip. A dog comes to say hello and then Bernadette, a former live-in, and her daughter Clara who's two join us.

'Aunty Sarah, Aunty Sarah!' the two-year-old girl shouts as she comes toddling into the art class. She approaches one of the core members, holds her hand and clambers up next to her. Sarah, who had been complaining about her weekend to a Franciscan friar who lives at the West Hill, a more typical L'Arche house, beams back.

'I'm Aunty Sarah,' she says, to make sure I'm clear. 'I was at her Christening.'

Although they are not involved in any formal way at L'Arche now, Clara and her mum regularly visit the art club to say hello. Part way through, a tea round is made and Sarah takes me and Clara to feed the fish. It's her responsibility and a role in which she takes great pride.

The live-ins are not saints here, and nor are they completely separate from economic priorities and pressures. Their funding comes from statutory contracts and so they still are essentially being paid by government bodies to run a service which takes place in the building of home.

There remains the tension that most of the core members will call L'Arche their home for decades and in that time see many different live-ins stay for just a year or two before leaving. Core members are also paying rent to be there in a way that live-ins are not. As much as the L'Arche houses seek to design in equality, core members will be accompanied by a rotating cast of house-mates each year. There is an inherent inequality in that core members themselves cannot choose to leave or decide who comes and goes into their house. They get who comes and lose them when they choose to leave.

The last few years have caused L'Arche to reflect on whether the equality of a housemate relationship fits comfortably next to care responsibilities too. Kirsty wondered if, in the future, personal care would be outsourced to assistants, leaving live-ins to focus on friendship with core members.

Time with L'Arche caused me to reflect again on the role that intentional communities can have modelling alternative ways of organising society. They use the critical mass of living together to create frameworks within which societal norms can be set aside and replaced with alternatives, better ones. Even with those constant tensions about how to truly live their values, the imperfection of any attempt to design in total equality, the understanding of how much learning disabled people have to offer society is so deeply held amongst past and present members of L'Arche communities that it's difficult not to absorb. You are swept in its slipstream as soon as you enter through their doors. You see the world differently.

The inclusive community they have built, which sought to remove barriers for learning disabled members has removed barriers to inclusion for everyone, barriers they imposed themselves or had been given by society. It gave Kirsty permission to remember her father alongside Marcus. It gave Anna a supportive framework within which to explore her sexuality; it gave Hugh a context in which he could feel free to be himself, unfettered by the suffocating constraints of masculine scripts; and it provided Hannah a context within which she could build a community, share poor mental health days and learn and grow as she sat alongside Maggie in her death. Changing the metrics against which people are valued provided metrics for everyone to thrive.

The question is, how do we replicate that values shift scaled up into our own homes, communities, families, workplaces and even supply chains? Is it even possible in a globalised capitalist world to live with integrity to our ideals within homes, communities and the world?

L'Arche live-ins don't have conventional jobs or families. It takes a huge amount of time to live the way they do. No one I know would consciously co-sign a culture in which disabled and elderly members are held in low esteem, in which we devalue those in marginalised groups who must prove themselves doubly to be held equally, in which we outsource our low-cost labour under the implicit understanding that the lives of workers in the UK are of more concern than those in Vietnam and Bangladesh. And yet it's a world that, by default, we're all participants in. These are the value systems which govern how we live. I'm no exception.

In large scale, this is a very draining thought, where each email we send, piece of clothing we wear, meal we eat and interaction we have on the street is a source of injustice. It's a bit sackcloth and ashes. Woe betide the person who gets seated next to the systemic justice warrior at a wedding.

In micro though, it's possible to challenge the value scripts we've absorbed by osmosis, and to project these out into the world through the pragmatic activism of daily life. Within our communities we can turn the dictates of capital on their head. We can seek out the opinion of the quietest person in the room, and celebrate the achievements of the most junior. We can recognise that wisdom rarely looks like letters after a name and give power to those with lived experience, even if that is a longer road. We can insist on broadening our frameworks for communication so that a wider number of people can be heard. Like Hugh, we can go the long way round. We can sit uncomfortably with thrown teapots, slowed down by a journey of speed bumps and round-abouts, knowing there is joy to be had in inefficiency.

CHAPTER 9

Together for success: hacker houses and the civic technologists

N EWSPEAK HOUSE OCCUPIES A LARGE building at one end of Brick Lane in East London. The area has long been a poster child for gentrification but also a centre for social change, innovation and entrepreneurship. It's a dynamic mix of long-standing Indian restaurants, Jewish salt-beef bagel shops and novelty cafes whose whole menu is just avocado or cereal. It's an area populated by people founding start-ups on their MacBooks and its lampposts are pinned with police notices asking for witnesses to a stabbing. There are fashion brands launching themselves in shipping container pop-ups, political street art climbs the brick walls and proper caffs serve fried breakfasts on Formica tables. It is a street in conversation with itself.

It strikes me as an appropriate setting for Newspeak House, a space where community is not held for its own sake but to host an ongoing discussion, a pressure cooker within which ideas are thrown and either honed or discarded.

Newspeak House is a co-housing project designed for 'socially conscious technologists' to live alongside other tech-activists whilst they develop ideas and work on projects which aim at strategic social change. They are intentional about including residents across the political spectrum so that ideas are developed in the context of a broad range of skills and experience rather than the narrow circuit of our individual ideological silos.

To understand how the house emerged and developed, its founder Edward Saperia tells me, you have to understand the context. It was 2011, when the effects of the 2008 financial crash were still filtering through to people. London felt bruised and was struggling to pick itself up after the knock-backs. Disillusionment with the financial systems that invisibly governed us had bedded in.

'This was before fake news,' Edward tells me. 'This is very early mobile, web 2.0. Social networking was relatively established but still quite primitive compared to what it is today. The tech sector was still in an exciting time where people would just make stuff and it would be new and it was very unclear what would happen, or even what the business models would be. Coupled with the recession there were loads of young people who had graduated, the job market wasn't great but they're smart, they taught themselves some technical skills and suddenly they found work and things to do.'

It was a utopian moment for the tech sector, when people knew the technology they were developing was going to change the world but the lines of that map had yet to be fully drawn. Most people felt that the tech sector and emerging online world would be a vehicle of positive change. The business model for the attention economy that would come to dictate social media interactions and stoke our outrage and division for profit, had yet to emerge.

It was almost an artists' collective at this point, Edward tells me, where creatives and like-minded tech enthusiasts lived together but no wider focus had emerged. The community's current identity was formed as it grew obvious that technology wasn't necessarily going to be the force for good that coder utopians had thought it might be. And so the need for a space where people could come together to design positive solutions grew. Civic technologists, who wanted to shape the tech space in positive ways, found a gathering point at Newspeak House.

Typically people live here for six months or a year. The house-mates are referred to as Newspeak House's 'fellows'. Upstairs it's a fairly standard co-living set-up. There's a kitchen, lounge, co-working space and large terrace that is shared by all the residents. A third floor houses private bedrooms and shared bathrooms. The communal space has quite a student-y feel. Past iterations of the communal area had more of a cyber theme, or included neon graffiti murals but currently the walls are painted over with chalk board paint, a move which reflects a house in flux.

The names of the current residents are chalked on the wall, in a grid made of salvaged picture frames, alongside their areas of interest. Amongst the listed interests of the cohort are refugee settlements, curiosity-driven fundamental research, Tofu (a cat), supply chains, Taxonomy crowdsourcing and inefficient markets (of which I could possibly define half).

What it's morphed into now, some years away from its more informal roots, is more of a learning institution, an incubation space for ideas. Although I get the sense after speaking to two others who have spent time there that if you asked each resident what Newspeak House is, you'd get a different answer.

They self-describe as a college, with Edward's job title as 'Dean', but the identity seems a little tentative, approximate. They have very little resemblance to the more prescriptive, bounded educational institutions I've been part of.

Edward's role there is also in a state of tension. He is, thanks to inherited wealth, the building's owner and the project's lead, and yet claims to be sceptical of top-down governance. He has quite specific ideas about what the space should look like and also talks about letting the space be shaped by those in it. He is, in equal parts, pastoral and provoking. He's anarchically in charge of Newspeak House, in disagreement with himself.

At street level, Newspeak House is an open shop-front and events venue which seats 120 people. They allow various groups and organisations to use it at no cost for events, discussion nights, political organisation and activism. These events are where most of the action happens; it's the meeting point between the soup of ideas in the residential space and the outside world. The events downstairs will often end in the lounge or on the terrace. They make the space feel very permeable. I wasn't even clear after an hour with Edward how many people actually lived on site.

The ongoing conversation there overlaps with the online world as well as those who flow through its events, so Newspeak House is orbited by many who feel the space is theirs regardless of whether they've ever lived there or even visited. In occupying the world of technology someone's presence there could be physical or virtual, members present in the building or across the world. Those living there were plugging themselves into the network in a very literal way, of course, but by no means the most significant or important one.

Conversation with Edward has a protracted, slightly infuriating quality, where the response to every question is an interrogation of terms or exploration of wider ideas. I keep wanting to say: 'Just answer the bloody question!'

Q: How did you start?

A: In answer to the question, perhaps we should look at the tech space in the early noughties.

Q: How is the space governed?

A: It depends what assumptions you're making about the concept of governance?

Q: So would you call Newspeak House anti-establishment?

A: I'm not sure it's a helpful term in so far as pop culture is typically anti-establishment but that doesn't tell us much about how it actually operates in relation to the establishment? Does it imply a degree of success or merely a posture?

I don't feel like I managed to clarify much about the routines of the space or how it was run during my visit.

'Did you not find it all quite opaque?' I ask a former resident over lunch. 'How did you know what you were joining?'

'In a way, yes. There's not an obvious hierarchy, not obvious systems for conflict or establishing priorities. But that's Edward's whole thing, that governance is an ongoing experiment,' he tells me, not surprised that my time there hadn't provided much clarity on the bones of the place. 'Pinning down concepts isn't always good because it closes off avenues.'

The rules are not concrete. They're shaped by the ideas that sit within the walls at any given moment. Its governance is not set out in policy documents but instead guided by an equilibrium when good ideas will trump worse ones. There's an adversarial element to it where paths are reached by a facilitated tug of war between perspectives and opinions. Unlike the hard-won consensus of so many of the other communities I've visited, Newspeak House thrives on dissonance, the clashing of ideas which allows thoughts to be tested, improved, and discarded, to sink or swim.

'The more coherent you want your worldview to be, the narrower and narrower it gets,' I'm told by the former resident over udon noodles.

The questions I'd been asking, looking to compare their way of life to other intentional communities I'd visited, were the wrong questions at Newspeak House. They didn't need algorithms for harmony, processes for consensus and a filtering system to ensure a cohesive group of residents. Its ends were not served by comfort and the building of predictable and consistent routines. It didn't even need to be a pleasant place to live. It's building community that will be a catalyst, rather than a sustainable framework.

In fact, at times it sounds like quite an annoying space to live. A resident described going to get a glass of water from the kitchen late at night and being asked abruptly to keep quiet so he did not interrupt an ongoing and animated discussion with Extinction Rebellion activists who didn't themselves live in the house but had found themselves there. 'I live here!' he told them, before returning to his room.

It may sometimes be an annoying place to live, but it's undoubtedly a productive one. Former Newspeak House fellows, whose ideas were formed around discussion tables and at events there, can be found dotted through government, business and the third sector. Fellows wrote the Coronavirus Tech Handbook,[1] a crowdsourced guide to pandemic adaption which was used by thousands of people and organisations looking for ways to adapt over the Covid lockdowns. The browser extension 'Who Targets Me?'[2] was developed there, allowing people to mirror the data tracking used by big tech and find out which political groups were targeting them with advertising. Open Access (OA.works)[3] was conceived and built at Newspeak House, a project which uses software to override paywalls on academic articles making scholarship open-source. Often these projects were produced at speed, in reaction to the newly realised demands of the pandemic or in anticipation of an upcoming election. The pace of their development was a product of the concentration of human energy within the space, a jostled together bag of stones, each rounding off the others' sharp edges.

What enables this kind of work is a great deal of failure. The projects above are the highlights. Many of those Newspeak House fellows whose interests are written up on the board will come away from their time there with precious little in the way of tangible achievement. Edward speaks very fondly of these discarded ideas and unreasonable proposals as though they were more vital to the lifeblood of the house than the success stories. There's a culture, typical of entrepreneurial incubation spaces, in which failure is seen as positive and dynamic.

The curated dissonance of Newspeak House, where those using the space are intended to absorb a spectrum of ideas, challenge their assumptions and discover new ways of thinking, involves the meeting of people from across the political spectrum. They've hosted both Extinction Rebellion meet-ups and a Conservative Party hackathon. In fact, they've hosted all the main political parties for hackathons. (Edward describes the activism of these established political parties as some of the least interesting activity that takes place there.)

'Hackathon' – for the uninitiated – is a portmanteau of 'hacking' and 'marathon'. I'd mostly heard the term 'hacking' in relation to Russian political spying or corporate blackmail but 'hackathons' aren't necessarily to do with forging a path into the back end of the web for nefarious ends. Instead they refer to a concentrated process whereby a group get together and collaboratively engineer solutions or improvements to problems over a fixed time period, like a race. The concept has grown wider than the computer programming events that birthed it. The goal of the hackathon could be to work out how to communicate an organisation's manifesto or to get an idea trending online, to create an app or to host two teams which competitively design viral memes. What makes it a hackathon is the concentration of energy and ideas, and the intent to achieve some goal in a short time period.

So much of how Newspeak House runs, the concentration of energy, its focus on problem solving using tech solutions, slightly anarchic governance, that it prioritises productivity over comfort and its culture of normalising failure, sets it firmly in the hacker-house tradition. Edward typically responds evasively to the suggestion that they might fit into the genre by asking questions about how one might define the hacker-house movement, but it has much of the same DNA as its less civic cousins which sprouted from Silicon Valley during that utopian period of tech development.

I can understand why Edward is hesitant about the term. Whilst Newspeak House is focused on engineering the tech space to serve humanity better, your average hacker house is about individuals mutually benefitting from one another to achieve individual success. In hacker houses, co-living isn't in itself the goal. It's a method by which a person can lower costs and share intellectual resources as a means to an end: success.

Residents of some of the early hacker houses talk about these spaces having a 'ride or die' culture where some housemates become billionaires and others spend their entire savings on an idea that fails. Rather than pull apart and interrogate the economic, political and technological systems we live under and trying to hack them to serve humanity more effectively, these hacker houses are about individuals trying to 'game' the systems we live in, to emerge as winners on the terms of those systems. Hacker houses produce billionaires and broken men. They are centres of cryptocurrency investment, hustle culture, high stakes start-ups and tech bro Live+Work incubation. Like Newspeak House, they normalise failure, rely on frantic short-term collaboration and achieve success through connection. Also like Newspeak, they're not always comfortable.

Accounts of the early hacker houses are fraught with cockroaches, bunkbeds and intellectual property attribution conflicts. They provided cheap bed space for those wanting to plug themselves into the tech conversation in the enormously unaffordable San Francisco Bay Area. It's the tech version of Hollywood hopefuls renting rooms during pilot season, hoping to hit the big time by immersing themselves in the swell.

The Negev was one of these houses, started by Alon Gutman, an early Google engineer and tech entrepreneur, in 2014. Early tenants describe a selection process where they were led to an abandoned pier and asked to scream out his name in the dark. There was often no hot water and 'not enough mattresses for everyone'. The Negev's alumni talk about how these sub-optimum conditions were actually part of what made them such productive space, the discomfort building brotherhood and motivation.

Yelp reviews range from 'Five stars – It's been one of the greatest years of my life. It's a house filled with talented, ambitious, friendly people' to 'One star – ceiling leaks, filthy house, tiny extremely overpriced rooms, trumped-up social environment that is actually very cliquish'.

Like Newspeak House's evolution, some of the newer iterations of the hacker-house ideal look more like college programmes or established incubation/co-living spaces.[4] As they've commercialised, there's less of a DIY focus on camaraderie in the squalor, and more on engineering the conditions for professional development. In the same way as commercial co-living uses data to achieve wellbeing outcomes, these spaces are designed to engineer financial success through networking. Some are more like standard co-living set-ups with co-working spaces attached, marketing themselves in the hacker-house brand to appeal to those wanting to join the slipstream of the tech gold rush; others offer short-term accommodation to tech interns.

HackerHome advertises their places to those heading to coding camps or needing temporary accommodation. Its bunkbed hostel accommodation reflects a need for flexibility, as well as a desire for those coming to immerse themselves in the tech space. HackerHome 'bridge your network' allows you to pay in Bitcoin.

In a slightly less transient iteration, nine 'Dead Houses'[5] are home for collectives of Stanford University post-grads and alumni seeking to continue their journey after studying in a co-supporting environment with like-minded individuals. Seven of them are on the same street, and a further two on the surrounding roads.[6] There are interconnecting gardens and an atmosphere that members describe as a 'village'. It's a way to elongate the benefits of being in Stanford's intellectual orbit once you're no longer eligible for their on-campus co-ops. Bobby Holley, a resident at Enchanted Broccoli Forest describes the 'bias toward action' that is the guiding principle of the houses. Members are encouraged to follow any idea they have unless it's harm inflicting.

The 'bias towards action' reminds me of an analogy we use to talk about the motivating power of community organising in the town where REfUSE, our community project, is based: When you take a burning coal out of the fire and put it on the cold hearth, it doesn't take long for it to dull black and lose its heat, but the moment you put it back into the fire, the heat from the other coals will colour it again, and the whole fire can generate more warmth. It's a facet of social connection that our behaviour is influenced by those we spend most time with, that our expectations for ourselves are shaped by what we see others doing. The lives of those around us becomes the reference point for our version of normal.

The logic of these hacker-house communities is to make sure those shaping their version of normal are the high achievers, the hustlers, the brightest and the best. It's a bias to action and 'good vibes only'. The mutual success model does not just occupy the start-up stage. Those looking to co-living to situate themselves in an engaged, buzzy network still benefit from this type of community once they've achieved relative success. Entrepreneurial co-living isn't necessarily bunkbeds and washing-up rotas.

Over the lockdowns the Savoy Palace, in Madeira's capital Funchal, hosted a community that was something of a grown-up cousin to the hacker house. In terms of its risk appetite, tech adjacency, bias to action and focus on mutually enabled success it very much followed in the hacker-house imprint, but there were certainly no cockroaches.

I came to know of the community because a friend of mine, a successful London-based lawyer went to Funchal for a two-week holiday and found such positive, free-thinking community there that two years later she still hasn't come back to the UK. She sold her London flat and is applying for permanent residency. I speak to Bogdan, a Ukrainian online marketer who helped to start the Funchal collective, to understand more about their community's organic growth.

Their community evolved alongside Portugal's wider identity as a tech centre enabled by low tax and incentives. 'It's really rare, nowadays, to find something that is realising its potential from nothing,' Bogdan tells me. 'And that's how I feel right now about community creation in Madeira.'

Before settling there, he'd spent the previous twelve years living in thirty-six countries and over 100 cities. During the

Covid tourism downturn, Bogdan negotiated a heavy discount on luxury suites at the hotel, allowing people to live there for between 1,400 and 1,600 euros a month. Because they were counted as a single household, this allowed them to avoid Covid restrictions and continue a regular social calendar of karaoke and yoga. Whilst, for most of us, our worlds became smaller over 2020, for the Savoy Palace community it was a time when their worlds expanded.

Their co-living experiment was coordinated via Slack channels. Members of the community were from thirty-three different countries and even included a baby, alongside mostly young professionals. 'The kind of person that is attracted to a co-living movement in a hotel has got to be quite free-thinking,' Bogdan tells me. 'As an open-source community, we're able to share that expertise from so many different sectors together.'

During the evening, cryptocurrency entrepreneurs ran workshops, teaching others how to mine their millions and wellness practitioners conducted regular sessions of yoga and breath work. There were sessions on tax efficiency for those hoping to settle permanently in Madeira, and group working sessions.

Bogdan tells me about how this environment has benefitted those who moved there: 'A couple of our guys received, I think, about half a million in investment for their start-up, just from the other guests. We have people creating businesses together. About 15 people are very big on cryptocurrencies. So there was this clip being shared around the hotel about a new cryptocurrency being introduced. A couple of guys were quick enough to get in on the deal. I think each of them invested $1,000, and made $300,000 in return, 300x within a week! There's a lot of interesting opportunities, a lot of interesting information floating around.

'It's not only financials or technical or crypto or IT people. We have two *New York Times* bestselling authors, we have people who are artists, we have designers, we have people from every scope of life.'

The community no longer lives exclusively at the Savoy Palace as the close of the pandemic saw tourism return the hotel to more normal rates and levels but the network remains in clusters across the island with many moving there permanently. Though there was some breakdown in relations with the hotel towards the end of their stay,[7] they provided vital financial support for the tourism-reliant town. Bogdan described the community's relationship with the town around them as positive.

Beyond the financial gains which Bogdan claims individuals made, the community was hugely beneficial for the mental health of its residents, individuals who would otherwise likely have found the period very lonely and isolating. For the time it ran, it gave those living there a space where they were built up, supported and encouraged, where they could share their skills for mutual benefit. In truth, any criticism I had would be tinged with jealousy.

Zooming into Bogdan's sun-drenched terrace where community drinks were about to start, the view from my sofa felt shabby and solitary. It did though, bring to mind what I was told by the former Mason and Fifth resident – 'It's easy to be nice when everyone is rich.'

What I found interesting, looking at the different iterations of the hacker model is that their success partially depends on building a public narrative of success. So much of what goes on with hacker houses and success networks is about attracting the brightest and most entrepreneurial members who will go on to found the next Facebook, make 1000% return on an unknown new cryptocurrency and join the ranks of mythic success stories. It's these stories that will attract the next cohort of entrepreneurs to the space, keeping it buzzy.

It's one of the things Saperia is hesitant about, the packaging up of their success stories up as jewels in their crown until they are currency. That's why he emphasises that a valuable time there could look like failure and learning as much as success.

Despite the rough and ready conditions, or even because of them, there manages to be a real pride and belonging in these networking spaces. Community identity is bound up in the mutual currency of sacrifice and framed by the stories of those whose footsteps they're following. This makes hacker houses masters of marketing.

The more commercial housing ventures particularly are pitched to new joiners in characteristic Silicon Valley jargon. They're spaces which are heavily documented online, on Reddit and YouTube particularly. Some of the content makes for fascinating watching, occasionally verging on satire. One resident, giving a video tour of her home at Serendipia Nest,[8] a co-living/working house in San Francisco, refers to Gandhi as an 'influencer' during her video tour without a hint of irony. Serendipia Nest self-describes as a 'home for change makers, tech entrepreneurs, crypto hodlers & buidlers,[9] artists, lifelong students and risk takers'.

This focus on external comms as a vital facet of hacker-house community building brings me to wider questions about how feeling a sense of pride in our social groups can help to sustain them, even in the moments where they take more from us than they give. Locally concentrated pride doesn't always have a healthy reputation. It can translate as exclusive and parochial, the preserve of the NIMBY crowd writing letters to the council about new social housing developments. A positive narrative about our communities, though, is the only way people will continue to invest in them and see value in them.

Selfish herd theory dictates that in order to be successful, our communities need to attract members. This is important not just to keep up the critical mass but also to engender pride, commitment and loyalty in existing members which, in turn, fosters cohesion. It's important that members are able to tell positive stories about their tribe. This is ever more important in an age where we're sharing stories as soon as they happen, when we are our own over-worked PR team.

Local, residential or tribal pride is the public face of a sense of belonging.

We're all involved in this kind of marketing exercise to some extent, every time we share photos of friends on Facebook, tag our colleagues on LinkedIn, wear a Bride Tribe sash on a hen-do or send a family Christmas newsletter. Pride in our tribe is the sentiment behind every 'Squad Goals' hashtag, reinforcing our sense of belonging within a social network by marketing it to the outside world.

Although it's made more obvious by the indivisible partnership with social media that you'll find in the hacker-house movement, every group I've visited has had some sort of external communications created by those inside which tells the world who they are and invites others who feel similarly about the world to add their name to the roster.

The most awful iterations of this kind of communication are perhaps 'hype houses', communal homes where influencers live together to create content, amassing and sharing their followers to widen audiences and, in turn, financial return. Members are literally there to boost the share value of one another's platforms.

Even really non-commercial community models tread a very fine line around authenticity as we reinforce the value of our social networks through communicating them with the outside world. Like with all social media marketing, there is a temptation for communities to edit and filter, leaving us with dominant narratives of their successes and minimising difficulty and failure.

I have personally contributed to the over-dominance of successful outcomes many times, both socially and professionally. I've simplified stories for an article or reduced someone's journey to a highlight reel case study for a funding application. It's partly a by-product of the platforms most of us are using to tell these stories about ourselves and our communities.

Social media platforms operate according to the principle of the attention economy, where equity is held by being effectively able to detain someone's gaze.[10] It leaves us labouring under a framework where attention is synonymous with value so we're taught to communicate in attractive easily digestible sentiments rather than the more laboured demands of accuracy and nuance.

In our community we called these dressed-down representations 'glory-stories' but more commonly, you might call it 'toxic positivity': smiling pictures of home-sprouted mung beans and oat milk with polystyrene-packed burgers out of shot; filtered stories where homeless Albert just happened to be in the background so everyone knows what a good person I am; humble-blogging about our asylum-seeking guests. At the time I saw this as a really positive way of sharing our life with others, puncturing some of the fear that comes with connecting across divides, breaking stereotypes and wanting others around us to know that there are more equal, connected and compassionate ways to live. It probably also had a lot to do with justifying my life choices to those around living nicer-looking lives. It was an effort to claim that we, too, were squad goals.

There is a huge responsibility for those telling the stories about our communities. These case studies have rightly come under scrutiny over the last ten years as we've grappled with the importance of who is controlling and shaping the narratives that define our communities. For example, third sector communications about community development have had a well-needed reckoning in tune with the Black Lives Matter movement. Boiling down lives into case studies that confine people within the roles of 'helper' and 'helped' has, for decades, left us with a Live Aid narrative of the African continent. The stories of whole communities have been told by snapshots of malnourished children with fly-covered faces as a shortcut to donations.

In L'Arche it could look like emphasising a narrative of harmony at the expense of telling stories about the cost of care. At the Bruderhof, it could look like sharing the stories of those who've found homes there much more loudly than those who've felt un-included. At Hacker Houses, it looks like perpetuating the legends of tech billionaires above the reality of loneliness and bankruptcy. For us, it looked like pinning people to their happy ending in a way which didn't reflect the ongoing struggle of finding recovery and stable housing. The stories of our guests, framed by the beginning-middle-end of their telling, would complete their narrative arc at the point they left our house and signed a tenancy or found a job. We'd be left to polish our shiny armour whilst the story continued unaware of its neat conclusion.

'Brilliant!' someone would say when I shared these tales about our communal life at a conference or event. 'Perhaps we'll move in together too and sign up to be emergency housing hosts.'

'Great idea!' I'd reply.

Perhaps they are now telling the same stories as I was, boiling down to case studies the swirl of joy and heartache that becomes more concentrated the closer we live together.

What I was most struck by at these networking communities is that they designed in an acceptability of failure. They manipulated the social norms in a small-scale setting so that people were encouraged to take risks, to try ideas and to not accompany failure with shame. The tension and intensity of these spaces across San Francisco led to the creation of billions in wealth. What if, like the fellows at Newspeak, community organising within our residential and local communities was able to find their energy in these kinds of spaces.

Ironically these 'bias to action' communities reminded me more of our own group in our twenties than many of the others I visited, even houses with more similar aims. The breathless hype of living with people who felt that they were able to effect positive change, and believed that you could too, created an energy which sponsored success and failure, where we founded projects and saw others die. The buzz and supportive atmosphere of the space, though not ultimately sustainable, for those years allowed our horizons to expand, and they made the bunkbeds and shared bathrooms well worth it.

So long as it's paired with a 'bias to empathy', I find the bias to action quite appealing. If we want our living spaces to be greener, more equal and more connected, then they've also got to be fun, attractive and energising. We've got to be able to tell stories about our localities that make us proud to belong to them, that disrupt the appeal of the greener grass on the other side. Co-livers can sometimes seem like a worthy lot, but there is no reason this should be the case. If connection is better for us, then it's also better professionally, socially and environmentally as well as societally. If this wasn't true, we wouldn't be able to sustain these spaces.

CHAPTER 10

Buddhist community: routine, rest and spiritual health

OMMUNITY LIVING, OR *SANGHA*, IS one of the three-fold refuges of Buddhism. Beliefs about the interconnectedness of humanity are at the core of the Buddha's teachings, built on a philosophy that we are not separate cells and instead are in unavoidable commune with one another.

The practices of Buddhist communities are perhaps the most familiar to us amongst the monastic traditions in that meditation, yoga, mantra and breathing disciplines have entered into mainstream Western wellness practices in a way that Catholic liturgy or Islamic Salat daily prayers have not. Buddhist monasticism is one of the oldest traditions of community life and yet its communal rhythms, though centuries old, are still kept beating at communities all over the UK and the world.

More formal Buddhist communities tend to be single-sex and take the form of either rural retreat centres which host permanent residents as well as guests or urban communities connected to a Buddhist Centre, like those in Birmingham and London. They're also, in line with historical monastic traditions, mostly populated by singles or at least singleness is very much more culturally acceptable within them.

Now in her fifties, Kalyanavaca has lived in Buddhist communities since she shocked her parents by moving into one at twenty-five. She's alternated between large rural centres which invite people to retreat from the busyness of city life, to smaller houses in the heart of the city. She's now resident at one of the women's houses connected to the London Buddhist Centre. There are four of them in a row in East London, housing between six and twelve residents in each house. These residents are the lifeblood of the Buddhist Centre, helping it to run courses, retreats and group meditation. Like residents at L'Arche, they receive a stipend according to need as well as living in the houses, but aren't paid a salary for their work there. As well as enabling the wider spiritual rhythms of the centre, each of the houses has its own practices, points of connection on which the rest of the life, work and leisure pivot.

These rhythms emerge in each house as agreed by those living there but centre on helping one another improve their following of the precepts of the Buddhist faith to their best ability. They have in common with the Bruderhof that the rest of their life is built on a foundational principle of being able to follow their religious beliefs as authentically as possible. In each house, residents have a private room and beyond that, the rest of the space is communal.

At Kalyanavaca's house the communal day starts with a 7am group meditation and is finished by a communal vegetarian meal in the evening. These aren't compulsory. Members can note on the house's board if they're out, or would like food saving to eat later and can choose to attend morning meditation or not.

'They can encompass all manner of difference,' Kalyanavaca tells me, 'but it wouldn't work if members weren't committed to their practice of Buddhism.' It's the foundation on which the whole thing is built. She tells me about another of the houses, where commitment to their spiritual practice together dropped off and their community, unhinged from those rhythms that were its beating heart, became a house-share rather than a community. The house ended up being dissolved in order to refocus it.

Without the intentional structures, focus and routines agreed upon by those living together, I suppose every community I visited would amount to a house-share. Intentional communities are only made such by the collective will of those who live there.

The houses and centre are part of the Triratna tradition, a more modern form of Buddhism centred on mindfulness and meditation. You won't see ritual costume, enforced celibacy or mandatory veganism. Rather than being isolated from the culture that surrounds it, they seek to be in community with the world around them, to speak the truths of their beliefs into the modern world.

It's one of the largest Buddhist movements in the UK, with around thirty urban and retreat centres.

Like many of the communities I've visited, these intentional homes sit in awkward adjacency to the cultures around them. Their life together is designed to give them a greater chance of following the teachings of Buddhism, to embody simplicity and stillness, to opt out of greed, over-consumption and the swirl of distractions that is the default of modern life.

The norms of consumerism, constant stimulation and pace encircle them, snatching at their edges as they seek to interact with the city around them. It's a relationship that's not always reciprocal. Buddhist practices, particularly over the last decade, have often been co-opted into the framework of a wellness industry which offers up mindfulness and meditation to people as tools with which they are able to sustain productivity, to press pause on the relentlessness of life just long enough to be able to go back to it.

In this setting, the wider heritage and communal context of these practices can be shaved away.

Buddhism focuses on a holistic reading of wellness where focus on the individual body is only relevant when set in the context of greater engagement with the community and world. As one resident of a Buddhist house put it, 'the call of Buddhism is to transform ourselves so that we might transform the world and challenge the three great evils of greed, hatred and delusion.'[1]

The Buddhism-lite offered on corporate team-days and hotel wellbeing bundles has been, for the most part, repackaged for Western consumers, trimmed of its challenge of community transformation, given hashtags and put to work towards ends of energy optimisation.[2] The face and identity of the Buddha himself is used to sell bowls of salad and garden-centre ornaments. His rounded cheeks are marketing shorthand to communicate that a product is healthy or wholesome. The Westernisation of Buddhism has become one of the most acceptable forms of cultural appropriation there is, where an idea is used without crediting or recompensing the cultural context which birthed it.

I speak to Kalyanavaca about how their community has dealt with tourists to their way of life. I expect her to be more cynical about those dipping their toes in, using Vinyasa yoga alongside party-pills and fast fashion. She surprises me though: 'Of course, it effects our wider community, but in a way we're part of that.'

She tells me about a project she helps to run trying to reach the local Bangladeshi community where their house is based in Bethnal Green, East London. Kalyanavaca is a breathworks teacher training others in meditation and mindfulness to help people with chronic pain and depression.

'We've made these workshops available for free in the local community,' she tells me. 'Because a lot of people could never be able to afford to come on one of these courses. We adapted it. We made it shorter. And we made the English a lot simpler because a lot of people don't speak English as their first language.'

Like the church-goers who welcome Christmas visitors, she seems quite happy to sit in this tension. 'We have thousands of people coming through the Buddhist Centre doors, you know?' she says. 'Not everyone will become Buddhists, but a lot of them do. And many, many more people will learn to meditate. It really helps them in their life.'

There is a simplicity, an evenness, in the way that Kalyanavaca talks that is replicated amongst all the Buddhists I speak to. Trev, who lives in a mixed Buddhist community in Salisbury, has the same tone. He tells me about the freedom of letting go of his smart apartment and collection of antiques, and the beauty of respecting those you're in disagreement with.

'How do you solve conflicts?' I ask Kalyanavaca.

'It's challenging,' she tells me, 'but we're all committed to practice. So we're committed to trying to sort things out, you know, when things go wrong.'

Trev responds similarly. 'Disagreement?' He waves a hand. 'Oh we've got no problem with that. We'll either resolve it or postpone it for another meeting. The key thing is having a non-prescriptive approach to dialogue that respects the person you're talking to.' He describes the agreed standard of coming to conflict conversations with a blank slate of assumptions about the other person, of treating their feelings and opinions with deep value, even when they diverge from your own.

One of the residents from an LBC's men's house puts it like this: 'Living here means you make that effort to move towards the life of another human being, which it sounds like a simple thing to do, but in practice that's a much more challenging thing to do. You're confronted with your own limitations, your own prejudice, your own views, and to really move out of that into the life of someone else takes effort and kindliness and open-heartedness and sometimes, anger. That's my vision of community.'

It's not necessarily a skill of mine. In fact, I feel a bit irritated when Trev suggests in a calm, considered voice, that my hunched-over posture might indicate some sort of tension or bad energy that I need to let go of. 'Yeah, maybe,' I tell him. 'Or maybe it's because I'm sitting on the stairs to get wifi signal.'

Even the manner in which they both speak involves a great deal of pausing for thought and slow consistent pace. I wonder whether Buddhist community attracts these even-tempered people or creates them, what it is about their communal life that forms this open, measured, calm approach to one another and the world outside.

Buddhists live in community as a precept in itself but also for the way in which it enables them to lead a certain type of life. Community forces us into a rhythm as we live in step with others, whether that's prayer, meditation and retreat or positive social time, exercise, hobbies and rest. Ideally there would be enough critical mass for there to be freedom within that rhythm, where members are able to come when they are able with the rhythms still beating time regardless.

Those members of the Buddhist communities in London may not always attend daily meditation and nightly meals but these things are a metronome, keeping pace in a world which wants us to spin faster.

Particularly for those without children and without offices to go to, these reliable markings of time passing are continually being eroded. We no longer mark the end of the week by gathering together with our local community at the parish church, with the reliability of a family Sunday lunch and a drink at Working Men's Club. Many of us do not sign off from work at 5pm on Friday and commence the working week again at 9am on Monday but allow work and rest to bleed into one another. We do not bring our bread to bake at the communal ovens or chatter with the greengrocer as we collect our weekly vegetables. The greater choice that modern life gives us, to live and work flexibly, can easily cut us loose from the steady markers of routine.

Dr Steve Orma, Clinical Psychologist and CBT practitioner, writes about how routine is one of the sharpest tools we have to help us manage anxiety, stress, depression and insomnia.[3] He says: 'To manage anxiety, you need to consistently check in with yourself about what you're worrying about and then address it.'

'Just as we create routines with exercise for our physical bodies, we should do the same for our mental health,' Orma advises. We should schedule moments of pause, 'thinking time' to bring to the surface any problems or worries weighing on us instead of letting them build up.[4]

It's easier said than done.

Although it's difficult to disentangle the factors that have contributed to a mental health epidemic amongst children, teenagers and young adults, the environment of immediacy and urgency we live in, particularly when time and money are tight, certainly exacerbates poor mental health, even if it's not the root cause. This immediacy is, of course, facilitated by the internet which means that so long as there is coverage, we are never truly out of the office, or detached from the incoming slew of world news, social interaction and product marketing. The amount of time we spend plugged into this data stream directly correlates with instances of depression. A study of young adults by the University of Pittsburgh school of medicine found that participants who reported most frequently checking social media throughout the week had '2.7 times the likelihood of depression compared with those who checked least frequently'.[5]

When it comes to our work lives, millennials report that on average they experience 'a great deal of stress' as part of daily life, 5.4 on a ten-point scale.[6] Some 76% of these respondents cite work as their biggest source of stress, with money, family and the economy coming in as close contenders. We are constantly under strain, staving off burnout with mindfulness, meditation, luxury retail and mindless Netflix watching, but without changing the underlying patterns.

The enforced breaks of monastic routine allow those that live within its bounds to extract themselves from this dynamic. As well as having positive effects on mental health, routine gives us a framework within which we can prioritise what we value. It marks out our priorities in calendar blocks. It says 'I'm not available to you.'

In the absence of this routine, it's easy to look back and realise that your time across a week has been spent on things that have demanded it the loudest. Rather than reflecting what we really want and need, our schedules can reflect what others want and need from us.

This dynamic is a very quick route to burnout.

New year resolutions are peppered with commitments to these routines that feed us, and those around us physically, emotionally and spiritually.

I'm going to call my mum twice a week.

I'm going to pray regularly.

I'm going to keep one evening clear a week for a hobby that brings me joy.

I'm going to value rest, not as an aid to productivity but as a positive thing in itself.

I'm going to make time for this friend I love and who brings me life.

I'm going to have a weekly date night with my partner . . . OK, fortnightly then.

I'm going to practise mindfulness every morning.

I'm going to journal, or paint, or run.

I'm going to eat breakfast with my kids, without looking at my phone.

I'm going to volunteer regularly.

So many of these fall by the wayside quite quickly. Even though we know they are good for us and the world around us, we don't live in set-ups that make these boundaries easy to achieve. Without the framework of a community to hold them in place, these resolutions are trumped by urgency. Individualised living does not always give us the tools we need to opt out of the productivity default.

Often, it's not even external factors that are to blame. As someone with appalling self-control, communal routines have also helped me override my anarchic self which decides at 9am that I absolutely would benefit from going for a walk before making an abrupt U-turn at ten past nine in favour of sitting on the sofa scrolling through Instagram.

The set-up that they have at the London Buddhist houses means that the group collectively decide which priorities are of importance to them, and then regardless of how they feel on the morning in question, those priorities will persist. In some ways, it's similar to the 'bias to action' principles that dictate life in the hacker houses, where residents put themselves around people that will match and multiply their motivation to achieve professionally and financially. Instead those in Buddhist community are seeking to put themselves into an environment where their spiritual and ethical preferences will be matched and multiplied. It's a 'bias to wellbeing' or a 'bias to meditate' perhaps?

Like those scheduling meditation in Kalyanavaca's Buddhist home, the accountability of a group setting can give us the tools to resist the urgency of the world around us. Committed communal routine can be a barrier to the path of least resistance. It gives an external source of routine which enforces its priorities through regularity, that can counter a world that needs all of you and needs it now. The critical mass of community can bed these boundaries in more heavily than we could alone. Solitude, with its lack of external accountability, relies on us alone to state our needs more loudly than the needs that compete with them. In community, the push back is collective, unable to be rewritten at a moment's notice because its lines are interconnected. The collective rhythm can shore up our defences, can give us the tools to resist the current of capitalism which values us for our productivity above our wellbeing.

Most of my conversations with those living communally have centred on addressing mental, environmental and societal health. Speaking to Kalyanavaca brings me to the question of whether more connected styles of living can help people nurture their spiritual health.

It's a question which, over my years of community living, has been quite central.

The practices that punctuate life together in these Buddhist communities can be found across mystic faith traditions, methods where the soul is fed by withdrawing from the rush of life and grounding yourself in your body, and in that moment. Sufism, Paganism and Celtic Christianity have for centuries included in their practices meditation, contemplation, movement and breath work.

Newer forms of communal living, which may seem as though they are inventing new ways of greener, more healthy and connected living, owe their lineage of intentional community to spiritual and religious communities who have been establishing these ways of life for millennia. Monasticism reflects this in its most acute form but communal structures are common across faith and spiritual traditions.

Of course, it's a flawed lineage too. Faith communities could write a long book on how not to conduct communal life – even the modern faith communities I've visited, of all faiths, have been the subject of accusations around moral control and hierarchy – but those forging new paths in intentional living would be remiss to not also ask what we can learn from religious communities about how to live in more connected and mutually beneficial ways.

How we can nurture our spiritual health, and learn from religious groups, are questions that, even a decade ago, I couldn't imagine asking. They are a reflection, I think, of a cultural shift to post-secularism, an acknowledgement that there are things we do not know.

Organised religion is absolutely in decline. Church of England data shows that less than 1% of Brits are church-goers and a third of those are over seventy. When the results of the 2021 British census are published, those identifying their religion as 'Christian' are expected to comprise a minority for the first time, dropping from 72% in 2001, with 'no religion' expected to be the most popular answer. Sociologist Professor Linda Woodhead conducted a study, published in 2016, looking in detail at those selecting identifying as having no religion, the 'nones'.[7]

She created what she called a 'Dawkins indicator', in reference to famous atheist Richard Dawkins, which measured indicators such as whether people identified as atheist and whether they felt negative about faith schools. It offered a sliding scale to register faith and allowed respondents to state their belief in the form of a God, higher power, energy or life-force. Those who came out as 'strongly secular' amounted to under 5% of the UK population.

'The growth of "no religion" cannot be conflated with the growth of the secularism championed by the "new atheists",' she writes. 'Indeed, atheism has not been growing anything like as fast as "no religion", and atheism does not share the youthful age profile of "no religion".'[8]

The ardency of Richard Dawkins' atheism has fallen out of fashion as people have realised that it's failed to answer all of our questions about who we are, collectively and individually. I think we've also realised that there was patronising Western superiority about in Dawkins' approach, which looked down on cultures that held dear religious and spiritual traditions and rituals or acknowledged the duality of body and soul. Younger generations are not abandoning logic and science, but rather widening the scope of what we mean by scientific study – curiosity about how humans and the planet work, an acceptance and comfortableness with the amount we do not know.

If we have not explored 80% of the oceans and do not yet fully understand how most of the human brain functions, surely there's an arrogance in claiming to pin down the intricacies of human spirituality. Of course this is not universal, but even my most anti-religious friends now find peace in breath work, astrology, prayer and meditation. It's a shift, though, which hasn't chimed in time with communalism. Although spiritual practices like prayer and meditation are present within the group identifying as non-religious, this doesn't translate to communal practices. Woodhead reported in the same paper that in the course of a month a quarter of those identifying as non-religious will take part in a spiritual or religious practice.

'What they absolutely do not do,' she writes, 'is take part in communal religious practices like church attendance and worship. Nor do they join religious groups. On the whole they do not much care for religious leaders, institutions and authorities, but they tolerate them.' In this we differ from our US neighbours, who are much more likely to take part in communal religious practices without having a belief and whose non-religious are much more likely to also slot into a wider left-leaning political identity (mostly Democrat), unlike the British data, which is spread across demographics.

This cultural shift to post-secularism has taken place in people's personal lives and within a context of personal wellbeing. This represents a break with much of religious and spiritual history which tends to frame spirituality as a communal pursuit. The Buddha's teachings speak of humans as deeply one and recommend that we seek enlightenment together; Jesus uses the analogy of a human body to speak about the church, where each body part must value and nurture the other or suffer as a whole; in Islam, community, 'Ummah', is what enables Muslims to best practise pillars of prayer and pilgrimage. The prophet Mohammed taught a deep sense of responsibility towards your community. Pagan spirituality is indivisible from people and place, grounded in the natural world and conjoined with the rest of humanity.

I think there is a huge amount to learn from collective spirituality that a 'wellness' reading of religious and spiritual practices edits out, that in looking at how we live together better, we can learn a lot from the example of religious and spiritual groups whether we're building in a context of faith and spirituality or not.

The patterns of ritual, retreat, pilgrimage and pause that religious, and particularly monastic, life is often built around can enable us to prioritise mental health within our communities. If the collective mass can make us feel like we have to put on a smiley front, operate a conversational currency of outrage, and be constantly online to make our jobs work, then the collective mass can also make mandatory the routine of rest. A local and regular weekly gathering which is a mix of age, income and ethnicity and provides time for reflection and connection is one of the best things about faith communities. Finding these kinds of spaces, whether that's meditation groups, community volunteering or communal worship, can transform the shape of your week.

Religious life does not allow us the illusion of self-sufficiency. It forces us to depend on others, the wider world and a higher power outside of ourselves. Never was this more obvious to me than when I spent time in the recovery communities whose acknowledgement of a higher power outside of themselves is a necessary part of self-love, healing and development and compassion for the outside world.

It's a perspective which bursts the swirling bubble of 'am I good enough?' and 'will I be able to do it all?' by answering firmly . . . 'well, no actually.'

Luckily there is no need for individuals to be self-sustaining, self-sufficient and all-encompassing. If written into the DNA of humanity is dependence on some life-force greater than ourselves and an unchangeable cellular connection with those around us, built to need one another, then the task of self-sufficiency is a pointless exploit. If, for you, theology and spirituality isn't the fertile ground in which this perspective can grow, then there are plenty of humanist ways to frame the idea in natural science or sociology. The cells that make us up also construct the ground beneath and the sky above us. Studies of healthy communities find that having lower levels of separation and inequality leads to higher levels of wellbeing throughout.[9] However you look at it, everyone is better off if we acknowledge our unavoidable part in a wider 'we' and engage with how we play our part in that.

In all versions of communal religious life there are points within the schedule where individuals reflect on what is meaningful, valuable and important to them and refocus on it. This could take the form of the Ignatian Examen,[10] a type of prayer which involves reflecting on the day gone by, noting points of joy, sorrow, anger and peace, and allowing yourself to find the divine within it. It could be Islamic Salat prayers, where the well-worn poetry of words refocuses Muslim followers on what they hold to be the most important and central truths they know, from which all else stems. It could be a moment at a Hindu shrine or site of ancestor worship devoting time to gratitude for the blessings of life, sharing hopes for the future and seeking comfort for pain. It could be the repetition of breath in Buddhist meditation grounding you in the cells of your body, recognising the value of your life and the world around you. With the exception of a quick round-table at Thanksgiving or Christmas, these contrived and very regular moments where we remind ourselves what is important to us, and redirect our energies towards them don't often happen outside of a professional 'goal setting' context. To force yourself to audit your priorities, to check again whether you're being able to centralise the things you value, can be incredibly powerful. These points of pause and review are so much easier to hold in place collectively.

Accountability amongst peer groups is the norm within faith communities. It's a two-sided coin, of course. Almost all forms of coercion start life in the guise of accountability, with others claiming to know what is best for you. In communities where it works well, though, it looks like asking questions about whether those in your community have what they need to be content and compassionate. If it functions well it is, of course, a norm that you've consented to. There's a certain amount of account-ability which is just a side product of proximity and trust. One of the residents of an LBC men's house put it well, talking about how living with others enables him to simplify and encourage his best tendencies: 'Community takes away some of the rubbish that I think I need but I don't.'

Groups which organise around faith and spirituality are not better, but they do tend to be the most enduring. This may be simply for the practical reason that there's an external reference point for disagreements which exists outside the group of people gathered at any one time, allowing groups to span different generations with relative ease. As Kalyanavaca explained, if the residents have in common a commitment to practise the Buddhist precepts, then it gives a focus which can encompass all other forms of difference.

Religious spaces have provided, historically, gathering points. Parishes have collected people into local areas, and provided a fixed point in the week where neighbours have been in the same space, where work has stopped and where individuals celebrate and mourn together across generational and income divides.

Even if we're building communities with no reference to spirituality, it's important to acknowledge that there's some heritage to the exercise of building intentional communities that is indivisible from religion, faith and spirituality. We can learn from this history both how community is built badly and how it's built well, we can look at what we've gained as a society by moving to a non-religious majority, and what we've lost.

Transgressive together: finding safety in numbers at the naturist community

R ULE THREE ON SPIELPLATZ'S CODE of conduct states 'nudity is expected at all times except during inclement weather'.

I'm en route there for a weekend and, frankly, feeling more concerned about the camping than the mandatory nudity. I've got a pull-along suitcase, an indoor sleeping bag with a broken zip and three-quarters of a camping stove, rendering the whole object, lugged from County Durham to St Albans, quite pointless. I'm six months pregnant and have arrived with a towel in lieu of a camping mat.

I have never been a natural camper. I wake feeling as though I've been zipped into a used sandwich bag, cocooned with my own sweat and exhaled air. The naturism though, will be less of a challenge. My family are mostly German which perhaps accounts for a more relaxed attitude to the naked human body. This is why I'm accompanied by my sister rather than my slightly more prudish husband.

The versions of bodies we see in the UK are mostly the kind that make it onto billboards and lads' mags; shiny, slim limbs advertising cars and moisturisers. They are, for the most part, young, waxed and tanned into ethnic ambiguity. In contrast, a less commercialised approach to nudity where the pool of images available to our brains includes a selection of unedited bodies along a spectrum of age, size and colour seems a far more sensible approach.

It's not the philosophy of naturism itself which piqued my intrigue for a visit but rather the question of what it is about the freedom to undress that has motivated the residents of Spielplatz to construct a world around it, a residential enclave where they are able to live the lives they want without judgement.

Naturist groups belong to a type of intentional community where those who have been viewed by society as transgressive in some way, or even dangerous, live together in freedom and safety. On the metric I gave you in the first chapter, they are protective, rather than proselytising. I asked the manager at Spielplatz whether they might try to convince those outside of the merits of their way of life, and he responded, 'There wouldn't be any point. People are too fixed in their views.' Instead, the community there build a wall of protection around their way of life. There's an element of sanctuary about it.

Groups that fit into this typology have historically pivoted on issues around sexuality, gender, ethnicity and culture. It might bring to mind queer chosen families or feminist squatters in the 1970s.[1] They can take the form of Romany traveller communities, indigenous groups and marginalised tribes. Equally, they could be polyamorous, or polygamous. They tend to form in response to societal prejudice, aiming to provide a place of refuge for those for whom the world outside can be judgemental and un-inclusive. They are set up to enable those within them to live freely the life they want.

I'm welcomed through the electric gates of Spielplatz remotely and am greeted at the entrance by Janet, a fully clothed receptionist. Although it's May, it is a fairly overcast day. I had been half expecting a cast of goose-pimpled staff huddled against electric heaters, and I have to admit that I'm quite relieved that I won't be expected to undress at the gate. I'm shown to our pre-erected tent which is thankfully already set up with camping beds and chairs and then Janet and her husband take me over to the clubhouse for a drink.

We are joined by others coming in for Friday night drinks so we sit and chat in the bar about how each person found themselves at Spielplatz. The group are almost all middle-aged and fairly middle-class. There is a psychologist, software designer, gardener, legal assistant, and personal carer, a gas engineer and many retirees. There are married couples wearing sensible sandals and men in their sixties sipping pints. Were it not for the common thread of naturism and the under-forties being notably absent, it could have been any village pub. Several naked men join us for a drink as they move between sauna and hot tub and I'm reminded that it's not.

The fact of their nudity, after an initial effort to maintain more-direct-than-necessary eye contact, becomes commonplace. 'New people worry about whether others are looking at them, but really everyone is just looking at themselves,' I'm told. They're

245

not wrong. The following day I have a half-hour conversation with a lady in the sun, both of us bare. I refer to being six months pregnant towards the end of our conversation and, despite the fact that my stomach has been protruding into our conversation, it is news to her.

Spielplatz is the longest-running naturist community in the UK, and the only one to host a full-time residential community. Because there are seasonal members who might spend nine months of the year there, the exact number of full-timers is difficult to pinpoint. It is currently around forty-five with around eight solo men, eight solo women, and the rest couples. The seventy plots have been built up individually and so host a range of ageing prefabs, new-build chalets, caravan pitches and luxury tiny homes. The site feels almost like an exhibition of compact living.

Spielplatz operates as a business rather than a cooperative so the homes are individually owned. Because of their varying shapes and sizes, they might retail for £15,000 or £250,000 and there's also a monthly ground lease paid to Spielplatz that pays for the communal areas. Alongside the private residencies there is the clubhouse and bar, swimming pool, playground, lawns, a sauna and a hot tub.

It is also, surprisingly, one of the oldest communities I've visited, only rivalled by the Bruderhof who were founded the previous decade. When the land was bought in the late 1920s by Spielplatz's founders Charles and Dorothy Macaskie, it was intended as a place for just their family and friends. The family sold most of their possessions to buy the land and arrived with just a bell tent and a few saucepans.

Charles, known as Mac, was notoriously naked. Even as a child growing up in Scotland he could not bear clothes and would tear them off as soon as he was put in them. Footage and photos of him shot over the years show him bearded, tanned mahogany all over and leaning on a spade.

It only became the business it is today, his daughter Iseult tells me over tea, because of the Second World War. It was a period when British beaches were littered with landmines following the anticipation of a Nazi invasion. Leisure space was hard to find and, more pressingly, many in British cities had been left without homes after the Blitz. Those in search of sanctuary were told by word of mouth that they could find it with the Macaskies and so in the period after the war their family's bell tent was joined by makeshift cabins, caravans and tents.

Although on opposing ends of the communalism spectrum, their history reminded me of the early years of the Bruderhof too. Their respective journeys to community building were both set firmly in the aftermath of a war which tossed people's lives into the air. Ideas around home and family were ransacked by the upheaval of conflict and its death toll. As the tossed fragments required piecing back together in the post-war period, they could be assembled into new combinations with new priorities. The Bruderhof and Spielplatz both offered freedom for those looking for a new life; freedom from war and violence, freedom from bombed-out cities, freedom from economic constraints and cultural restraints. Freedom to cover up from head to toe or to air your buttocks to the wind.

Iseult was born at the Spielplatz community in 1932, just a few years after its conception so remembers her childhood in this setting. She's eighty-nine now and her short-term memory is dappled by dementia. She rarely leaves her home but her hair is still set in a Barbara Windsor beehive and accompanied by frilled clothes and wonderful stories. Every surface of her home is covered in framed family photos and doilies. She's iconic – if you research the history of British naturism then it will not take you long to come across black and white photographs of her, with her hair set in 1940s waves, dressed only in a ribbon of lipstick.

Though I'm told that the present week's activity would likely have become dislodged in her mind, her memories of growing up at Spielplatz and the glory days of the seventies and eighties are still vivid. People used to ask her, 'Why are you a naturist?' And, like her father before her, she'd reply, 'Why do you wear clothes?' She tells me about her childhood there, in a small, close-knit community with other families, running around without clothes in the sun. When she was fifteen, in 1947 she took her first job as a typist in a nearby electrical factory.

'I got asked out a lot because people heard I was a naturist and thought I was easy,' she said. 'They got a shock though because I was, in fact, very difficult! Far from being easy an upbringing like mine taught you that your body is private, not to be touched by others.'

The story speaks to the ongoing tension with how Spielplatz relates to mainstream society, how the story that the community tell about themselves and the story told about them have always sat unallied. A pamphlet published in 1957 describes journalists visiting the community in the 1940s and 50s: 'Even hardened journalists from National Newspapers, anxiously seeking a sensational story for the next edition, have come away from nudist gatherings despondent; they realised in a flash that here was not the sensation they sought but just a crowd of naked people behaving naturally and sensibly.'[2]

The conflating of ideas that she describes amongst the men in the electrical factory in the 1940s, where sexuality and nudity are treated as two sides of the same coin, is as much a topic of conversation amongst members today as it was for her in the 1940s. It's a narrative which casts the community at Spielplatz as sexual deviants or at the very least weirdos.

An Instagram poll I shared before coming to Spielplatz revealed that the biggest thing that put people off naturism was the perception that it is pervy. That particularly women stripping off would be subject to the unwanted male gaze or sexual approaches. Given that British naturism is more commonly a male pursuit, I can understand their concerns.

The link between naturism and sexual kink is pretty well documented. There is certainly some overlap between naturism, sexual voyeurism and swinging culture, for example. Cap d'Agde, in France, one of Europe's largest naturist resorts where a number of the Spielplatz members holiday, has a family beach at one end of the sandy coast, and further down the rather brilliantly nick-named 'porky end', which serves as an arena for public sex, partner swapping and spectating audiences.

Spielplatz occupies a more purist form of naturism where communal nudity is valued, in part, because of how it de-sexualises the human body and treats it as natural and shame-free. It advertises as a family friendly space and regularly has children present, although none live here now. It is a school of thought

249

more akin to naturalism, seeing bodies as part of the natural world. It's well summarised in their 1956 pamphlet which describes Spielplatz as 'a group of people who wish to live in harmony with nature, and in the costume that God gave them'.

If you take into account the different ways that the naked human body has been viewed across cultures and thousands of years of history, it's not really a particularly controversial view. But why have those living there shaped their lives around this particular freedom, rather than freedom from other dysfunctional norms that we live with like economic systems, supply chains, moral norms? What is it about the freedom to bare skin that makes it the foundation for a communal life?

I share a cup of tea with Tom and Victoria, a couple in their forties who've been living at Spielplatz for five years. Tom is a true naturist. He opens the door to invite me in for tea without a scrap of clothing on, despite the drizzle and, for the duration of the weekend, I don't see him wearing clothes. Victoria is a textile designer and artist and Tom is a former university lecturer and life model. Above the door in their wooden chalet is a sign which reads 'Nude is normal'.

Their house is in homage to the naked body, each wall hung with life drawings and paintings of men and women in their natural state. Tom speaks of naturist theory and easily dips into philosophies about the human body and study of its form.

'That immediate association of the naked body with sex happens all the time,' he explains. 'Everybody says it. Simplest way for me to reduce my feelings about naturism is that it's about respect. And respect covers a lot. It's about respect for each other, respect for different genders, respect for different wishes. The typical naturist will say respect for wildlife, the environment. Babies would love to stay out of clothing, they often resist being put into it but society wins out. You're so young, you don't know better, and you grow up with it. There is no need to directly associate the naked human body with sex but the associations culturally, of the last several hundred years, have made that the default norm. Not previously, but that gets lost in history. And people don't want to look that far back or attempt to understand.'

He goes on to talk about how reframing our relationship with the human body shapes how those at Spielplatz relate to one another. 'So many barriers that one considers standard drop away in an environment where you are looking at people as individuals, you can't judge someone, whether they are astronaut, or politician or merchant or a gardener, when they have no clothes on. There is no uniform. You are an individual, you're a person. And that is a special thing.'

I'm not so sure about his theory that nudity here has led to equality. I hear the same conversational prejudices at Spielplatz as I would have at any other village pub, generational divisions and suspicion towards other cultures. There are village cliques by the pool and class divides in the clubhouse. But certainly, a far-reaching positivity around human bodies is borne out visually. Disability, mastectomy, the gravity of age, wrinkled bodies using mobility aids and stomas and genitals of all shapes and sizes are in evidence.

Tom's commitment to naturism is almost ideological. He, like Iseult and Mac, asks us to question the societal norms which have sexualised the body and hidden it away. His nudity is the logical conclusion. Victoria, though, already having an appreciation of the human form through art, came to naturism through Tom. She enjoys the option of being without clothes and the pace of life here. Its network of others has suited her Multiple Sclerosis, which leads to bouts of exhaustion and pain. She describes where they lived before moving to Spielplatz, a suburban semi where neighbours didn't know one another. We talk about Spielplatz as a 'safe space' for those who think like Tom, for the human body, and for those that see naturism as part of who they are.

I find the terminology of 'safe spaces' interesting here. Those I spoke to over the weekend viewed naturism in a number of different ways. Some described it in an ideological sense, like Tom, where nudity was the natural summation of a set of beliefs about the world, others saw it as a lifestyle choice or hobby, but for many there, it formed part of their core identity that they'd be unable to change.

For this group naturism allows them to freely express very deeply held truths about who they are, and who they had been born as. They speak about their yearning to live without clothes in the same terms as you might speak about sexuality; they knew from a young age that they had naturist leanings, that they were different from others around them; they hid this part of themselves in order to conform to prevailing norms; they came out to friends, colleagues and family; they were able to live freely once they had found acceptance amongst other naturists and allies. For this group, living in a society which saw their true selves as transgressive was a painful experience, akin to being closeted.

252

I ask one man, who considered himself innately naturist, and at odds with the very 'textile' family that brought him up, if he could describe the feeling of being wholly naked. He tells me that the sensation of air on his genitals made him feel complete, that in that setting he could connect with his whole body and his masculinity. 'This is the kind of thing the *Daily Mail* would jump on,' he adds, 'layer their own assumptions on top of so it sounded sordid. I've said it aloud to very few people and I'd never want this attributed to me. I'm not talking about a sexual experience, but it is a deeply sensual one.'

In the open air he experiences a moment of union with his body, of feeling at home in his male identity, of complexities dropping away. I can understand why he would worry about publicly coming out with the 'air-on-the-genitals-makes-me-feel-complete' line but in some ways, his description reminds me of how the Buddhists I met spoke about mindfulness. In the same way as Buddhist communal life allowed them to build in rhythms of union with their bodies, this unnamed man was granted that experience of bodily connection by naturist communal life.

We keep in touch and later he sends me a radio programme featuring Frankie Boyle speaking about alcoholism. Boyle says, 'I remember having my first drink at 15 and going, "Yeees. Yippeee. This is it." There is something they say in addiction therapy, there is a feeling sometimes that addicts get that this substance "completes" them. That is what it was for me. Oh, this is the real me.'

'What struck me,' the man reflected, was that, 'it is the very word I use to describe naturism to me. It makes me "complete". How fortunate it is not alcohol.'

Not everyone feels that way of course. For others, naturism tells a wider story of being able to opt out of cultural norms. It provides a backdrop against which they can be themselves completely in other ways.

'We're all the black sheep living together,' one of the single women tells me. 'It's like a big fuck off to the world which has always judged us.'

Janet mentions to me as we chat in the clubhouse that there is a trend of those coming to Spielplatz suffering with poor mental health for whom the freedom of naturism was part of their journey with depression and anxiety. Their acceptance of one another in their barest form provides a context in which they can fully show themselves in other ways too.

Neuro-diversity here is over-represented too. Nicola, a child councillor and long-term resident describes an overlap she'd observed between Spielplatz and the autistic community. 'I do think there are a lot of people on the spectrum here, especially men,' she explains. 'I think it's got a lot to do with the hyper-sensitivity that can affect people with autism, the aversion to the feeling of fabric on skin, or physical constraint.'

Over the course of the weekend several people describe themselves and their peers as being autistic and tell me that Spielplatz is an environment where they can live outside of not just physical but also social expectations. 'People can live without the constraints of clothing, sit in company but not talk, or opt out of certain social set-ups altogether, and they know that nobody's going to bother them.'

I wanted to avoid the weirdos narrative, but in one sense, they are a group of weirdos, people ill-fitted with the culture they were living in in mainstream society, grouped together in order to find greater freedom.

These two groups provide an interesting contrast with the hobbyists.

Amongst the cast there are weekend caravanners, and skinny-dipping enthusiasts, retired couples who have come to Spielplatz to find fun and friendship. 'You could go to work, retire and spend the next decade doing nothing new, going on the same holiday and doing the garden.' By coming here, one of the weekenders explained, you could put on silly parties, wear fancy dress, and sing karaoke naked. Where else would a couple in their fifties or sixties get together with friends and just have fun? Throw their inhibitions to the wind.

Holding these groups together in one residential space is complex.

For those who have found in Spielplatz a safe space to live freely in a marginalised identity, including hobbyists risks building a slippery slope to textile living. One of the units has even been bought by a textile, someone whispers to me by the pool, because he wanted to live in a low-cost, green environment and had a naturist girlfriend. What does that mean for protecting their way of life?

The dress-up parties, for some, represent an erosion of the ethos. A naughty nightie evening and 'Back to School' dress-up are loved by some, and left others feeling uncomfortable, the sexy implication of the themes sitting uncomfortably against the 'nude is normal' philosophy.

I can understand why individuals feel protective about their way of life but the practicalities of protecting it are complicated.

Should management confront members about not removing their clothes enough? How does it interact with consent? Particularly for women, this would obviously strike an uncomfortable tone as nudity and vulnerability are unavoidably intertwined.

One of the single women shared that after a boundary dispute with a neighbour became nasty, she no longer felt comfortable to be naked in certain areas.

'Why does it matter if someone else is naked or not, as long as you can be?' I ask one man who was firm in his views that nudity should be expected of all members where possible.

'There's a mutuality to it,' he shares. 'However permissive the culture is to your own nudity, if you're the only one naked, something about the camaraderie of a minority group, or minority culture is compromised.'

As a millennial, I find it an interesting space. I'm used to the conversation about protecting minority identities being necessarily if imperfectly intersectional, meaning that there's a general acceptance that all forms of discrimination are linked. Those who engage in advocacy, if they're doing it right, need to be concerned with all forms of oppression. Single-issue advocacy where you might be a feminist, but not an active ally with Black women, is out of date.

Spielplatz have, for almost a hundred years, been operating in a protective way. Those who visited the space in the seventies and eighties when its pool and lawns were filled to the brim are still the same people who are there now. In some ways they fit neatly into how I'd talk about other minority groups facing oppression, and in some ways, they're outside that conversation. The language and culture there is noticeably old-school.

I mention at the clubhouse on that first night, for example, that I won't use the sauna because of my pregnancy and, misinterpreting my reaction as shame, a man in his eighties tells me that I ought not to feel self-conscious because, in fact, he thinks pregnancy would make my body more attractive.

Even though I could appreciate that he was trying to alleviate what he had heard as low self-confidence, I felt quite taken aback that in this vulnerable context a man might make a comment about my body. Likewise, naughty schoolgirl dress up would now be considered at a University Freshers week . . . slightly inappropriate, out of step with the realities of schoolgirl grooming.

The reality is that their community is ageing. In being a protective space, perhaps it is harder for new demographics, language and ideas to circulate. Or maybe that's a deeply patronising and needlessly woke response towards a community that are happy in their skin?

My sister and I have a wonderful time sunbathing and swimming in clothes-free freedom. We experience the pleasure to just be ourselves that others describe, the collective care for one another, the openness and kindness, the gorgeous liberty of sun and water unencumbered on bare skin, but it doesn't necessarily ever feel like somewhere that could be ours, where we'd be able to carve out a feeling of belonging. During our visit we are the youngest people there by at least a decade. Spielplatz is a business, the last bastion of a way of life that will only survive if it attracts younger people. The need to appeal to new audiences is pressing.

The tension between protection and welcome would be drawn in different places by those different groups. In the past, they have been able to extend invitations to visitors quite freely, but now they must come with a personal recommendation. There are DBS checks and interviews to make sure people are not coming for the wrong reasons. Strict rules about sexually inappropriate behaviour have had to be enforced a few times, I'm told, and safeguarding policies have been strengthened to try to keep out those who might fetishise naturism or come to view them as a novelty without sharing the ethos.

I get the sense that these threats are more keenly felt for the women. It's not surprising. Grant, Iseult's son, who is currently managing the site, tells me that their applications from single men are weighted ten to one compared with single women. It's a common problem in the naturist movement and one of the main gate-keeping roles is to ensure that the balance is kept in such a way that makes the space not feel intimidating for women. There is some huffing and puffing about this by the single men I speak to for whom access to these spaces is harder, but the even mix makes a huge difference to how I feel walking around the site in bare skin, even though I know that it might make the space un-inclusive for men who would love to be there.

Like in many communities which house subcultures, their life together is marked by hyper-specific patterns of activity, social codes, norms of behaviour and language. The place has an indigenous lexicon. I could be a 'textile' because I accept clothing norms or a 'nudist' if I enjoy a clothing-optional lifestyle but don't feel it is a core part of my identity. The identity marker 'textile' is used in the same way as my generation might use 'cis' to describe someone who identifies as the gender they were assigned at birth. It's a linguistic marker which disrupts the implication that one state of being is 'normal' (cis or textile) and the other is 'divergent' (trans or naturist), by giving a name to each.

In addition to these language markers there are also culturally naturist activities. Almost everyone swims – there's some shared heritage with skinny-dipping – and 'mini-ten' is the standard game, played on a miniature tennis court, completely without clothes when possible. It's a bizarre game which simply does not exist outside of naturist circles, played with 'thugs' which hit the ball across a net. These are square wooden boxes held by an internal handle which resound a mighty thwack around the court as they send the ball back and forth. I find this oddness, their drive to build a world which does not accept cultural norms just because they're norms, admirable. Naked box tennis, why the hell not! Paint with all the colours of the wind, you crazy cats.

Although I'm sure neither will be entirely flattered by the comparison, the culture at Spielplatz reminds me again of where I started at the Bruderhof, meeting those holding together minority cultures, negotiating the tension of welcoming in those from the outside, but also needing to protect a way of life they've fought for. Within their matching electrical gates are a set of cultural norms, a code of belonging that new people join and reform, idiosyncratic language marking the edges of their communities.

There is something about the external threat which for both communities has been quite bonding; building a protected world has allowed a supportive network to grow within it. It's much less marked at Spielplatz of course, residents have vastly more connection with the world outside of it, they have jobs externally, holidaymakers visiting and social circles outside. For some people Spielplatz is their centre of gravity and for others an escape from the expectations of the world for a few weeks each summer.

Even hearing about the internal tensions and cliques, it's not hard to see why people would want to live there. The fifty or so residents are not a group you would ever put together. They are musicians and gas engineers, swingers and asexual, young and old, on low and high incomes, and yet they are drawn together at the meeting point of the naked body. For those that see naturism as an enjoyable pastime the meeting point could, perhaps, have been something else, but it wasn't. The feeling of sun on bare skin has had a small village built around it. Even those who were open about disliking other members, or feeling at odds with them, told me how important it was that if they needed help, they could find it. If they needed company, they could come to the clubhouse or the lawn and if they needed to be their weird, wonderful and black-sheep selves, they'd be left in peace to do just that. I wouldn't be tempted to join Spielplatz, my conditions for belonging are found in different places, but I'm glad they exist, the last bastion of old school naturism, providing a sense of home for those that might otherwise feel at odds with the world around them.

CHAPTER 12

Can we live in more connected, greener, healthier and kinder ways?

Y SISTER AMI, WHO ACCOMPANIED me on the final visit to Spielplatz, said something whilst we were there that I've thought about a lot since. That it's much easy to start from a point of community, and make friends within that, than start with friends who can be scheduled in and commuted to and try to turn them into a community, a group with whom you'll share your day-to-day living space, eating, childcare and health, whose fortunes are bound up with your own.

Ami works in London and lives just inside the M25. She has plenty of friends and a full social schedule but to translate those relationships into the supportive web of community is not an easy task. We no longer live in a world that is set up for it. Her reflections echo the experience of so many of my peers. None of us are short of people to arrange drinks out with or have round for dinner, but physical distance, time shortage, individualised consumption patterns, and the cost of housing, mean that these relationships aren't always providing the interwoven baskets which can hold the rest of life within them.

The same week I left for the final visit, we moved out of our semi-detached house on the edge of the city, gave away the things we didn't need and moved the rest of the boxes into the community farm. My great-grandfather's sofa which I've patched with suede scraps now sits alongside bamboo chairs, a cacophony of mismatched styles brought by each of us as we moved in together from three separate self-sufficient households. I'm still not sure whether this will become our way of life for good, these six people committing to one another, the land, its guests and the local village, but we felt it was worth a try.

I went into this process thinking that I'd emerge convinced that we should all live communally, that individual family homes were no longer fit for purpose, but in fact it wasn't the sharing of space that emerged as the most important factor to building supportive, inclusive community. In every case, these spaces were built by intention, more than they were by bricks and mortar. Those living in cooperatively built blocks in Stuttgart could simply choose to disengage, the Women's Buddhist house that dissolved were still sharing their home, but without the rhythms of communal life being maintained. It didn't work, regardless.

Pooling space, food and material goods gave those I've visited a framework which could help reduce the cost of living and carbon footprint, that could provide a natural backdrop for connection, but what helped people feel that they were living positive, equal and healthy lives was all the stuff which happened within that framework; little Ollie being picked up from school by some of the older women at Old Hall so that his mum could go back to work; the non-profit financial structure at LILAC meaning that residents could opt out of the pressures of full-time work; the weekly sessions at the Mehrgenerationenhaus where the residents came down to read to the kindergarten children; the children of the Bruderhof singing outside the window of a dying woman; the impromptu baking at Mason and Fifth where residents shared fresh cookies and conversation; the crypto tips shared open source which meant that more people could benefit from individual knowledge; the cheer that erupts at the recovery centre when someone collects their one-day token; the trips over speed bumps and round roundabouts that Hugh drives every week.

All of this stuff we can plan into our lives as they are.

What intentional communities do is to scaffold these inter-actions so that they can occur organically within its bounds, so that the building blocks of life are tipped to favour them. Positive community is designed in rather than left up to individuals to prioritise and instigate. Each community I've met with has designed different facets of connection and inclusion into being, has been built around different priorities and ideas, but there are some threads that have run through them all, common approaches for a life more communal.

1.   Structures are positive. Those I saw creating really inclusive places of connection were doing so in quite contrived ways. They were organising intergenerational meet-ups in the community centre, starting a nappy library for new mums and facilitating arduous stakeholder consultancy evenings to design cooperative community spaces. As physical structures have given way to

technological ones and those communal spaces lost, it's far harder for this sharing to happen organically – the path of least resistance is to collect in like-minded groups or fortify our individual or family resources.

2.   Sharing resources provides a touch point. Like the communal bread ovens in County Durham terraces providing a meeting place for local households, collaborative ownership creates space for positive interaction. The environmental cost of extensive individual ownership in any case is increasing, but aside from that, in every community I visited shared kitchens, tool libraries and community repair cafes were hubs for connection. The sharing economy will not just reform how we understand ownership, but how we relate to others who we might have nothing in common with beyond needing a drill or wanting to swap our children's toys for the next age bracket.

3.   Intentional communities make visible unspoken social dynamics. This meant that neuro-diverse individuals were over-represented in every community I visited. Speaking to the councillor at Spielplatz about the overlap between autism and naturism made me reflect back on all the communities I visited and people I spoke to. From the tech-activists of Newspeak House to the crypto entrepreneurs in Madeira, the assistants at L'Arche and Buddhist monks, so many did not colour inside the lines of normativity. Without the structure of a village, or social club, rules of social interaction are really opaque. My mum was on the autistic spectrum and often felt like she was excluded socially without quite having understood why, as though she had

missed a mark that she couldn't see and no one had explained was there. She was always drawn to environments like churches and art clubs which demystified the terms of social engagement through structures, schedules, manifestos and codes of conduct.

By demystifying the lines of participation through communal structure, stating in black and white the expectations of inter-actions, intentional communities make accessible the conditions of social inclusion. You're not required to be hilarious, interesting, socially adept, cheerful and conversationally competent in order to qualify for community inclusion.

From a different angle, as someone who had an ADHD diagnosis as a child, sharing the emotional labour of running a household is also a huge perk when I feel that my brain is already over-full with administrative tasks. Community life has allowed me to reduce the swirl of responsibilities jostling for space in my head, alternately being neglected. Instead a much smaller number of items are allocated to me on a larger scale. I cook and shop regularly but in return, not a single energy or council tax bill comes into my inbox. I have no idea who insures us or who mended the lawnmower. I've probably de-skilled myself to the point of incompetence but it does wonders for my available head-space.

4. Communalism is, for the most part, still extremely middle-class. Space sharing, cooperative ownership and resource pooling could have the power to release individuals and families from the grip of the rat race, from the constant worries over rent, mortgage payments and the bills. It could help to provide solutions to those suffering most from the soaring cost of living. It

could give people the space around them to decide how they want to spend their time and then do it. Conversations about communalism are often quite academic though. We're all talking about how to make our conversations more inclusive, how to invite those to join whose lives it might change, but in that word 'invitation' is the problem.

Our conversation, and I say 'our' because we have also just moved into an over-academic, white and middle-class communal home, reminds me of bell hooks talking about the white-dominant feminist movement. 'Many white women,' she writes, 'have said to me "We wanted Black women and non-white women to join the movement," totally unaware of their perception that they somehow "own" the movement, that they are "hosts" inviting us as "guests".'[1]

Community-led housing needs to burst out of its bubble if it's going to have the impact it needs to. It needs to scale, and snowball until it becomes so normal that it can be a solution to the housing crisis rather than a special interest subject for optimists and utopians. Like in Amsterdam, wider state systems need to make it much easier to do, so that the space isn't largely occupied by those with PhDs in community cohesion and time to battle with planning departments.

5.   Communalism and absolute personal rights aren't easy bedfellows. Every community I went to involved some agreement to 'prefer the other'. Individuals living there had committed to laying down their own will and preference for the sake of a wider group. For the Bruderhof, this was made obvious in its extremity, with individuals sacrificing career ambitions, choice

266

of clothing and romantic partner but even in fairly informal low-control communities like LILAC, residents were sacrificing growing their capital investment, for example, for the sake of including others. Of course there were communities like Mason and Fifth, or the Madeiran Savoy Palace crew where there was no explicit ask to sacrifice individual rights, but they weren't seeking to build in longevity or affordability.

It's become popular to say, 'you don't owe anyone your time', 'no one has the right to your energy' or in the case of explaining your experience to others 'you don't owe them an education'. Of course, this is an important point when applied to putting the burden on minority groups to solve oppression. It has been co-opted in a much wider sense than that though, borrowed from helpful therapeutic dialogue and repurposed by individualism where it's used to abdicate responsibility to live in communication with those around us.

Community is reciprocal, and in fact we do owe something of ourselves to our local communities, just as they owe us something of their selves. Inclusivity can be tiring. Connecting across divides involves putting yourself second and sometimes having to communicate across gulfs of perception and understanding. If we edit out the difficult and energy-sapping parts then we'll struggle to build anything worth keeping.

6.   The most powerful way we can foster connection is to take a lead in saying 'I'm doing very badly thank you. I'm weak and failing and feeling disappointed.' The rehabilitation communities I visited taught me more than anyone else about how to foster mutually beneficial connection quickly and effectively, by having

the courage to walk failure-first. In the spirit of the exercise, let me have a go.

- I'm supposed to be a vegetarian and tell everyone how bad meat eating is for the planet but I ordered a steak in a restaurant last week because I fancied it.
- I perform and exaggerate in social settings and then at night replay the things I've said and wonder when people will find out how much less interesting and impressive I am than my first impression implies.
- I put my phone on flight mode this afternoon so I could avoid a friend who is having a mental health dip and might want support.
- Part of me wishes I hadn't written a book about communal living in case it all goes tits up in a public sphere. I'm already finding living with others a bit annoying and my internal narrative on the matter very rarely includes any admission of my own flaws.
- Reading back on my own writing, I often think how insufferably self-righteous I sound.

Your turn.

7. We are inseparable from the world around us, the flora, fauna and individuals.[2] It won't help us to pretend this isn't the case. Connection with others and the world is our natural state. We share the cellular make-up of every other living thing. Our health and wellbeing is interdependent with the health and wellbeing of the people and planet. Living communally is just

one way to recognise this dynamic, there are plenty of others. What won't work is to imagine that our wellbeing exists in isolation, that we can give our lives a positivity trim until we're surrounded by good vibes only. Your fortunes will still be interconnected with the world around you, your health invariably connected with your community's health.

8. The only way people are going to feel like they belong is to feel like they can contribute. This, again, was borne out at every community. Even for those living at relatively wealthy communities like Mason and Fifth and the Funchal digital nomads, where members' contributions were not rooted in necessity, giving something of themselves, their interests and skills embedded a sense of belonging far more than being on the receiving end. People, at their core, want to give. We are yearning to find a home for our time and skills which will build others up.

9. Communalism is still the best chance we have to pilot change in the micro. Any communalism project, even ones knitted to ancient traditions, are ultimately pilot projects. It could go terribly wrong, and leave you feeling like you want to never speak to other people again, but it could also demonstrate in small scale how we could build better systems than the ones we've got. Each time a group of people get together to collectively opt out of food systems, moral norms, housing markets, economic structures, social assumptions, unequal power dynamics or gender confines, they show it's possible. They demonstrate that we are not powerless pieces of data slotting into columns on a graph we haven't seen, but that systems are just made by people, and can be un-made

by people. I didn't want to join those communities I visited,[3] but in each case, I was glad they existed, glad that these groups of people had said, 'No thanks, I think we'll do it differently.'

We are hoping, in some small way, to do the same. To rebuild our space so it better reflects the ways we want to live, trying to design in connection, sustainability and hospitality. We've drawn out dreams to open up the land as community gardens, to provide space for young people, to provide a small oasis for women at crisis points, to bring up our daughter where she'll meet people from all walks of life, to reduce our carbon impact, to grow the food we eat on the land we're standing on and share it with others. These dreams are two-dimensional at the moment. They are so far away from being realised that they feel fictional, but the first step towards them is to plant our own feet in the soil, to build our pram in the hallway.

The repurposed corridor, bathroom and two bedrooms we are having to assemble into our family space will not fit the furniture we've been used to. The baby's nursery, until she needs it, will double up as a spare room and living space. Our first house meeting, discussing how we'll arrange our finances to make the space accessible to our varying incomes, and allocate the different jobs, ran for several hours. The list of other things to discuss ran to several pages.

Alongside learning to live with others again, we're working out what it means to be locally rooted.

The thing I loved most about our previous house was how quickly you could leave it – just nine minutes to Newcastle!

Forty-five to York! You could be in Kings Cross door to door in under three hours! We've got into the habit of constant motion, of always looking for the next exciting place or thing. It was a tiring way to live, sure, but how we've always been and in some ways, we love it.

Now we're playing pool at the Working Men's Club on a Friday. I'm helping to make the sandwiches for the village's Jubilee party which we've planned with the residents association. There was a meet-up of my university friends in London planned after we'd written out the list of sandwich flavours and I genuinely found it challenging to not duck out of the sandwich making and head there instead.

Living in a more rooted way will require intention, damming the flow of the river I've always followed. I've deleted the Right Move app which I browse as a pastime. I'm typing this chapter with soil under my fingernails after planting out our spinach seedlings and have been offered a couple of spare hives so we can start keeping bees. Our spoilt urban cat is struggling to live peaceably alongside the seven feral ones which came with the barn.

Moving out of our cosy, private house, I must admit, gave me cold feet about our new community life. There was a frustrating morning last week when my husband Sam had failed to assist in mending the lawnmower urgently required by our unintentionally re-wilding fields. He appeared, oil-covered and cross and asked me, 'Do you think it's too late to change our minds?'

What will it be like sharing those initial vulnerable weeks after birth with others, including a couple we don't yet know well? How will hosting those coming at crisis points fit together with our family life? How will we decide what food to buy in the weekly shop?

In truth, we don't know; only that if there's a way of shifting our normal, it's worth a go.

Acknowledgements

A huge debt of gratitude goes to all the communities who opened up their lives and homes to me over the last year and trusted me to share their stories. I left each one having learned more about living in kinder, greener and more connected ways.

Likewise a huge thank you to all the people that we've lived alongside in our own journey; our first community Number 25, where we learnt the ropes of vulnerability, activism and communalism and felt loved enough to fail; the community which grew from it whose weekly rhythms of prayer and food have provided touch points ever since we moved out; the REfUSE volunteer family who have taught me what true acceptance looks like, even when it's messy and costly; and to the residents at the farm whose commitment to the slow plod of building community we've been so blessed to join in with and benefit from.

To all those who made writing *Living Together* possible.

Nelle Andrew, who went above and beyond to find the right home for the book. She's incredible and I still pinch myself that I get to work with her.

The Footnote team, Vidisha, Candida, Dave, Kwaku, Grace and Sara, who stitched together my stream of consciousness into an actual book and supported me through my doubts.

Tom and Esther deserve a special mention for endless cheer-leading, Em for providing a 24-hour voice note helpline and Nikki for picking up my slack at REfUSE whilst I gallivanted around the UK and Europe. She's objectively the best person in the world.

And lastly to Sam, a man who makes taking big decisions and big risks feel feasible because I know he's on my team. If it all goes tits up, we'll live on a train playing Bananagrams and it'll still be a nice life.

Notes

INTRODUCTION

1 www.bls.gov/news.release/pdf/tenure.pdf
2 Research conducted by Corgi Homeplan.
3 www.ons.gov.uk/peoplepopulationandcommunity/
birthsdeathsandmarriages/families/bulletins/familiesandhouseholds/2020
4 www.pewresearch.org/fact-tank/2020/03/31/
with-billions-confined-to-their-homes-worldwide-which-living-
arrangements-are-most-common/
5 The Loneliness Experiment (2018) Largest global study on loneliness,
Radio 4 and the Wellcome Collection, 55,000 participants. www.bbc.
co.uk/mediacentre/latestnews/2018/loneliest-age-group-radio-4. Later
published as a paper: Manuela Barreto, Christina Victor, Claudia
Hammond, Alice Eccles, Matt T. Richins and Pamela Qualter,
'Loneliness around the world: Age, gender, and cultural differences in
loneliness', *Personality and Individual Differences* 169, 2021.
6 https://today.yougov.com/topics/lifestyle/articles-reports/2019/07/30/
loneliness-friendship-new-friends-poll-survey
7 https://mcc.gse.harvard.edu/reports/loneliness-in-america
8 www.theguardian.com/society/2019/oct/08/
millennials-social-media-loneliness-epidemic
9 www.independent.co.uk/voices/here-s-proof-british-mental-health-worse-
ever-a6876921.html. www.ons.gov.uk/peoplepopulationandcommunity/
wellbeing/bulletins/youngpeopleswellbeingintheuk/2020
10 https://mhanational.org/issues/state-mental-health-america
11 www.camh.ca/en/driving-change/the-crisis-is-real/
mental-health-statistics
12 www.adb.org/sites/default/files/institutional-document/633886/
adou2020bp-mental-wellness-asia.pdf
13 www.theguardian.com/society/2016/may/09/

self-harm-the-biggest-killer-of-people-in-their-early-20s-in-the-uk
14 www.thelancet.com/commissions/adolescent-health-and-wellbeing
15 www.theguardian.com/commentisfree/2016/oct/12/
neoliberalism-creating-loneliness-wrenching-society-apart
16 www.sciencedirect.com/science/article/abs/pii/S0031938416305583
17 https://heart.bmj.com/content/102/13/1009
18 www.kcl.ac.uk/policy-institute/assets/divided-britain.pdf
19 https://therestartproject.org/podcast/
restart-radio-top-5-good-news-stories-of-2015/
20 www.thetimes.co.uk/article/
people-living-alone-blamed-for-increase-in-wasted-food-sqqf2j92rdl
21 www.ic.org/directory/
22 Jacqueline Kent-Marvick, Sara Simonsen, Ryoko Pentecost and Mary
M. McFarland, 'Loneliness in pregnant and postpartum people and
parents of children aged 5 years or younger: a scoping review
protocol', *Syst Rev* 9: 213, 2020. https://doi.org/10.1186/
s13643-020-01469-5

CHAPTER I
1 www.mms.com/en-gb/
2 www.independent.co.uk/money/spend-save/generation-rent-now-what-
millennial-lifetime-renting-property-a8579951.html
3 https://fullfact.org/economy/employment-since-2010-zhcs/
4 Interviewed by Andrew Marr on *Start the Week*. www.bbc.co.uk/
programmes/m000my6r
5 www.bbc.com/worklife/article/20201230-why-are-we-learning-
languages-in-a-closed-world
6 www.independent.co.uk/news/business/news/british-workers-hours-put-
longest-hours-eu-study-finds-a8872971.html

CHAPTER 3
1 *Communal Village*, 1959, Pathe: www.youtube.com/
watch?v=dRxk2RRR5zY
2 Chris Coates, *Communes Britannica, History of Communal Living in
Britain 1939-2000*, Diggers & Dreamers Publications, 2001.
3 Incidentally, the gates were installed by my brother-in-law a few years
earlier. 'One of the weirdest jobs I've been sent on,' he told us.
4 www.bruderhof.com/en/life-in-community
5 @DrRonx and @56blackmen are my favourite of these in case you could
also do with a Shutterstock reset.
6 www.bruderhof.com/en/our-faith/foundations
7 Lewis V. Baldwin, Paul R. Dekar, *In an Inescapable Network of Mutuality:*

Martin Luther King, Jr. and the Globalization of an Ethical Ideal, Cascade Books, 2013

8 Luisa Marcela Ossa, Debbie Lee-DiStefano, *Afro-Asian Connections in Latin America and the Caribbean*, Lexington Books, 2019

CHAPTER 4

1 Diana Lind, *Brave New Home: Our Future in Smarter, Simpler, Happier Housing*, Bold Type Books, 2021.

2 There is, by the way, a literal 'WeWork of bedspace'. 'WeLive' was a residential extension of the company, billed by its now-ousted founder Adam Neumann, as a project which would globally revolutionise our living and working environments. It went the same way as the now derided WeWork and never expanded from its original bases in New York and Virginia. In 2021 the sites were handed over to other co-living operators and the spaces officially divorced themselves from WeWork.

3 Kelly Watson, 'Establishing psychological wellbeing metrics for the built environment', *Building Services Engineering Research and Technology* 39(2), January 2018.

CHAPTER 5

1 www.theguardian.com/housing-network/2012/jan/13/housing-cooperatives-affordable-alternatives

2 www.theguardian.com/society/2019/mar/27/can-co-ops-solve-the-housing-crisis

3 www.local.gov.uk/about/news/lga-430-increase-bb-spend-people-who-are-homeless-reveals-urgency-more-social-housing

4 I should mention here that Sam, my partner, visited LILAC and I joined him virtually so any well-observed notes on their community are his rather than mine.

5 LILAC's 'mutual home ownership society (MHOS)' model was drawn up by the New Economics Foundation. A fuller legal document explaining the terms of its lease, including the specifics around how their system relates to high earners and low earners and the ways that the equity is held and extracted can be found on the LILAC website, searching 'Schedule 6 LILAC lease agreement'.

6 His book, *Low Impact Living: A Field Guide to Ecological, Affordable Community Building* (Routledge, 2014), goes into much more detail about their start-up process and financial model should you want to read more.

CHAPTER 6

1 www.nationalreview.com/magazine/2019/06/03/britains-socialist-seventies/

2 Published by Old Hall, 2000, edited by Brenda Gamlin.

3 www.iucn.org/resources/issues-briefs/peatlands-and-climate-change

4 Steven Ruggles, 'Intergenerational coresidence and family transitions in the United States, 1850–1880', *Journal of Marriage and Family* 73(1): 138–148, February 2011.

5 Diana Lind, *Brave New Home: Our Future in Smarter, Simpler, Happier Housing* (p. 149), Bold Type Books, 2021.

6 www.lovemoney.com/news/14690/multigeneration-households-near-victorian-levels

CHAPTER 7

1 Russell Brand, *Recovery: Freedom from Our Addictions*, Henry Holt and co., 2017.

2 Brené Brown, *The Power of Vulnerability: Teachings on Authenticity, Connection, and Courage*, Sounds True Inc., 2013.

3 Brené Brown 'The Power of Vulnerability', TedXHouston, www.ted.com/talks/brene_brown_the_power_of_vulnerability/transcript

4 Karen Slater, *My Journey Through Hell*, Fortis Publishing, 2020.

CHAPTER 9

1 https://coronavirustechhandbook.com

2 https://whotargets.me/en/

3 https://oa.works

4 Rise is a classic example of this more formal college-like conception of the same idea. They run a Live+Work accelerator available to people across Europe where entrepreneur hopefuls spend eight weeks working on their start-up ideas in the hope of jump starting their business ideas.

5 They're all named after Grateful Dead songs, of which their founder Rob Levitsky, a microchip specialist, is a fan.

6 https://stanforddaily.com/2014/03/12/palo-alto-dead-houses-provide-an-off-campus-community-for-students/

7 www.gq-magazine.co.uk/lifestyle/article/remote-working-zoom-island

8 www.facebook.com/serendipianest/

9 HODL stands for Hold On For Dear Life, it's a crypto investment tactic. BUIDL refers to the practice of building and developing within the crypto space rather than just accumulating currency. Reddit reliably informs me that I should be HODLing my Bitcoin and BUIDLing my Ethereum.

10 https://econreview.berkeley.edu/paying-attention-the-attention-economy/

CHAPTER 10

1 Shuddhakirti, Birmingham Buddhist Centre, 'Danger, Community Living Could Change Your Life'. https://thebuddhistcentre.com/birmingham/danger-community-living-could-change-your-life
2 https://tricycle.org/magazine/buddhism-and-yoga/
3 Dr Steve Orma, *Stop Worrying and Go to Sleep*, www.drorma.com
4 www.headspace.com/articles/the-secret-benefit-of-routines-it-wont-surprise-you
5 Based on report by University of Pittsburgh, School of Medicine, www.upmc.com/media/news/lin-primack-sm-depression
6 American Psychological Association, *2012 Stress in America: Stress by Generations*, https://www.apa.org/news/press/releases/stress/2012/generations
7 Based on a UK study which excluded Northern Ireland.
8 Linda Woodhead, 'The rise of "no religion" in Britain: The emergence of a new cultural majority', *Journal of the British Academy* 4: 245–261, 2016. DOI 10.85871/jba/004.245
9 Kate E. Pickett and Richard G. Wilkinson, 'Income inequality and health: A causal review', *Social Science & Medicine* 128, 2015.
10 Named, unsurprisingly, after St Ignatius.

CHAPTER 11

1 https://womenslibrary.org.uk/2021/08/18/feminist-housing-activism-in-the-1970s-1980s-2-building-it-ourselves-building-it-together/
2 Charles Sennet, *Nudist Life at Spielplatz: The Story of a Modern Experiment in the Art of Living*, The Naturist, 1941.

CHAPTER 12

1 bell hooks, *Feminist Theory, From Margin to Centre*, Pluto Press, 2020.
2 In case you thought I was going to take a break from sounding insufferably worthy.
3 With the possible exception of Old Hall where I would hone my cheese-making skills.

Index

and Buddhist communities 226
children 49, 54, 56, 57, 66, 68,
  141, 263
diversity and unity of views 61–2
factory 47–8, 50–1
farm 49, 50
and gender roles 58–9
and individual identity 64–6
Kaiya 60, 64–5
kitchen and 'stores' 52–3
leaving the community 66–7
library 55, 56
and mainstream culture 70–1
and marriage 57–8
and mental health 67
and Nazi Germany 46
outposts 46
radical Christianity 50
and self-denial 59–60, 266–7
and socialism 52
and Spielplatz 246, 247
technology 54–6
teens 56–7
videos of 45, 50
vow of poverty 46–7
website 46, 51–2
women 48–9, 58–9
and clothes 56, 60–1, 68
and young people 66
Buddhist communities 225–43,
  262, 264
bias to wellbeing 235
and the Brudenhof 226
Buddhism and Western
  consumers 227–9
commitment to Buddhist
  practices 227
Kalyanavaca 226–7, 229–30, 235,
  242
London Buddhist Centre 225,
  226, 230
meditation 226, 227, 228, 229,
  231, 235

and mindfulness 227, 253
and modern life 231
and monastic traditions 225–6
routines 231, 235
and the Triratna tradition 227
and Western wellness practices
  225
burnout 233
Burns, Rebecca 121

Canary Wharf
  the Collective 74–8, 81, 82, 84,
    86, 87, 91, 119
Carroll, Louise 115, 116–19
cars 10
Celtic Christianity 236
census data on religion 236–7
Chatterton, Paul 108–9
children
  at the Bruderhof 49, 54, 56, 57,
    66, 68, 141, 263
  at Old Hall Farm 140–4
  disabled 150
Children of God cult 33–5, 39
Christian communities see the
  Bruderhof
Christian cults
  the Children of God 33–5, 39
  Coulsdon Christian Fellowship
    35–8
Christianity 236–7, 239
Cirillo, Chris 117, 118, 119, 120
Clark, John G. 30
Clark, Penny 78–9, 79–81, 120
class
  and garden cities 90, 109
  and luxury co-living 90
  and naturist communities 245
  and urban co-living 110–11, 112,
    113, 114
climate crisis 11, 18, 109, 154
  and luxury co-living 79
Cold War 125

282

285

289